B.J. DANIELS

OUTLAW'S HONOR

HQN™

HQN™

ISBN-13: 978-0-373-80198-5

Recycling programs
for this product may
not exist in your area.

Outlaw's Honor

www.HQNBooks.com

Printed in U.S.A.

OUTLAW'S
HONOR

CHAPTER ONE

DARBY CAHILL ADJUSTED his Stetson as he moved toward the bandstand. The streets of Gilt Edge, Montana, were filled with revelers who'd come to celebrate the yearly chokecherry harvest on this beautiful day. The main street had been blocked off for all the events. People had come from miles around for the celebration of a cherry that was so tart it made your mouth pucker.

As he climbed the steps, Darby figured it just proved that people would celebrate anything. Normally, his twin sister, Lillie, attended, but this year she was determined that he should do more of their promotion at these events.

"I hate it as much as you do," she'd assured him. "But believe me. You'll get more attention up there on the stage than me. Just say a few words, throw T-shirts into the crowd, have some fry bread and come home. You can do this." Clearly, she knew his weakness for fry bread as well as his dislike of being the center of attention.

The T-shirts were from the Stagecoach Saloon, the bar and café the two of them owned and operated outside of town. Since it had opened, the bar had helped sponsor the Chokecherry Festival each year.

He heard his name being announced and sighed as he made his way up the rest of the steps to the microphone to deafening applause. He tipped his hat to the crowd, swallowed the lump in his throat and said, "It's an honor to be here and be part of such a wonderful celebration."

"Are you taking part in the pit-spitting competition?" someone yelled from the crowd, and others joined in. Along with being bitter, chokecherries were mostly pit.

"I'm going to leave that to the professionals," he said, reaching for the box of T-shirts, wanting this over with as quickly as possible. He didn't like being in the spotlight any longer than he had to. Also he hoped that once he started throwing the shirts, everyone would forget about the pit-spitting contest later.

He was midthrow when he spotted a woman in the crowd. What had caught his eye was the brightly colored scarf around her dark hair. It fluttered in the breeze, giving him only glimpses of her face.

He let go and the T-shirt sailed through the air as if caught on the breeze. He saw with a curse that it was headed right for the woman. Grimacing, he watched the rolled-up T-shirt clip the woman's shoulder.

She looked up, clearly startled. He had the impression of serious dark eyes, full lips. Their gazes locked for an instant and he felt something like lightning pierce his heart. For a moment, he couldn't breathe. Rooted to the spot, all he could hear was the drumming of his heart, the roaring crowd a dull hum in the background.

Someone behind the woman in the crowd scooped up the T-shirt and, scarf fluttering, the woman turned away, disappearing into the throng of people.

What had *that* been about? His heart was still pounding. What had he seen in those bottomless dark eyes that left him…breathless? He knew what Lillie would have said. Love at first sight, something he would have scoffed at—just moments ago.

"Do you want me to help you?" a voice asked at his side.

Darby nodded to the festival volunteer. He threw another T-shirt, looking in the crowd for the woman. She was gone.

Once the box of T-shirts was empty, he hurriedly stepped off the stage into the moving mass. His job was done. His plan had been to have some fry bread and then head back to the saloon. He was happiest behind the bar. Or on the back of a horse. Being Montana born and raised in open country, crowds made him nervous.

The main street had been blocked off and now booths lined both sides of the street all the way up the hill that led out of town. Everywhere he looked there were chokecherry T-shirts and hats, dish tow-

els and coffee mugs. Most chokecherries found their
way into wine or syrup or jelly, but today he could
have purchased the berries in lemonade or pastries
or even barbecue sauce. He passed stands of fresh
fruit and vegetables, crafts of all kinds and every
kind of food.

As he moved through the swarm of bodies now
filling the downtown street, the scent of fry bread
in the air, he couldn't help searching for the woman.
That had been the strangest experience he'd ever had.
He told himself it could have been heat stroke had
the day been hotter. Also he felt perfectly fine now.

He didn't want to make more of it than it was and
yet, he'd give anything to see her again. As crazy
as it sounded, he couldn't throw off the memory of
that sharp hard shot to his heart when their gazes
had met.

As he worked his way through the crowd, following the smell of fry bread, he watched for the colorful scarf the woman had been wearing. He needed
to know what that was about earlier. He told himself he was being ridiculous, but if he got a chance
to see her again…

Someone in the crowd stumbled against his back.
He caught what smelled like lemons in the air as a
figure started to brush by him. Out of the corner of
his eye, he saw the colorful scarf wrapped around
her head of dark hair.

Like a man sleepwalking, he grabbed for the end

of the scarf as it fluttered in the breeze. His fingers closed on the silken fabric, but only for a second. She was moving fast enough that his fingers lost purchase and dropped to her arm.

In midstep, she half turned toward him, his sudden touch slowing her. In those few seconds, he saw her face, saw her startled expression. He had the bizarre thought that this woman was in trouble. Without realizing it, he tightened his grip on her arm.

Her eyes widened in alarm. It all happened in a manner of seconds. As she tried to pull away, his hand slid down the silky smooth skin of her forearm until it caught on the wide bracelet she was wearing on her right wrist.

Something dropped from her hand as she jerked free of his hold. He heard a snap and her bracelet came off in his hand. His gaze went to the thump of whatever she'd dropped as it hit the ground. Looking down, he saw what she'd dropped. *His wallet?*

Astonishment rocketed through him as he realized that when she'd bumped into him from behind, she'd picked his pocket! Feeling like a fool, he bent to retrieve his wallet. Jostled by the meandering throng, he quickly rose and tried to find her, although he wasn't sure what exactly he planned to do when he did. Music blared from a Western band over the roar of voices.

He stood holding the woman's bracelet in one

hand and his wallet in the other, looking for the bright scarf in the mass of gyrating festival goers.

She was gone.

Darby stared down at his wallet, then at the strange large gold-tinted cuff bracelet and laughed at his own foolishness. His moment of "love at first sight" had been with a *thief*? A two-bit pickpocket? Wouldn't his family love this!

Just his luck, he thought as he pocketed his wallet and considered what to do with what appeared to be heavy cheap costume jewelry. He'd been lucky. He'd gotten off easy in more ways than one. His first thought was to chuck the bracelet into the nearest trashcan and put the whole episode behind him.

But he couldn't quite shake the feeling he'd gotten when he'd looked into her eyes—or when he'd realized the woman was a thief. Telling himself it wouldn't hurt to keep a reminder of his close call, he slipped the bracelet into his jacket pocket.

MARIAH AYERS GRABBED her bare wrist, the heat of the man's touch still tingling there. What wasn't there was her prized bracelet, she realized with a start. Her heart dropped. She hadn't taken the bracelet off since her grandmother had put it on her, making her promise never to part with it.

"This will keep you safe and bring you luck," Grandmother Loveridge had promised on her deathbed. "Be true to who you are."

She fought the urge to turn around in the surging throng of people, go find him and demand he give it back. But she knew she couldn't do that for fear of being arrested. Or worse. So much for the bracelet bringing her luck, she thought, heart heavy. She had no choice but to continue moving as she was swept up in the flowing crowd. Maybe she could find a high spot where she could spot her mark. And then what?

Mariah figured she'd cross that bridge when she came to it. Pulling off her scarf, she shoved it into her pocket. It was a great device for misdirection— normally, but now it would be a dead giveaway.

Ahead, she spotted stairs and quickly climbed a half dozen steps at the front of a bank to stop and look back.

The street was a sea of cowboy hats. One cowboy looked like another to her. How would she ever be able to find him—let alone get her bracelet back given that by now he would know what she'd been up to? She hadn't even gotten a good look at him. Shaken and disheartened, she told herself she would do whatever it took. She desperately needed that bracelet back—and not just for luck or sentimental reasons. It was her ace in the hole.

Two teenagers passed, arguing over which one of them got the free T-shirt they'd scored. She thought of the cowboy she'd seen earlier up on the stage, the one throwing the T-shirts. He'd looked right at her.

Their gazes had met and she'd felt as if he had seen into her dark heart—if not her soul.

No wonder she'd blown a simple pick. She was rusty at this, clearly, but there had been a time when she could recall each of her marks with clarity. She closed her eyes. Nothing. Squeezing them tighter, she concentrated.

With a start, she recalled that his cowboy hat had been a light gray. She focused on her mark's other physical attributes. Long legs clad in denim, slim hips, muscular thighs, broad shoulders. A very nice behind. She shook off that image. A jean jacket over a pale blue checked shirt. Her pickpocketing might not be up to par, but at least there was nothing wrong with her memory, she thought as she opened her eyes and again scanned the crowd. Her uncle had taught her well.

But she needed more. She closed her eyes again. She'd gotten only a glimpse of his face when he'd grabbed first her scarf and then her arm. Her eyes flew open as she had a thought. He must have been on to her immediately. Had she botched the pick that badly? She really *was* out of practice.

She closed her eyes again and tried to concentrate over the sound of the two teens still arguing over the T-shirt. Yes, she'd seen his face. A handsome rugged face and pale eyes. Not blue. No. Gray? Yes. With a start she realized where she'd seen him before. It was the man from the bandstand, the one who'd thrown the T-shirt and hit her. She was sure of it.

"Excuse me, I'll buy that T-shirt from you," she said, catching up to the two teens as they took their squabble off toward a burger stand.

They both turned to look at her in surprise. "It's not for sale," said the one.

The other asked, "How much?"

"Ten bucks."

"No way."

"You got it *free*," Mariah pointed out only to have both girls' faces freeze in stubborn determination. "Fine, twenty."

"Make it thirty," the greedier of the two said.

She shook her head as she dug out the money. Her grandmother would have given them the evil eye. Or threatened to put some kind of curse on them. "You're thieves, you know that?" she said as she grabbed the T-shirt before they could take off with it *and* her money.

Escaping down one of the side streets, she finally got a good look at what was printed across the front of the T-shirt. Stagecoach Saloon, Gilt Edge, Montana.

LILLIE CAHILL HESITATED at the back door of the Stagecoach Saloon. It had been a stagecoach stop back in the 1800s when gold had been coming out of the mine at Gilt Edge. Each stone in the saloon's walls, like each of the old wooden floorboards inside, had a story. She'd often wished the building could talk.

When the old stagecoach stop had come on the market, she had jumped at purchasing it, determined to save the historical two-story stone building. It had been her twin's idea to open a bar and café. She'd been skeptical at first, but trusted Darby's instincts. The place had taken off.

Lately, she felt sad just looking at the place.

Until recently, she'd lived upstairs in the remodeled apartment. She'd moved in when they bought the old building and had made it hers by collecting a mix of furnishings from garage sales and junk shops. This had not just been her home. It was her heart, she thought, eyes misting as she remembered the day she'd moved out.

Since her engagement to Trask Beaumont and the completion of their home on the ranch, she'd given up her apartment to her twin, Darby. He had been living in a cabin not far from the bar, but he'd jumped at the chance to live upstairs.

Now she glanced toward the back window. The curtains were some she'd left when she'd moved out. One of them flapped in the wind. Darby must have left the window open. She hadn't been up there to see what he'd done with the place. She wasn't sure she wanted to know since she'd moved most everything out, leaving it pretty much a blank slate. She thought it might still be a blank slate, knowing her brother.

Pushing open the back door into the bar kitchen, she was met with the most wonderful of familiar scents. Fortunately, not everything had changed in her life, she thought, her mood picking up some as she entered the warm café kitchen.

"Tell me those are your famous enchiladas," she said to Billie Dee, their heavy-set, fiftysomething Texas cook.

"You know it, sugar," the cook said with a laugh. "You want me to dish you up a plate? I've got homemade pinto beans and some Spanish rice like you've never tasted."

"You mean *hotter* than I've ever tasted."

"Oh, you Montanans. I'll toughen you up yet."

Lillie laughed. "I'd love a plate." She pulled out a chair at the table where the help usually ate in the kitchen and watched Billie Dee fill two plates.

"So how are the wedding plans coming along?" the cook asked as she joined her at the table.

"I thought a simple wedding here with family and friends would be a cinch," Lillie said as she took a bite of the enchilada. She closed her eyes for a moment, savoring the sweet and then hot bite of peppers before all the other flavors hit her. She groaned softly. "These are the best you've ever made."

"Bless your heart," Billie Dee said smiling. "I take it the wedding has gotten more complicated?"

"I can't get married without my father and who knows when he'll be coming out of the mountains."

Their father, Ely Cahill, was a true mountain man now who spent most of the year up in the mountains either panning for gold or living off the land. He'd given up ranching after their mother had died and had turned the business over to her brothers Hawk and Cyrus.

Their oldest brother, Tucker, had taken off at eighteen. They hadn't seen or heard from him since. Their father was the only one who wasn't worried about him.

"Tuck needs space. He's gone off to find himself. He'll come home when he's ready," Ely had said.

The rest of the family hadn't been so convinced. But if Tuck was anything like their father, they would have heard something from the cops. Ely had a bad habit of coming out of the mountains thirsty for whiskey—and ending up in their brother Sheriff Flint Cahill's jail. Who knew where Tuck was. Lillie didn't worry about him. She had four other brothers to deal with right here in Gilt Edge.

"I can see somethin's botherin' you," Billie Dee said now.

Lillie nodded. "Trask insists we wait to get married since he hopes to have the finishing touches on the house so we can have the reception there."

Trask, the only man she'd ever loved, had come back into her life after so many years that she'd thought she'd never see him again. But they'd found their way back together and now he was building a house for them on the ranch he'd bought not far from the bar.

"Waitin' sounds reasonable," the cook said between bites.

"I wish we'd eloped."

"Something tells me the wedding isn't the problem," Billie Dee said, using her fork to punctuate her words.

"I'll admit it's been hard giving up my apartment upstairs. I put so much love into it."

"Darby will take good care of it."

She couldn't help shooting a disbelieving look at Billie Dee. "He'll probably just throw down a bedroll and call it home. You know how he is. Have you seen what he's moved in so far?"

Billie Dee gave her a sympathetic look. "I know it was your baby, but once you took out your things, it didn't feel so much like yours, right?"

Lillie nodded. "Still, it was my home for so long. I thought maybe Darby might need my help decorating it."

The cook laughed. "I'd say 'decorating' is probably the last thing on his mind. So how is the new home?"

"Beautiful. Trask is great about letting me do whatever I want. But it still isn't like my apartment. I put so much of myself into that place. I miss it."

"And you will put so much of yourself into your home with Trask. It's going to take time. How long did it take you to get the apartment upstairs to your liking?"

"Years."

"Exactly." Billie Dee studied her for a moment. "You aren't gettin' cold feet about the weddin' and marryin' Trask, are you?"

"No." Lillie shook her head adamantly. "Never." She thought of the day when she and Trask would have a family and she wouldn't even be working at the bar anymore, but pushed that away. "I guess change is hard for me. I feel like I'm giving up the bar even though I'll still be half owner and still work until the babies come."

"Babies?"

"I'm not pregnant yet but Trask and I want a big family."

"So who is coming to your weddin'? I'm still waitin' for you to introduce me to some big, strong Montana cowboy," Billie Dee joked as she had often before. "I want one like Trask."

"Who doesn't?" Lillie said with a laugh. Trask was handsome as the devil, sweet, loving, wonderful. "Guess I'll have to rope you up one."

"I can do my own ropin', thank you very much. Just point me at one."

"You have someone in mind?"

"Might. Ain't tellin'." She gave Lillie a knowing wink.

"By the way, speaking of handsome cowboys,

where is Darby? I thought he'd be back by now from the festival." She'd barely gotten the words out when they heard a vehicle pull up under the tree next to the building where Darby always parked. A few moments later, her brother came in the back door, took a whiff and said, "Billie Dee's famous enchiladas."

She and the cook both laughed. "Don't worry. We left plenty for you and our customers tonight."

Darby tossed his hat onto the hook by the back door and hung up his keys on the board along with the extra keys to the bar and the upstairs apartment. Not that Lillie would need to use the spare key. She still had an apartment key on her keychain. She just hadn't used it.

"I was just asking Billie Dee if she'd seen what you've done with the apartment," Lillie said.

Her twin brother scoffed. "If you're so curious, go on up. But I warn you, you won't like it."

"Why?"

"Because I'm a firm believer in less is more."

She groaned. "You haven't done *anything*."

"I wouldn't say that. I have a bed, chest of drawers, the lamp you left me, the television you left me and a chair I bought for myself."

"That's it?"

"That's all I need, little sis." As he took off his jean jacket and hung it, Lillie heard something make a clinking sound in one of the pockets. He heard it too and reached into the pocket to pull out his cell phone and shove whatever had "clinked" deeper into the pocket.

He really was handsome, she thought as she studied her brother. A real catch for some woman. The problem was Darby. She got the feeling he was open to a relationship, but that he hadn't found a woman who interested him.

The cook motioned toward the stove. "Help yourself. But I thought you would have eaten at the festival."

"Wasn't hungry," he said, his back to them as he pocketed his phone and went to the stove to fill a plate.

Both women looked at him in stunned silence, then at each other. Darby was *always* hungry. He stayed too busy to gain weight, but there was never anything wrong with his appetite.

"You didn't even have any fry bread?" Lillie asked. "That doesn't sound like you."

He shrugged, still not looking at them.

She felt a stab of guilt for making him go to the festival. In truth, she could have covered it. But she thought he ought to start doing it since she didn't know how long she would be able to. She and Trask were planning to start a family right away.

"That was the only thing I was looking forward to," he said. "But the line was too long." He looked away.

Lillie wondered what her brother was leaving out.

He never missed a chance to have fry bread. "But otherwise everything went all right?"

"I said a few words. Tossed the T-shirts into the crowd and got out of there before I had to take part in the pit-spitting contest," he said as he stabbed a bite of enchilada. He mugged a face at her. "Did you know they were going to try to rope me into the pit spitting?"

She laughed. "No, but I would have paid money to see that." Still as she studied her twin, she got the feeling something had happened to upset her usually unflappable brother. She and Darby had always been close. They'd shared the same womb. But she couldn't put her finger on what it was about him that made her think he wasn't telling her everything.

"Did you run into our brothers while you were there?" she asked.

"Didn't see Hawk or Cyrus, but Flint was walking around looking like a Western lawman," Darby said.

"He *is* a Western lawman," Lillie said of her brother Sheriff Flint Cahill, the black sheep of the family. Flint had always played by the rules, while the rest of them had never minded bending the rules or the law. Now he followed the letter of the law. Needless to say, they often butted heads over it—especially when he arrested their father on those occasions when Ely came out of the mountains and had too much to drink.

"Hawk and Cyrus stopped by earlier," Billie Dee said as she got up to put her plate in the dishwasher.

"They said they were moving cattle today and skipping the festival and all that craziness. I asked if they were going to the dance tonight. No surprise, they weren't."

"They are going to stay old crotchety bachelors forever at this rate," Lillie said, and then she saw that her brother had stopped eating. He was picking at the spicy pinto beans distractedly, frowning as if his mind was miles away. Or maybe just back downtown where the festival was still going strong.

Lillie felt worse about making him take care of their promotion at the Chokecherry Festival. Now something was bothering him that hadn't been this morning before he'd left.

"Is everything all right?" she asked bringing him out of his trance.

Darby smiled, complimented Billie Dee on the food and dug back into his meal before he said, "Couldn't be better."

But she sensed that wasn't true. Something was definitely different about him.

SINCE HE AND Lillie had traded shifts today, Darby had the rest of the day off. He almost wished he was working though. At least that would help keep his mind off the woman at the festival.

"Thanks for dinner," he said to Billie Dee as he put his plate into the dishwasher. "You sure you can handle it tonight without me?" he asked his sister.

"It will be slow with everyone at the festival and street dance," she said. "I'll probably close early, but thanks for the offer. What are you going to do the rest of the day?"

He shrugged. "Probably just take it easy." Retrieving his Stetson and jacket, he headed upstairs, glad his sister hadn't asked to see what he'd done with her old apartment. As he unlocked the door and looked around, he admitted there wasn't much to see.

When it had been Lillie's, the place had such a homey feel. Now it was anything but. He'd bought a bed, taken his chest of drawers from his room at the ranch, complete with the stickers from his youth on the front, and found an old leather recliner at a garage sale.

Other than that, the apartment was pretty sparse. Fortunately, Lillie had left the curtains, the rug on the living room floor and a couple of lamps, along with a television. The place was definitely nicer than the old cabin he'd been living in before, so it was just fine with him. More than fine. He'd never needed much for creature comforts.

As he closed the door behind him, he felt bad though. He'd have to be a complete fool not to know that Lillie was dying to help him "decorate." He cringed at the thought. She'd fuss and bring in plants he'd forget to water, a bunch of pillows he wouldn't know what to do with and knickknacks he'd end up breaking. No, she had her big house on the ranch to do her magic on. He wouldn't bother her. At least that would be his excuse.

He hung up his hat and was about to do the same with his jean jacket when he remembered the bracelet. Taking it out, he turned it in his fingers. It was fancy looking enough. Heavier than it appeared too, the surface buffed to a rich patina. He brushed his fingertip over the round black stone on one side of the wide cuff bracelet. Probably plastic, the whole bracelet no doubt made out of some cheap metal and not worth anything. Otherwise why would the woman have to resort to stealing?

As he started to put it down, he noticed that the clasp was broken. It must have happened when he'd pulled it from her arm. With a start, he remembered the tan line on her wrist, a wide white patch of skin where her bracelet had been as she was hurrying into the crowd. Surprised, he realized this was a piece of jewelry she wore all the time. If it was nothing but cheap costume jewelry, then it must have sentimental value. He frowned, as curious about the bracelet as he was the woman who'd worn it.

His mind whirling, he looked at his phone to check the time. The local jewelry store was still open. If he went the back way and entered the store from the rear, he could avoid the crowds still on the main street.

There was, of course, a temptation to look again for the woman. But he told himself that she wouldn't have hung around. After what happened, wouldn't she be worried that he'd alert the sheriff about her?

Now that he thought of it, why hadn't he? What if she'd been picking pockets all day at the festival? He let out a groan, realizing that he'd been so captivated by her that he hadn't even thought about reporting her.

He didn't think she would try to pick anyone else's pocket after what had happened with him. More than likely, she'd expect him to notify the sheriff. If he was right, there would be no reason to look for her in the crowd because she would have left, thinking the law was looking for her.

Darby knew he was making excuses for not notifying his lawman brother. He'd been embarrassed by the whole incident. And yet he was still curious about the woman who'd worn the bracelet. Still curious and still shaken by the effect she'd had on him for that second when their eyes had met.

The piece looked unusual enough, he told himself. The fact that it must have been a favorite of hers piqued his interest even more. He stuffed the bracelet back into his jacket pocket and, Stetson on his head, headed for the door.

THE ELDERLY JEWELER put the loupe to his eye and slowly studied the bracelet Darby had handed him. "You say you picked it up at a garage sale?"

He wished now that he'd come up with a better story. "In Billings."

"Interesting."

Darby waited as jeweler John T. Marshall went over every square inch of the bracelet. "It's just costume jewelry, right, John?" No answer. The piece couldn't be *that* interesting, he thought.

John finally put the bracelet down along with the loupe. He shook his head, seemingly unable to take his eyes off the piece. "It's not costume jewelry. It's fourteen-karat yellow gold."

That explained why it was so heavy. With a start, Darby realized it could have more than just sentimental value to the woman. "So what can you tell me about it?"

"The gold alone in weight is worth several thousand dollars, but its real worth is that it is a rare piece of vintage Roma jewelry."

"Roma jewelry?"

The jeweler nodded. "I've only read about it. This type of cuff was once made for the whole family including men and children, and was usually worn in pairs, one on each wrist. This bracelet is definitely rare."

"You're saying it's *old*?"

"In this country, most surviving pieces date from 1900 to 1930." He picked up the loupe again to look at the round black stone at the center. "The Roma almost always used synthetic stones because of the difficulties of verifying a gemstone's authenticity, unlike real gold, which cannot be faked easily."

"So the stone is what? Plastic?"

"In this rare case, a valuable gemstone—onyx. This is an amazing find. I've never seen any original Roma jewelry before. It's quite remarkable." He picked up the bracelet again and began to point out the designs on it.

"Look at this profiled face of a beautiful woman, possibly a Roma queen."

"What exactly is Roma?" Darby asked.

"Often called Gypsy jewelry. The word *Gypsy* is a misnomer though. The Roma were called Gypsies because they were believed to have come from Egypt. But they were actually part of an ethnic group whose ancestors left India a thousand years ago. Many of them still called themselves gypsies, though many Roma consider it a derogatory term."

Darby thought of the woman he'd seen at the festival. Was she Roma?

The jeweler was still inspecting the bracelet with a kind of awe. "Flowers and stars are common, along with a horseshoe for luck. It is always worn with the horseshoe up so the luck doesn't spill out." He traced a finger over one of the designs. "The filigree is so delicate." He met Darby's gaze. "I'd say this bracelet is worth from ten to twenty thousand dollars."

Darby was taken aback. He'd almost thrown the piece away. Worse, he hadn't picked it up at a garage sale. He'd torn if off a woman's wrist—admittedly she was trying to pick his pocket at the time, but still...

"And you say you paid fifty cents for it? The person who sold it must not have known its real worth." John shook his head. "If you're interested in selling this piece—"

"No," he said quickly. "If it's that rare, I think I'd like to keep it. But I do want to get the clasp fixed."

The jeweler nodded. "I don't blame you. It will only take a minute."

Darby stepped to the back of the shop to watch as John worked. He couldn't believe this. He'd really thought the jeweler would tell him it was nothing but junk. He thought about the woman who'd been wearing it and found himself even more intrigued.

"It's a shame how much of this jewelry has been lost," the jeweler was saying as he worked. "Much of it was melted down in the Great Depression, even more recently with the price of gold up like it has been. For the wearer, the jewelry was like a portable bank account."

So why hadn't the woman sold it if her situation was dire enough that she had to steal? Or was it possible that, like him, she'd underestimated its value since maybe she'd stolen it herself?

"You are wise to keep this," John was saying. "According to superstition, Roma jewelry is very good luck to have, but bad luck to sell. You wouldn't want to sell off your good fortune, now, would you?"

CHAPTER TWO

AFTER A NIGHT of weird dreams, Darby had awakened, his heart racing as if the woman had been in the room with him. He'd half expected the bracelet to be gone—the whole episode at the Chokecherry Festival only a figment of his imagination.

But there sat the bracelet on his bedside table where he'd left it last night—proof that the woman had been real. The sun gleamed off the gold—and the round dark circle of onyx. It gave him a small thrill at the same time it sent a chill up his spine. He felt like a thief. He'd taken the woman's very expensive bracelet. Worse, last night in his dream she'd confronted him, accusing him of stealing her luck—and, in her fury, had put a curse on him.

Shaking off the dream and the guilt, he reminded himself that she'd been the one trying to steal from him. That rationale didn't help that much as he stepped into the shower. The warm water chased away the remnants of the dream, leaving him feeling a little better.

He knew why he couldn't get her off his mind. The woman had been mysterious and exhilarating.

He reminded himself that he was talking about a thief. But for too long he'd felt antsy, as if he needed a change, but he couldn't bear the thought of leaving his sister alone to run this place.

He'd thought he needed a change of scenery, but maybe it had been something else entirely. This morning he felt amped up as if he'd been hit with a jolt of electricity that had awakened something deep inside him. He felt…different. And all because of a woman he'd seen in passing. A thief who could have been using one of his credit cards right now if he hadn't grabbed her to talk to her. He let out a laugh. Talk about luck…

With a sudden chill, he glanced at the bracelet.

What if it *was* cursed?

That made him laugh at his own foolishness as he dressed and went downstairs. It was hours before the bar opened, but he felt even more restless than usual. Needing fresh air, he raised the windows and even propped open the front door. This was Montana—the only place to be this time of year since the temperature was as perfect as it could be.

He breathed in the mountain air scented with pines and rushing creek water and felt as if he'd been given a shot of vitamin B. Still, at the back of his mind he debated what to do with the bracelet as he busied himself washing bar glasses.

If only it was just costume jewelry. He would toss it in the trash and put the whole episode behind him. And yet, he didn't want to put it behind him. He wanted to savor that excitement even as he felt it slipping away.

Engrossed in this work and his thoughts, he didn't hear her. Nor did he pick up the scent of her perfume. Instead, he sensed her and looked up to find the woman standing in the open doorway of his bar like an apparition.

At the sight of her, the soap-slick glass slipped from his hand. Without looking, he caught it with his other hand before the glass shattered in the sink.

"Good hands," the woman said from the doorway, sunlight spilling around her, making her appear ethereal. But there was nothing angelic about her from her obsidian black hair that was loosely braided over one shoulder to the mystery behind her dark eyes as she stepped in.

His tongue felt rooted to the roof of his mouth for a moment. "Thanks." He had thought that he'd never see her again. But now he realized how foolish that had been. The bracelet was worth too much money for her to simply walk away from it. But the realization that she'd tracked him down sent a chill up his spine to raise the fine hairs at the back of his neck.

His gaze moved from her face to her wrist and the band of pale skin where the gold cuff had been. She wore jeans, biker boots and a black leather jacket. With a start, he recognized the T-shirt beneath the jacket. Stagecoach Saloon. One he'd thrown to the crowd yesterday?

Seeing his apparent interest in her T-shirt, she opened her jacket wider and smiled. "Nice place you have here," she said as she sidled up to the bar.

That's when he noticed the backpack slung over her shoulder. He wouldn't have been surprised to find out there was a gun inside it. Or that she was about to pull it on him.

"Thanks." He fought to rein in his pulse as he waited for her to get down to the business of her visit since they both knew what it was. She had come for her bracelet. He didn't have to wonder too long how she'd found him. He'd hit her with one of the T-shirts promoting the place. Maybe the one she was wearing right now.

He waited for her to ask, though, curious how she was going to explain taking his wallet. "We don't open until eleven," he said, finding he had to fill the deathly quiet that had fallen over the bar.

Tantalizing whiffs of her citrusy perfume drifted to him as she set her backpack on a stool and slipped onto the one next to it. She was taller than he remembered, slimmer, but no less striking. As she looked at him, he caught a flash of something at her neck. A gold pendant lay against her glowing olive skin. In its middle was a dark circle of black onyx—just like the one on the bracelet.

As she crossed her long legs and reached into a

side pocket of her backpack, he put down the glass in his hand, slowly dried his hands and waited, the baseball bat he kept behind the bar within reach.

"I was hoping you might have a job opening," she said as she took out a tube of lip gloss and applied it to the deep pink of her full lips.

Darby stared at her for a moment, uncomprehending. *"You want a job?"*

She gave him an amused look before she glanced around the bar, taking it in with a professional air. "I have experience."

He just bet she did. Was it possible she didn't remember him from yesterday? He certainly remembered her. No, he thought, she knows exactly what she's doing. "Experience? As what? Bartender, waitress, barmaid?"

Her gaze settled on him with an intensity that made his pulse jump. "All three." She said it with such confidence that he had to call her on it. Most of his patrons ordered a draft beer, a glass of wine or possibly a margarita. Every once in a while, someone would order something more upmarket, but that didn't mean he didn't know his cocktails or how to make them.

"Great," he said. "Step behind the bar and make me a…mojito."

She laughed, a pleasant tinkling sound that filled the empty room. "You call that a challenge?" she said, slipping off the stool to come around the end of the bar, forcing him to move down a few feet.

He watched as she nimbly picked up a clean glass, spun it in her fingers and reached for the fresh mint he had growing in the window. She adroitly used a pestle to muddle the mint to release its flavors, then added sugar and fresh lime juice, squeezing the lime with one hand as she poured rum with the other.

She didn't measure the alcohol but he could see that it was dead on. Just like the soda water she added as well as the ice. As she poured the mixture into a shaker and gave it a few hard shakes, her gaze returned to him. Bartenders hated mojitos because they were time consuming, but she'd managed to make it in no time without even one misstep.

He watched her pour the drink into a glass, add the slice of lime garnish as well as another mint leaf, and set it on a bar napkin in front of him.

Her questioning gaze rose to his. "Aren't you going to try it?"

"I don't drink."

She cocked her head at him, surprise in her expression.

At the sound of car doors slamming, they both turned as three twentysomething females came in. "Is it too early to get a drink?" one of them called out.

He started to say they didn't open for another hour or two, when he felt her touch his arm. She motioned the women in with, "We don't open for a while, but I could make you something."

She moved to take their orders, performing the

task with such efficiency that he couldn't help but be impressed. He noticed that she also had a way with the customers. She was a born con artist, he thought, reminding himself how they'd met and what was at stake. She was only here for her bracelet.

The smartest thing he could do was to go upstairs, get her bracelet and send her on her way.

"So do I have the job?" she asked as she came back down the bar to where he stood.

Was that the way they were going to play this? He couldn't help but be intrigued. His earlier feeling of excitement had reached a fevered pitch. He was having fun and enjoying himself.

She picked up the wet cloth, wrung it out, wiped down the bar and turned to look at him. Those dark eyes were killer. As his blood suddenly ran cold, he reminded himself that this woman could be something more dangerous than a pickpocket.

And yet, he knew he was looking at the most exciting woman he'd ever met. His heart pounded. His skin tingled. His pulse thrummed under his skin. This woman fascinated him and that was no small matter. All he could wonder was how far she would take this.

No way was this one of those stranger-than-fiction coincidences. She'd come here with only one thing in mind. Getting her bracelet back. So why not waltz in here and simply demand it?

Because, he thought as he looked into her eyes,

she preferred subterfuge. She was a game player, and this was one game she apparently thought she could win. The woman had grit, he'd give her that.

His every instinct told him not to do it. "You want a job?" he repeated, knowing he'd be a damned fool to hire her. He'd have to watch her all the time to make sure she didn't carry off the place. Or cut his throat in the middle of the night.

"You won't be sorry."

He wouldn't bet on that. "I can only offer you four days a week, but no promises," he said, telling himself he was taking one hell of a risk. "Let's just see how it goes. Swing by tomorrow before noon and you can fill out the paperwork and start the next day."

"Mariah Ayers," she said holding out her hand.

"Darby Cahill." He felt a jolt as he took her warm, silken hand in his. Her grip was strong, self-assured—just like her.

She smiled, her eyes glittering with challenge.

The game had begun. As he let go of her hand, he feared he was a poor opponent compared to her. But at the same time, he felt as if he'd been waiting for this—for her—his whole life. *Bring it on*, he said to himself as he returned her smile. He felt more alive than he had in years.

MARIAH'S HEART THUNDERED as she walked out of the bar. She'd done it. There was no doubt that he'd recognized her right away. She'd seen it in his gray eyes—and his reaction. But he'd still hired her. Either the man was a fool or crazy like a fox. Or both.

She kept her back straight, her head high, knowing that he would be watching her from the window. With practiced ease, she swung a leg over her motorcycle, adjusted her backpack and kick-started the engine. It rumbled under her, throaty and loud just the way she liked it. She hit first gear and took off in a cloud of dust and exhaust. She desperately wanted to look back, knowing the cowboy would be there watching her, wondering what she was up to.

Instead, she concentrated on the narrow paved road that curved through the rolling hills toward town. She hadn't gone far when she saw the for-rent sign. Unfortunately she'd been going too fast to get to a stop in time.

She hit the skids, sliding a little as she got the motorcycle stopped and turned around to go back. The bike throbbed as she slowly pulled in front of the old log cabin—and the for-rent sign. Shutting the engine, she climbed off and peered into one dusty window.

The cabin was what some might call rustic. She called it cheap and quickly dialed the number printed under For Rent. The call was answered on the third ring.

"I'm inquiring about the cabin you have for rent, the one outside of town on the Maiden Canyon road. What are you asking for it?" She listened. "I'd like it. How soon can I move in?" She frowned and stepped to the door. Just as the woman on the other end of the line had said, the key was under a rock by the door. "I'm new to the area but I just took a job at the Stagecoach Saloon."

Mariah listened to the woman go on about how nice Lillie and Darby Cahill were, how good the food was and how convenient the cabin's location would be for her.

She interrupted her to ask, "Do you take cash?"

"YOU HIRED ANOTHER WAITRESS?" Lillie asked, frowning as she perused the schedule and then her brother.

He kept his gaze elsewhere. "With things picking up this time of year, I thought we could use her. She'll work the nights I work and Kendall will work with you."

Lillie's eyebrows shot up. Since Kendall Raines had been hired, Lillie had hoped that her brother would ask the woman out. She was blonde, blue-eyed, cute as a button, a great waitress and loved by everyone. Well, almost everyone. When asked, Darby had said she wasn't his type. Kendall was every red-blooded American man's type.

"Has Kendall done something wrong?" she asked, afraid whatever had happened, that Darby planned to let her go. "You do realize she is a favorite around here. If she leaves—"

"Nothing happened. I don't want to lose Kendall

either. I just want to give this woman who came in looking for a job a chance."

Lillie realized her brother hadn't made eye contact once. She studied him openly for a long moment. "Why do I feel like there is something you aren't telling me?"

He chuckled as he came over to take the schedule from her and put it back on the wall of the kitchen. "Because you have a suspicious mind."

"True," she admitted.

"Did I see the old man's Jeep parked in front of his cabin?" Darby asked frowning. "I thought he was still up in the mountains." Most of the time, when their father came down, he headed straight for the bar and trouble. That's how they found out he was in town—their brother Flint would call her to let her know so she could bail him out.

"I haven't seen him." The whole family was worried about Ely. Flint was convinced their father was losing his mind, although most people in the county thought he'd lost it years ago. Ely still claimed that in 1967 he was abducted by aliens.

What made Ely's claim more terrifying was what was hidden underground in the back pasture of the Cahill Ranch. The alleged abduction had taken place near one of the more than two hundred missile silos that sat in the middle of farm and ranch land across Montana. Back in the late 1950s, Flint's grandfather had signed over a two-acre plot of land in the middle of his ranch to the US government in perpetuity for national defense.

The US Air Force buried a thousand Minuteman missiles three stories deep in ranch land just like theirs. A missile, which was on constant alert and capable of delivering a 1.2 megaton nuclear warhead to a target in thirty minutes, was still buried in their backyard. The program was called MAD, mutually assured destruction.

On the night Ely claimed he was abducted by aliens, the Air Force reported seeing a UFO hovering over several of the missile silos—including the one on the Cahill Ranch. Suddenly the missiles began to shut down, going off alert. It caused a panic with the military but no one had known about it until years later when the information was declassified.

A few months ago Ely had sworn something was going on at the missile silo.

"Maybe I'll swing by Dad's place later after work," Darby said.

Lillie saw that her brother was purposely trying to change the subject. Did he really think he could distract her that easily? "So this Mariah Ayers you hired, what is she like?"

"She's…" He seemed at a loss for words for a moment. "You'll see for yourself. She's coming in tomorrow to fill out the paperwork."

"Where is she from?" Lillie asked.

"I didn't ask."

"Well, you must have asked about her other jobs."

"Actually, I didn't. I had her make me a drink. A mojito."

"You don't drink."

"It wasn't for me," he said, turning to look at her with impatience. "I wanted to see if she was as good as she said she was. She was."

"Hmm," Lillie said, still eyeing him suspiciously. This wasn't like him. He was the one who asked a lot of questions when hiring anyone. So what was different this time? "I can't wait to meet her."

CHAPTER THREE

MAGGIE THOMPSON RAKED her fingers through the teenager's long hair, looking for a spot she might have missed before picking up her scissors again.

The girl wasn't paying any attention. She was on her phone texting and had been since she'd walked in the door. Next to her at the only other chair in the shop, Daisy Caulfield, her other stylist, was visiting with a regular, Irma Tinsley.

Maggie drew out each side of the teen's hair, eyeballing the lengths colored a bright pink. Last week it was purple. Before that, green.

She'd begun cutting her friends' hair at the age of eleven. Now at thirty-three, sometimes she felt as if she could do it in her sleep. She snipped a little more before putting down her scissors and picking up her blow dryer.

"Don't need to dry it," Astoria "Tori" Clark said, already slipping out of the chair before Maggie could turn on the blow dryer. "I've got to go. My mom called with the credit card number, right?" she said over her shoulder.

"She did," Maggie said, but not before the girl was gone.

"There a fire somewhere?" Daisy asked from the next chair, where Irma was getting foil pulled out from her highlights.

"I don't understand this new generation," the elderly Irma said. "Did you see her, thumbs just a flying on that phone of hers. What in the world does she have to talk about nonstop?"

Maggie laughed. "It's the way to communicate now."

"First they did away with teaching cursive writing in schools," Irma said. "Next it will be diagramming sentences."

Daisy laughed. "I think they've already done away with that."

"See what I mean? And you call that communicating?"

As she began to sweep up around her station, Maggie realized that she'd never seen Irma so worked up.

"People don't talk to each other anymore, let alone write more than a tweet or a text or some fool thing. When I think of the wonderful letters my husband wrote me—" She stopped abruptly as if choking on her words.

Maggie stopped sweeping to look over at the woman. "Irma?"

The elderly woman was in tears. "I'm sorry. It's

just… You probably haven't heard. My house was broken into. Not much was taken because I don't keep valuables there. But the letters from my husband… they were in a jeweled box of my grandmother's."

"The thieves took it?" Daisy said, stopping pulling foil from the woman's hair to stare at her in the mirror. Her gaze was full of sympathy. The more Maggie learned about her employee, the more she suspected the young woman was a true romantic.

Irma nodded. "It broke my heart. I would have rather they have taken my mother's pearls." She touched the strand at her neck. "But the thieves didn't even know that the pearls were worth money while the jeweled box will be next to impossible to pawn and the letters only mean something to me." She shook her head.

"I'm so sorry, Irma," Maggie and Daisy said almost in unison.

"Oh, the letters aren't gone exactly," the elderly woman said, brightening. Irma was one of those people who looked for silver linings. "I've read them so many times that I have them memorized. Still, it's not the same, you know."

"The sheriff will find out who took them and they'll be punished," Daisy said. "Maybe they won't have gotten rid of the letters."

Irma smiled up at Daisy and reached back to pat the younger woman's hand resting on the back of the chair. "Thank you, dear."

Maggie finished sweeping up as her next client came in. She was glad she didn't have time to think about Irma's loss—or Sheriff Flint Cahill. She just hoped Daisy was right and Flint would find the thieves—and the letters.

Even the thought of Flint though made her heart ache. They'd dated for a while and were getting serious when... She shook her head, refusing to even think about what—*who*—had broken them up because it made her so angry. She'd had a crush on Flint from as far back as she could remember. But then he'd married. Even after his divorce, Maggie hadn't thought there was any hope that he might notice her. When he did...

It hurt too much to think about. She missed him and couldn't help but wonder if he ever thought of her, as she greeted her next client.

FLINT KNELT DOWN next to the footprints in the soft earth outside the window.

"I'd say that's how the little bastards got in," Undersheriff Mark Ramirez said behind him. Mark had taken the call and was still angry, Flint could tell.

"You took photos of the shoe prints?" he asked, knowing that his undersheriff would have taken care of it, but still double-checking.

"Nothing distinct about the tracks unfortunately. Looks like new tennis shoes, no unusual wear, hardly any wear at all, actually, on either of the two pairs of shoes. Interesting, but there must be dozens of tennis shoes like them, right? But from the size, I'd say two kids."

Flint figured the same thing. When the first couple of houses had been broken into, he'd thought it was just kids up to pranks since the only things that were taken were alcohol and junk food.

"Sandra's sure nothing other than her iPad was taken?" Flint asked.

Mark nodded. "She doesn't keep money or jewelry in the house. Doesn't even normally lock her door, but she knew she was going to be gone for the night…"

Flint rose and studied the rough edge of the screen where it had been cut—rather than torn like the second break-in—allowing access into a spare bedroom. "Who all knew she was going to be gone for the night?"

His undersheriff frowned. "I'll ask her if she mentioned it to anyone. But you know how this town is. Everyone knows everyone else's business."

Flint nodded and stepped away from the window. This was the fourth break-in in a matter of days. The first one had been during daylight hours. The burglars had gone through the screen door into the kitchen and taken a six-pack of beer, some candy bars and a bag of potato chips. The second one was more of the same except that a screen had been torn out of a window to allow access.

"It's got to be the same ones, don't you think?" Mark said.

Flint nodded again. What disturbed him was that for this one the thieves had broken in through a window at night and, as at Irma Tinsley's, the thieves had taken more than snacks.

BACK AT THE Stagecoach Saloon the next day, Mariah took a seat at one of the tables in the corner to fill out the paperwork Darby had given her.

She could feel his gaze on her, a mixture of curiosity, puzzlement and worry. She smiled to herself. He *should* be worried. But given that, why had he hired her?

"Not sure what to put down for my address," she said, looking up at him to catch him staring at her. He quickly glanced away, adding to her amusement.

Last night, after she'd moved into the old cabin, she'd stood outside staring up at the stars and questioning what she was doing here. The smart thing to do was to keep moving. The thought made her smile since being a nomad was in her Romani genes. And like her ancestors, her reasons were much the same. She had to keep ahead of her past and the people who wanted to destroy her.

"I'm staying in that cabin down the road. I don't think it has an address."

Darby looked surprised. "That's where I was staying up until recently. Now I live upstairs here." He stopped as if he hadn't meant to be that forthcoming. "Unless you need to get mail, you can leave that blank. I will need a forwarding address when you leave, though."

She smiled. "Don't you mean *if* I leave?"

He nodded. "Right."

She finished and took the papers with her social security number on them over to him, pulling up a stool.

He looked through them, stopping occasionally to glance up at her. "You don't stay long at any one place."

Mariah shrugged. "Maybe I'm looking for the place I want to settle down."

"Apparently you haven't found it yet."

"No," she agreed. "But I like it here so far."

"Guess we'll see how you feel in a few days," Darby said.

"Guess we will." She slid off the stool. "So, you sure you don't want me to start tonight?"

"No, my sister, Lillie, is working along with our other barmaid and waitress, Kendall Raines."

The words were barely out of his mouth when a dark-haired beauty with her brother's gray eyes came in from the kitchen. Those gray eyes widened when she saw Mariah.

"You must be our new waitress," the young woman said, holding out her hand as she stepped to Mariah. "Lillie Cahill," she said, smiling as she shook her hand. There was more than interest in her inquiring gaze.

"Mariah Ayers." They were about the same height and close in age. She felt a connection that surprised her. Another strong, determined woman. Mariah didn't have her grandmother's clairvoyance, but still she could tell that Lillie was very protective of her brother.

"I was surprised to hear my brother had hired someone," Lillie was saying. "But he said he was impressed with your skills."

"Did he?" she asked, raising a brow as she shot Darby a look. With amusement, she saw that the cowboy looked as if he wanted to throttle his sister.

"And he already gave you a Stagecoach Saloon T-shirt."

"Actually, I picked this one up at the Chokecherry Festival yesterday," Mariah said.

"Lucky you." Lillie cut her eyes to her brother. "So is that where you two met?"

Mariah smiled at Darby and waited.

"We might have crossed paths at the festival," the cowboy said. "But we didn't meet until yesterday when she came in looking for a job."

"What a coincidence," Lillie said, still studying her brother and no doubt wondering why he looked flustered. "And so lucky we had an opening."

"Lucky for all of us," Mariah said.

She told herself that this would be fun for the short

time it would last and then she'd be gone again. She couldn't stay long in any one place. Not if she hoped to stay a step ahead of her past.

"I see you didn't put down a cell phone number in case I need to call you," Darby said to her as he busied himself with her paperwork again.

"If you need me, you know where I live," she said. "Otherwise, I'll be here."

They all turned as a blonde, blue-eyed young woman wearing jeans, a Stagecoach Saloon T-shirt and boots came in. The blonde stopped as if she thought she might be interrupting something.

"Kendall, this is Mariah, our new alternate waitress. Kendall Raines, Mariah Ayers."

Kendall frowned. "Oh." She took a few steps forward to shake Mariah's hand. "I didn't know you were thinking about hiring another waitress."

"She'll work my schedule," Darby said, making Kendall raise a brow.

"With the busy season ahead, it will give us all more flexibility," Lillie said, clearly bailing her brother out.

Mariah watched the interactions with interest. Her hiring had shaken things up around here. Kendall didn't look pleased. Was there something going on between the young waitress and the cowboy?

She met Darby's gaze, saw his disinterest in Kendall Raines and was surprised. Apparently he didn't go for cute, blonde and blue-eyed. She realized she liked him better because of it and quickly she reminded herself why she was here. Also she warned herself that this wasn't some easy mark. This cowboy was on to her. He'd caught her red-handed at the festival and yet he hadn't gone to the law. Why was that? More to the point, what happened now?

He'd be watching her, that was a given. He probably expected her to steal from the cash register like a common thief. He had to know that she was here for her bracelet. But he wasn't about to just hand it over, was he? She got the feeling he was waiting to see how far she would go to get it back.

Clearly, he was waiting for her to make the next move. She didn't plan on disappointing him, she thought as she flashed him a smile and saw his eyes narrow.

DARBY SADDLED UP his horse, anxious to clear his head. After Mariah had left the saloon, he'd felt too antsy to stay upstairs in the apartment. And there was no way he was going to hang out at the bar. His sister wouldn't shut up about the new hire. She was more curious about Mariah than he was—and that was saying a lot.

He swung up into the saddle and reined the steed toward the rolling foothills past the ranch. He'd been riding horses since he was a year old, but he hadn't taken to it like Lillie—until recently.

This feeling of being closed-in had been bothering

him for a while. He'd been so excited about opening the Stagecoach Saloon with Lillie. That had kept him busy for a while. After it was a success, though, he'd felt antsy again as if uncomfortable in his own skin.

"You need a woman," their cook Billie Dee had told him one day when he'd paced around the kitchen for no good reason.

"What?" Her words had taken him by surprise.

"Your symptoms. I've seen them before. Anxious, bored, unhappy, restless. Haven't you realized you're missin' somethin'?"

He'd shaken his head. "I'm fine."

Billie Dee had given him one of her don't-try-to-con-me looks. "You're going to need a special woman, the way I see it. Someone who challenges you. Someone who keeps you on your toes. Someone who puts the light back into those eyes of yours." She'd looked remorseful. "Haven't seen her yet, but if I do, I'll send her your way."

He'd told himself Billie Dee didn't know what she was talking about. But sometimes he thought he couldn't breathe until he was out here—away from everything. He'd look to the horizon and want to just keep riding off into the sunset as if the answer was just over that next mountain.

Fortunately, he was smart enough to know that the grass wasn't always greener over that next mountain or even up the road. Until he'd seen Mariah at the

Chokecherry Festival, he'd thought the last thing he needed for his malady was a woman.

Now all he could think about—even on horseback and away from it all—was Mariah. It was like she had put a curse on him.

When she'd shown up at the bar, looking for a job, he'd been amused. He'd actually wondered if it was a joke.

But when he'd realized she was serious, he saw it as a contest. He'd hired her out of curiosity, telling himself he was up for a game. What had he set himself up for? He could never trust her. Instead, he'd have to watch her like a hawk otherwise she might try to rob them blind.

He had a crazy thought. What if she turned out to be the perfect employee? He chuckled at that. He'd be surprised if she even made it a week. Maybe even less than that. Hell, she was probably upstairs in his apartment right now taking anything of value—and looking for her bracelet.

He was glad he'd moved it. Let her ask for it back. Let her apologize for trying to steal his wallet. Then, and only then would he hand the bracelet over.

At least that's what he told himself as he rode up through the ponderosa pines. They shimmered in the afternoon sun, a silken green. The air had that smell of summer that he loved in the mountains. The peace and quiet should have lulled him, should have silenced his thoughts about anything but the beauty of the place.

He reined in at the top of the rise and breathed in the warm spring air, trying to find the contentment he'd always found here. Montana's big sky was a clear blinding blue with only a few clouds huddling on the horizon. He smiled. It had been a beautiful eventful day. He felt…good.

The thought made him laugh. He knew why he felt like this. Mariah. She was enigmatic, exhilarating, enthralling…dangerous.

What had he been thinking hiring her? If Lillie found out the truth… He'd opened the door to this stranger, knowing what kind of woman she was.

No, he corrected himself. He didn't know just how dangerous she could be—but he might find out the hard way. He knew he had to try to find out everything he could about her before it was too late. He couldn't jeopardize the saloon because of some silly infatuation with an outlaw. Even one as beautiful as Mariah Ayers.

And yet as he started back toward the ranch, he couldn't wait until tomorrow when he and Mariah would work together for the first time. His heart began to pound. He kicked his horse into a gallop. He liked flirting with danger. He only hoped it didn't get him robbed—or worse—killed.

CHAPTER FOUR

THE NEXT DAY, Darby heard the rumble of Mariah's motorcycle coming up the road. He glanced at his watch. She was early for her first shift.

He had to admit he was a little surprised she'd taken the ruse as far as she had. He'd thought that once she had her foot in the door—knew he lived upstairs over the bar—she would break in and take the bracelet. If she could find it.

Because of that, he'd taken it off his bedside table and hidden it in a place he thought she'd never think to look. He told himself she could have it back anytime. All he wanted was for her to ask for it—and to give him some kind of explanation. In truth, he knew that as long as he had the bracelet, Mariah Ayers wasn't going anywhere and he liked that for now.

Last night, though, he'd lain in bed waiting for her. He'd opened the windows and left the back door unlocked, and then he'd lain awake, listening for the sound of her motorcycle in the distance until he'd fallen into a restless sleep and awakened with a start at the sound of the back door slamming.

His heart had taken off at a gallop, thinking it was

Mariah. Instead, he realized it was morning and the sound he'd heard was Billie Dee coming in early to get her lunch menu planned.

Now, showered and ready, he stood behind the bar, waiting for Mariah to park her bike and come in the back door. He actually felt nervous. When he felt a draft from the back door being opened, he waited for the sound of Mariah's voice. Instead, he heard Lillie's.

What was *she* doing here? As if he had to ask. She'd come in because this was Mariah's first day. He shook his head. What did she think? That he would hire someone just because she was a beautiful woman?

"I see you're ready for work," Lillie said as she slipped up on a stool. "Just heard Mariah pull in. Is that motorcycle her only means of transportation?"

"I wouldn't know." But he suspected it was.

"Going to make it hard to commute come winter—if she's still here," his sister said.

He didn't take the bait. "We mostly need her for this summer and fall so it should be fine."

She was eyeing him again as if trying to see into his brain—or was it his heart?

"What are *you* doing here?" he asked, sounding more irritated than he meant to.

"Can't a loving sister stop by the business she owns with her loving brother?"

"You and I both know why you're here," he whispered as he heard Mariah come in the back door. He hurried off to introduce her to Billie Dee, but when he reached the kitchen, the two were already in deep conversation about cooking.

"This girl knows her hush puppies," Billie Dee said with a laugh as she turned back to the stove.

"We were talking about those little round cornmeal dough balls they'd cook and toss to puppies," Mariah said.

"I know what hush puppies are." He sounded even more irritable.

"Sorry, you were frowning at me so I thought you were confused." A smile played at the corners of her mouth. "Rough night?"

He wasn't going there. "I just wanted to make sure you knew which locker was yours and check to see if you needed anything before your shift."

Mariah looked toward the metal lockers in the corner. "I'm betting the empty one without a name on it is mine."

He sighed.

"Thanks for trying to make me feel comfortable on my first day, really. But I have what I need." She indicated her backpack, the same one she'd brought with her that first day. The same one he thought might hold a gun. "Well, almost everything," she added and met his gaze.

"So have you ever had Texas gumbo?" Billie Dee was asking Mariah.

"With okra and tomatoes and big, fat shrimp in a rich brown file broth?"

The cook laughed. "You have been to Texas."

"I've been a lot of places."

Darby, seeing that Mariah was making herself at home, said to no one in particular, "I'll be in the bar."

"I DIDN'T ASK YOU what I should wear for work," Mariah said as she entered the bar a few minutes later. The cowboy looked as if he hadn't slept much last night. That should have made her feel better than it did. After all, she wasn't innocent in all this, was she?

"I went by what all of you were wearing yesterday. Is this okay?" Holding out her arms, she turned in a circle, knowing she looked good in the Stagecoach Saloon T-shirt and slim blue jeans that hugged her curves. From the look in Darby's eyes, he thought so too.

She'd pulled her wild mane of dark hair up and wrapped it with the colorful scarf she'd been wearing at the Chokecherry Festival. She couldn't miss that split second of recognition she saw on Darby's face. Like yesterday, she wore the pendant with the circle of black onyx in the center of the gold at her throat. It was something else that she never took off.

Her hand went to her bare wrist and she quickly pulled it back, the missing bracelet an ache. When she saw the cowboy looking at the pendant, she lifted it from her skin to turn it in her fingers. "You like it?"

"It's pretty. Onyx, right?"

She nodded, still running her fingertips over the stone. "My grandmother gave it to me. For luck. And," she said with a laugh, "to ward off the evil eye."

"The evil eye?" he repeated.

"I come from a very superstitious family. If you wrong someone they can put the evil eye on you. Once the curse is on you, well, it's almost impossible to get it removed. Often you take it to your grave. At least according to my grandmother. Just better to always wear the evil eye pendant to counteract evil."

"*Almost* impossible?" he said, looking as if he wasn't sure he believed any of what she was saying.

She laughed. "Do you have a curse you need removed?"

"Maybe."

"I'm afraid I can't help you. I should get to work," she said as a pickup pulled up out front.

"You can put your name on your locker," Darby said as if uncomfortable with the topic of curses. "You might want to get a lock for it if you're worried about someone taking your things."

She laughed. "Strange, but few people steal from a Romani. The consequences, you know…" She touched the pendant again. Her laugh echoed through the bar as she went to unlock the saloon's front door for their first customers.

FLINT STOPPED BY the clothing store—the only place in town that sold the type of tennis shoes that had left the tracks outside the latest crime scene. What made the tread unique other than the pattern on the bottom was that both pairs worn by the culprits appeared to come from brand-new shoes that showed no wear at all.

It didn't take him long to find the ones he was looking for. He was surprised by both the type of tennis shoe—and the price. But the biggest surprise was yet to come.

"Do boys buy these?" he asked the owner of the store.

"They're women's sneakers," she told him.

"Have you sold many of them?"

"They're really popular with teens."

"I need to know who in town has purchased them. Is that possible?"

The owner shook her head. "I wasn't here. Maybe the clerk might remember who bought them."

He was still processing the fact that his thieves were more than likely girls. "Is the clerk around?" he asked.

The owner hesitated before she said, "In the back helping with the shipment we got this morning. I suppose you could talk to her. If it doesn't take too long.

I have customers coming in. They've been waiting for some of the new dresses."

"I'll be brief," he promised as he grabbed one of the tennis shoes and stepped back into the employees-only area. It was dusty and a little dark back there, the area crammed with loaded shelves. He found a young woman tearing into a stack of boxes by the open back door.

"Sheriff?" Finn Marsh said in surprise as she looked up.

He hadn't realized she was back in town since, not only had he gone to school with her, she'd also dated his brother Hawk. "Finn, I didn't know you were working here."

"Again," she said ruefully. "Just like in high school."

He knew she'd gone away to college and gotten a job. He couldn't remember doing what. Strange that she was back, he thought. "I know you're busy. I just need to ask you if you remember selling three local girls these shoes?"

Finn smiled and nodded. "Funny you should ask. They bought them at the same time. The reason I remember is that Tori and Wendy used their mother's credit cards and the other girl paid with what looked like her piggy bank money—mostly small bills and coins. It was painful to watch."

"Is that unusual for a kid to pay with money they've saved?"

"No, but it was strange. I got the feeling that Tori and Wendy were forcing her to buy the shoes." Finn shook her head. "I know it sounds crazy, but I was thinking they might be bullying her since the girl wasn't one of them, you know what I mean?"

"Who was the girl?"

"Laralee Fraser."

He knew the Fraser family. The father was a truck driver on the road a lot. The mother took in laundry. The family barely scraped by. So what was Laralee doing buying expensive tennis shoes with Tori and Wendy? He didn't like the sound of this at all given that the shoe prints had turned up at three of the four break-ins. This sounded like the three were in some kind of cahoots. Or that the two were setting Laralee up to take the fall for the break-ins.

He thanked Finn and walked back up front to replace the tennis shoe he'd borrowed.

"I don't think they have those in your size," said a familiar female voice behind him. He turned to find his ex-wife, Celeste, smiling up at him.

One of the things that had attracted him to her in the first place was that she was adorable, from her button nose and her big green eyes to her bow-shaped mouth and her blond bob. Celeste had been a cheerleader, one of the popular girls in school, the girl most likely to marry well.

Her only misstep had been marrying him. But she'd rectified that by having an affair with Wayne

Duma, one of the movers and shakers in town. The now Mrs. Wayne Duma was the last person he wanted to see.

"Celeste."

"It's good to see you, Flint. I've been thinking about you a lot."

This was definitely not what he wanted to hear.

"I didn't like the way we left it, the last time we saw each other," she said, actually sounding nervous. But that, like so much of her, could be an act.

Keeping his voice down, he said, "The last time we saw each other, I made it clear I wanted nothing to do with you."

"I know you were angry—"

"Celeste, why can't you leave me alone?"

Her eyes filled with tears. "You really don't know?"

"I know you can't stand the thought that I might move on, might find some happiness with someone other than you."

"You can't think you'll find happiness with Maggie" She scoffed at the idea.

What had it been about Maggie that had made Celeste come after him again? He'd dated other women and Celeste hadn't seemed to care one way or another. But Maggie had set her off. Was it because she saw that he had true feelings for the woman?

"I'm not discussing this with you. I can be with anyone I want."

"But *Maggie*? She's so wrong for you."

He glanced toward the owner of the store, knowing she was probably listening to all of this. He lowered his voice. "It's none of your business, but I'm not seeing Maggie anymore."

Celeste looked as relieved as if he'd told her his cancer was in remission. "I think that's for the best."

He shook his head in disgust. "I don't care what you think. It's none of your damned business." He'd raised his voice again. Out of the corner of his eye, he saw the owner shoot them a glance.

"See, now you're getting angry again."

"Celeste." He wanted to wring the woman's neck. "Leave. Me. Alone. Stay out of my business. Stay out of my life." He turned and stormed out of the store, but he could feel her gaze boring into his back—along with that of the owner of the store.

Just saying Maggie's name made his heart hurt. He hadn't seen her for months—as badly as he'd wanted to. He couldn't explain it to himself. It wasn't because he still felt anything for Celeste other than a growing hatred and fear. Fear of what Celeste might do if he were to start seeing Maggie again.

The thought made him wonder if he was as crazy as his ex-wife. What did he think Celeste would do?

But look what she'd done in the past. Interrupted his last two dates with Maggie and come between them. He feared there was something terribly wrong with his ex-wife and he didn't want her near Maggie.

Or was that exactly what Celeste wanted him to

believe so she could control him and keep him away from the one woman he might find happiness with?

THE WORKDAY PASSED quickly since it was summer and the saloon was busy the whole time. Darby did his best to watch Mariah and still hold down the bar. What he did see was efficiency. She was even better at this than Kendall, which was saying a lot. He couldn't help being impressed.

"Do you have a tip jar behind the bar?" she asked as she handed over the money with her first order. Clearly she knew he didn't trust her and wanted to make sure every transaction was taken care of right away. She wasn't going to give him any reason to mistrust her.

When it got so busy even he was having trouble keeping up, Mariah came behind the bar and got her own beer and even helped make a couple of the more time-consuming drinks.

When he did have a moment to think, he thought about what she'd said about stealing from a Romani.

"You're really good at this," he said as the last patron left and he was able to bolt the door closed for the night and turn out all but the lights behind the bar.

"Thanks." She sighed as if tired. He knew *he* was. But she didn't look tired. She looked…beautiful. A lock of her dark hair had fallen down to curve around her high cheekbone. It made her eyes look even darker. For a moment, their gazes met. He felt his breath escape him. That feeling he'd had at the Chokecherry Festival of being shot through the heart was mild compared to this one. He was right. The woman had put a curse on him, he thought as he dragged his gaze away.

"Give me a minute and I can settle up with you on the tips."

"Don't worry about that tonight." Her voice was low, sultry in the empty bar, darkness deep against the windows. "But I would love a glass of wine. Red. Something cheap and sweet would be wonderful."

He laughed as he looked at her again. "I took you for something more exotic. Champagne, maybe."

"Really?" She moved with fluid grace to the bar, slid up on a stool and, dropping her elbows to the bar top, cupped her chin in her hands as she settled her gaze on him. "Was it my backpack with my entire life in it? Or my bike?"

"I haven't seen a bike like yours before."

"You know motorcycles?"

"I know horses, but I can appreciate a vintage bike like that," he said as he poured her a glass of wine and himself a diet cola.

"It was my father's. It has a 750 cc V-twin engine so it moves. Gets good gas mileage. I can go over three hundred miles on a tank of gas." She shrugged. "It gets me where I want to go."

"And where is that?" he asked, seeing her obvious love of the bike that had belonged to her father.

She smiled, lighting up the darkened saloon. "Wherever the road takes me."

"I'm envious." He could see it surprised her.

"But you have everything here."

Darby had to chuckle at that, remembering what Billie Dee had told him was wrong with him. "Not everything."

Mariah's eyes narrowed. "You really think you could get on a bike and just go and leave all of this behind?"

"Some days I definitely do. But then I remind myself that most places are pretty much the same. I don't think what I'm looking for is over that next hill."

She cocked her head, studying him. "What is it you're looking for?"

He shook his head and glanced away. "That's just it, I don't know. Excitement. Adventure. A challenge. Hitting the road like that sounds almost…"

"Romantic?" She scoffed. "It's not."

"What are *you* looking for?"

Mariah frowned. "I'm not. I'm just…going."

They drank in companionable silence for a while. It was a quiet dark night outside the saloon. Even the earlier traffic on the road had stopped. Darby felt as if they were the only two people left on Earth.

He kept thinking about what it would be like to

get on that motorcycle parked outside and just go. "Is there any place you haven't been?"

"A few." She shrugged as he refilled her glass and his own. She stared at the wine for a long moment and then, lifting the glass carefully, took a sip.

"You're right though," she said quietly. "Most every place is like another." When she raised her gaze, he saw sadness there.

"Earlier did you say you were a Romani?" he said, changing the subject. He hadn't wanted to make her sad. He loved her smile too much.

She nodded. "My grandmother was Romani and determined to keep the culture and traditions of her people. She came to this country as a young girl in the 1930s, hoping to find a better life." Mariah met his gaze. "She thought it was just a matter of luck. Unfortunately, she also believed there was a curse on our family."

"Even if you wear the evil eye necklace?" he asked, half joking.

Mariah smiled. "You don't believe in curses?"

"No, but lately…" He shook his head, sorry he'd brought it up as she finished her wine and slid off the barstool. He thought she might bring up the bracelet.

"I should get going. What do I owe you for the drinks?" She looked at him in a way that made his heart beat faster.

"It's on the house."

"Sleep well, then."

Her words brought a chill of both excitement and anxiety. Was she trying to warn him that tonight would be the night? "You too."

She started out but stopped in the kitchen doorway to turn as a vehicle roared past. Darby looked up from behind the bar to find Mariah silhouetted against the kitchen light. He stared at her profile with both shock and admiration.

The image of the Roma Queen on the bracelet. Mariah looked exactly like her before she stepped outside into the darkness.

CHAPTER FIVE

MARIAH PACED THE small cabin. She should have finished this days ago and moved on. Staying in one place was dangerous—even in such a small town so out of the way in a remote part of Montana.

Her first week at the Stagecoach Saloon had gone by in a blur. Each day, she told herself that she needed to get her bracelet and move on. Each day, she found another excuse not to do what had to be done.

These nights working with Darby… She shook her head. The work kept her busy. It was afterward, after they closed the bar, when they visited over something to drink. When they talked. When she looked into the cowboy's gray eyes…

Shaking her head now, she told herself that she didn't like the way being here made her feel. She didn't like the way Darby made her feel. Had she forgotten how dangerous all this was—and not just for her?

Mariah stopped in front of the cabin window that looked out on the rolling hills and the town of Gilt Edge in the distance. What *am* I still doing here?

What if Darby had gotten rid of the bracelet? Just tossed it out like a piece of junk? Or had it appraised and sold it? That was another possibility.

Why don't you just ask him for it?

She knew that was what he was waiting for. Was that why she hadn't done that the first day she'd walked into the Stagecoach Saloon? What was the worst he would have done? Accuse her of taking his wallet? She'd seen him pick it up after she'd dropped it. He couldn't prove she'd tried to take it.

But after she'd heard that his brother was the sheriff… She didn't want any trouble. And she could hide out here a while just as easily as anywhere else. If Darby Cahill was going to call the sheriff on her, he would have that first day when she'd asked for a job. He could have laughed in her face. He could have sent her packing.

So why hadn't he?

Was it possible he hadn't remembered her?

No, she thought, thinking back to their conversations. He was curious about her. Curious about her evil eye pendant. Curious no doubt what she was waiting for. And him? He was waiting too. Waiting to see what she was going to do.

It was time to end the suspense. She needed to get the bracelet back and move on.

Her cell phone vibrated in her pocket. She quickly checked it since only one person had the number.

She'd lied to Darby about not having a phone, always leaving it behind when she went to work.

Taking a shaky breath, she answered the call, knowing it would be bad news. "Yes?"

"He was here looking for you."

"Did you talk to him?"

"No, of course not. Auntie handled it. She wouldn't let him inside. He wanted you and then he asked for me. Auntie told him neither of us had been around."

"You know he'll be back. It isn't safe—"

"I had Auntie whisked away in the dead of night. I got word that she is safe."

"What about you?" Mariah hated the fear she heard in her voice.

"I left, as well, when it was safe. No one saw me leave, so don't worry. Anyway, I can take care of myself."

Not against this man. "You know what he's capable of." There was silence on the other end of the line. "Maybe you should pick up another phone."

"I won't call unless…well, you know."

She did know. Tears filled her eyes. Her hand went to her wrist to stroke her grandmother's bracelet, only to remember it was gone. The loss hadn't hurt as badly as it did at that moment. "Please be careful. I know you don't believe in the evil eye—"

"I'm wearing my pendant," her best friend, Serra, said. "Why not? We both need all the luck we can get and our grandmothers lived to ripe old ages—maybe we will too."

Mariah disconnected and tucked the phone behind the pillow on her bed. She had to end this and get moving again. He wouldn't quit looking for her.

But she wasn't leaving without her bracelet. Her friend was right. She needed all the luck she could get.

Tonight, though, she needed to clear her head and there was only one way. She grabbed the key to her bike. When she got like this, the best thing she could do was hit the road, let the motorcycle run and push away all the crazy thoughts.

Slipping on her jacket, she stepped outside. The moon peeked over the mountains, a brilliant glowing sphere that gilded the landscape. The air felt chilly and wonderfully scented with pine.

Swinging up onto her bike, she started the engine, loving the sound of its throaty roar, and turned toward the highway out of town. Once she hit the wide pavement, she opened it up and let it run. There was no traffic on the highway this time of night. It was just her and the road. The speed blew back her long hair in a dark wave. She breathed in the night. She was Mariah Ayers, granddaughter of a Roma queen. Nothing could stop her. Not even Darby Cahill.

The thought of the handsome cowboy with those dark-fringed gray eyes and easy smile made her even more restless. He was a temptation, one she couldn't afford. If she stayed here much longer—

She took the next curve too fast. The bike leaned dangerously, but she managed to pull it back out as the road straightened again. Her heart was pounding. Darby and this place, this feeling, were dangerous. They made her reckless.

Mariah slowed the bike to turn around and head back, feeling as if now she could get some sleep. It was time to move up her plan, time to put Gilt Edge and Darby Cahill behind her. Tomorrow night.

"SOMETHIN'S UP," BILLIE DEE whispered and pointed toward the bar.

"Something like what?" Lillie whispered back. The two of them had been in the kitchen talking while Billie Dee made cornbread to go with her pot of Texas ham and beans cooking on the stove.

"Your brother and Mariah."

Lillie's attention perked right up. "Like what?"

"I can't put my finger on it, but they act very strange around each other. Kinda too polite and yet I see each of them watchin' the other."

"She's new. Darby probably just wants to make sure she does a good job. And she's probably self-conscious knowing he's watching her."

Billie Dee laughed. "That woman is anything but self-conscious. She knows exactly what she's doing—driving your brother crazy."

"What?"

"He has it bad. Haven't you seen how off-center he is around her? He's not his usual cool self."

Lillie thought about it for a moment. "You're right. He hasn't been himself since the Chokecherry Festival. Do you think they met there and don't want us to know?"

"Why would they do that?" the cook asked frowning.

"Maybe because my brother doesn't like anyone to know his business. Do you realize he hasn't even invited me up to see my apartment?"

"You mean *his* apartment?"

"Whatever. But I think you're right," she said, watching Darby behind the bar as Mariah came up to place a drink order for one of her tables. "He's definitely interested in her. So why hasn't he asked her out?"

"Because he's Darby. Or because she works for him. Or because—"

"If he's really interested, then none of that matters. Maybe there is something we can do to help them along."

Billie Dee was already shaking her head. "No way," she said, heading for the stove to stir the beans. "I'm not gettin' involved in that."

"I thought you were a romantic," Lillie teased.

"I keep my nose out of other people's business. I suggest you do the same."

Lillie laughed. "You know me better than that. But first I need to know more about this woman."

"WHAT IS THIS obsession with Mariah?" Darby asked after being confronted by his sister when he came downstairs to the kitchen the next day. "So what if she doesn't have a Facebook page? A lot of people don't."

"She has no online presence at *all*," Lillie said from the table where she sat with her laptop propped open. "How is that possible in this day and age?"

"Maybe you haven't noticed, but the woman travels by motorcycle and lives out of a backpack. She doesn't even have a cell phone."

"Exactly. That's not…normal."

He laughed. "It sounds great to me."

His sister shook her head in exasperation. "I saw the paperwork on her. She hasn't stayed at any job more than a few weeks. What do you even know about her?"

"I know she's a good waitress. That's all I have to know about her. And if she doesn't stay around long…well, that's fine too since mostly we need the help through these busy weeks of summer."

Lillie mugged a face at him. "So you expect her to leave soon too."

"Based on her past employment, probably. She says she's looking for a place to settle but hasn't found it yet. I really doubt that place is Gilt Edge."

"Why not?"

He groaned. "If you're looking for an argument—"

"It's not like you to hire someone off the street."

"We hired Billie Dee and Kendall that way," he pointed out.

"So you're telling me that's all that's going on?" Lillie pressed.

Darby did his best to look innocent. "What else?"

"I don't know. I just get this feeling that you're interested in her but…"

He rolled his eyes. "You and your feelings. Or maybe you just need something else to occupy your mind other than your wedding and furnishing your new house and starting your new life. By the way, Dad's definitely back at his cabin. I saw his Jeep parked out front in a different spot. It's strange though that he hasn't contacted one of us. I wonder why he came out of the mountains so early?"

She sighed. "Mariah is sure beautiful, but kind of secretive too."

He cut his eyes to her. *"Seriously, you're that determined to talk about her?"*

"Okay, I'll lay off, but I think there is more to the story."

Darby was saved as Billie Dee came in the back door singing about saints marching in.

"CAN I GET A color this week?"

Maggie looked up from her scheduling book in

surprise to see Wendy Westbrook standing in front of her. She glanced around expecting to see Tori Clark with the girl. The two were inseparable. Across the street, she spotted Tori with her little sister Quinn. The younger one seemed to be arguing that she wanted to leave, but Tori was holding tight to the back of her sister's hoodie.

"Did you have a day in mind?" Maggie asked, noticing that Wendy was trying to read the schedule book upside down.

"I don't know. What do you have?" the teen said around a wad of gum.

"I would imagine you'll need it after school—"

"No, it doesn't matter. During the day is fine. Maybe…" Her gaze was on the book in front of Maggie. "Wednesday's good at nine. I don't have a class until after lunch that day."

"Fine, I'll pencil you in. You'll let me know if you change your mind." Maggie had dealt with these girls when they were younger.

"I won't," Wendy said, and she popped a bubble with her gum as she turned and left.

Across the street, Tori Clark finally let go of her little sister as Wendy streaked across to join them. She watched for a moment as the two friends put their heads together, then laughed, but they were soon chasing after Quinn who was a half block away.

Maggie wondered for a moment what she'd just

witnessed. Then she picked up the phone and called Wendy's mother.

Rachel Westbrook answered on the fourth ring. She sounded out of breath. "Yes?"

"I'm sorry, this is Maggie Thompson at Just Hair. Did I catch you in the middle of something?"

"Yoga."

"I'll let you get right back to it. Wendy was just in and scheduled—"

"Do you need my credit card number right now?" She still sounded out of breath. Also from some distance, a male voice said, "Hang up. Buy something later," then laughed.

"Not necessary. Sorry to interrupt." Maggie hung up, telling herself that if Wendy didn't show for her appointment, she thought Rachel would be happy to pay anyway since everyone in town knew that her pilot husband, Don, was away flying the Seattle–New York route for the next two weeks.

DARBY REALIZED THAT every day Mariah was scheduled to work, he found himself listening for the rumble of her motorcycle. Today was no different. And every day he knew that he might not hear it. He might not hear it ever again.

Would she just give up and leave? That he doubted. No, he thought she would come for the bracelet. He just didn't know how—or if she would have help. So far he hadn't seen her with anyone. Men hit on her at the bar, but she brushed them off like flies. No, he didn't think she would enlist anyone to help her. Mariah was too independent for that.

Darby had watched her rub her bare wrist sometimes as if it hurt. As if the bracelet was a missing limb. We should stop this, he thought. End this before it goes any further.

But this past week, he'd awakened every day with excitement in his belly. He'd looked forward to the days that he worked with Mariah. There was an anticipation in him that made the food that Billie Dee cooked taste even more amazing.

Darby couldn't explain this feeling. All he knew was that he didn't want to go back to the days before Mariah.

It was crazy and he knew it. His sister was right. He still had no idea who the woman really was. Or what she was capable of. But as insane as it seemed, that was part of the excitement.

At the growl of her motorcycle engine, he felt himself relax. It was just another day at the saloon. But at the back of his mind, he wondered how long this could last. How long she was going to let it?

"SORRY ABOUT EARLIER," Lillie said as she plopped down at the bar several hours later. "I didn't mean to give you a hard time about Mariah." She glanced over her shoulder to make sure the woman couldn't hear, but Mariah was busy with a group that had just come in. "I hate this new schedule. I never see you anymore. I miss talking with you."

"I miss you too. But soon your house will be done, you'll be happily married and summer will be over. Things always slow down in the winter. But right now, you have a lot on your plate."

She groaned. "Don't remind me."

"Oh, come on—it can't be that bad."

"Ha. Like you know anything about it. What kind of decorating have you done with the apartment?" she asked.

He laughed. "You can't stand it. You want to see upstairs, don't you?"

"I just want to see what you've done."

"Lillie, you know me. I haven't done anything."

"I could help you."

He shook his head. "Don't look so disappointed. I love you, but the apartment will never be as nice as when you lived there. I like things…simple."

"It wouldn't hurt to add just a few things. Maybe some pillows or a wall hanging or—"

"Lillie, what is going on with you?"

"I could ask you the same thing," she snapped as she got up to come around the bar and poured herself a cola. "I will never understand you. Kendall was all wrong for you, according to you. But Mariah? What are you waiting for?"

He looked across the room at the woman taking orders from the large table. Mariah made it look easy.

She made a lot of things look easy and appealing. He liked the way she smelled, that citrusy perfume she wore. He liked the way she moved, like a sleek cat. He liked the way she smiled, her dark eyes gleaming.

"She likes you, so what is the problem?" his sister demanded quietly.

He chuckled. "You're sure it's me she's interested in?"

"What? You think she wants the bar?" Lillie shook her head. "I've seen the way she looks at you."

"Really?" he asked, turning to gaze into his sister's beautiful face. "And how exactly does she look at me?"

"Like a woman who is trying to figure out a man. But it is more than that. She looks at you like she has feelings for you and she wishes she didn't."

Darby laughed. "All that in a look?"

"Make fun, but it's true. And you know what? I can tell that you are interested in her. I've seen you watching her." Lillie grinned as if she'd discovered a truth that he'd tried hard to hide. "Admit it."

"I'm fascinated by the woman," Darby confessed.

"I knew it. So ask her out."

He shook his head. "Fascinated from a distance, a *safe* distance. Like you pointed out before, what do we know about her?"

"You're going to let fear stand in your way?" She sounded appalled. But then again, she was an engaged woman in love.

"Nothing wrong with a good healthy dose of fear." He had good reason to fear Mariah's motivations—and her interest in him.

MARIAH CAME BACK to the bar with her order. Darby had his arm around his sister as the two stood together laughing.

"You just need to settle into your new lifestyle," Darby was saying to his sister. "Once the wedding is over and the house is done, you'll be just fine. Trust me."

Lillie smiled up at him. "I do trust you. Trust me. Take a chance."

He laughed and gently pushed her away. "Go, bride-to-be. The sooner this wedding is over, the happier we will all be."

As Mariah watched Lillie leave, she felt a pang of envy at how close Darby and Lillie were. She'd never had a sibling. Never had anyone who cared the way he did for his twin except maybe her grandmother, but no one since. Maybe things would have been different if she'd had a brother to look after her. She quickly shoved that thought away.

She'd never been one to live in the past. It did no good to spend her time going over the what-ifs. Things were the way they were. She had to deal with them.

The clock was ticking. She'd been here too long. She couldn't stay much longer. So what was holding her up? She knew staying here was dangerous. But she couldn't leave without her bracelet.

That was the only thing keeping her here, she told herself as Darby smiled as he took her drink order. She felt that tug at her heart, the one that told her she'd put off the inevitable too long. She had to end this.

IT WAS A busy night. Darby had spent it behind the bar, trying to keep up with drink orders. Mariah had kept up well with the demand on the floor. He had to hand it to her, she really was good at this.

When she came in for a drink order, he slipped her a water while she waited. She looked surprised, took a drink and said, "Thanks." For a moment their eyes met. That thrill he'd felt that first day rippled through him.

He started to lift one of the drinks he'd made up to her tray. At the same time, she reached for it. Her fingers brushed against his. He felt a jolt and dropped the glass. It hit the edge of the bar and shattered, glass going everywhere along with the bright colored liquid.

"Are you cut?" Mariah asked, looking alarmed. "I'm sorry. I shouldn't have reached for it." She quickly grabbed his hand, turning it this way and that to see if there was any blood. The bright red of the grenadine had splashed over his skin, but he could see that he hadn't been injured.

Still she didn't release his hand. She turned it palm up. He watched her trace a finger along one of the lines and then another.

"What do you see?" he asked, stunned by the shock of her touch. A current ran through his veins, racing toward his heart at a gallop.

"You've never had your heart broken," she said studying his hand with utmost seriousness. "You will have only one love." Her finger traced a line across the center of his palm to his wrist.

He felt a shiver he tried to rein in, but he knew she hadn't missed it. Her gaze came up to meet his.

"I see a long life if you aren't foolish, if you don't fall for the wrong woman before you find your true love." She let go of his hand.

"How will I know?" he asked pretending to play along.

"The wrong woman could get you killed."

He nodded as he wiped up the broken glass and replaced the drink he'd spilled. "She sounds dangerous. But exciting. You're sure she's that wrong for me?"

Her dark eyes locked with his. "Positive."

He placed the new drink on her tray and she started to turn away. "You do know that not all Romani are fortune tellers or—" she hesitated a moment "—thieves."

"So I shouldn't put much stock in what you read in my palm."

"Oh, that was all true. Didn't I tell you? My grandmother had the sight. It runs in my family." With that she took her tray of drinks and left.

He watched her go, his heart still pounding. She'd tried to warn him about her. He almost laughed out loud. He'd been doing the same thing himself. And yet, he found himself wanting her more than his next breath.

Glancing down at his palm, he touched the skin where she had only moments before and told himself she was right. He'd be a fool to take this any further.

So why did he feel filled with expectation and excitement? He'd never been one to take risky chances. Until now. He was completely enthralled by her. He wanted to know this woman in every sense of the word—no matter how dangerous it was.

THEY'D BEEN ABOUT to close for the night when the two men came in. Darby felt his stomach drop. Hadn't he been expecting this? If not, he should have.

He glanced behind the bar where Mariah was cleaning up the last of the glasses. She looked up at the sound of the door. Her expression mirrored his own. Trouble had just walked through the door. The question was, though, had she—unlike him—known it was coming?

Her gaze shot to him and he thought he saw something in it… Oh hell. He felt his heart drop. This was her doing. She was finally going to take back her bracelet—one way or another.

How foolish of him to think that she wouldn't change the unwritten rules of this challenge and bring in reinforcements.

The men were scruffy-looking, the kind he often saw hitchhiking through the state. They moved through the bar slowly, calculating every move. Darby swore under his breath. He should have closed fifteen minutes ago. But Mariah had distracted him. Now he thought he knew why.

The second man closed the door behind him and locked it as the first moved to the bar and pulled a gun. He pointed it at Mariah.

Darby's heart began to pound. He'd been hesitant to keep a gun behind the bar. That had always seemed like a bad idea before. Instead, he kept a baseball bat where he could get to it. He'd thought the biggest worry he would have was breaking up a bar fight.

These two were more than your average armed robbers. They were here for more than what little cash was in the register.

CHAPTER SIX

"NOT LOOKING FOR TROUBLE," the man said as he motioned for Darby to stay where he was. "We'll just take the money and be gone. No one gets hurt."

Darby looked at Mariah. She hadn't moved, didn't seem alarmed to have a gun pointed at her head.

Anger rushed through him—more toward himself than at Mariah or these men. He'd let this happen. His foolishness had caused this. Lightning bolt, love at first sight, infatuation be damned. He started to step toward the bar, determined to put an end to this, but the second man stopped him as he also pulled a gun.

"Let the little lady handle it," the second man said. They all looked toward Mariah, who nodded and moved to the cash register, opened it and began to take out the money.

Both men seemed to relax. The one at the bar stepped closer, watching as Mariah pulled out the bills. "What's that around your neck?" the man asked.

Her free hand went to the pendant. "It's to ward off the evil eye."

The man laughed. "*The evil eye?* You hear that,

Carl? You've got kind of an evil eye." He turned back to the woman, all humor gone. "I'll take it. You got any more of that evil eye stuff around?"

Here it comes, Darby thought. He'd walked right into this, lulled by the calm before the storm.

"Sure," Mariah said. "I keep a trunkful of it around."

"You live upstairs?" He didn't wait for an answer. "Carl, take a look upstairs."

"Why me? Lou, you always send me off to—"

"*I* live upstairs," Darby said, as if Mariah and these men didn't know that. "But there is nothing up there that would interest you." His gaze was on Mariah. She looked up. For a moment their eyes locked. Hers were unreadable.

"Go!" Lou ordered, scowling at his accomplice.

Carl, still mumbling to himself, grudgingly headed for the kitchen and the back stairway that led up to the apartment.

Darby simmered to a slow burn. Carl wouldn't find anything. Then what? Would they tear the bar apart looking for the bracelet? Or would they hold a gun to his head? Right now, he thought he'd rather die than give her the bracelet. All she'd ever had to do was ask. Not rob his damned bar.

He looked at her. She didn't look scared or worried. But then why would she? This was all part of her plan, one he hadn't seen coming. Without even being aware of it, he took a step toward her.

"You move again and I'll shoot you." Lou moved

so he had a clear shot at either of them. "You really don't want to do anything stupid. You either," he said, swinging the gun barrel back in her direction. "Hurry up, Carl!"

Darby could hear the second man's footfalls overhead. It wouldn't take long to search since there was nothing worth stealing. What the man wouldn't find was the bracelet.

Had Mariah thought it would be that easy?

He saw now how her plan could have worked. Have it look like a robbery so she would never be suspected. Get her bracelet back and disappear again. No one would be the wiser. Except Darby and he wouldn't be able to prove a thing.

"Speed it up, sweetheart," the man said to Mariah. "It doesn't take that long to empty a cash register."

Darby watched her start to hand over the money and stop. Her gaze darted to him and what he saw there sent his pulse into overdrive and made his stomach roil. Was it possible he could be wrong and she hadn't set this whole thing up?

"Just give him the money," he heard himself say. "It isn't worth getting killed over."

"You want the change too?" she asked the gunman. "I can put it in a sack." She bent down as if to reach for a sack.

Except there was no sack under there. The man was watching her, leaning over the bar a little, anxious for the money.

"Don't forget the necklace," the man said, seeming to enjoy the view of her cleavage as she bent over in the V-necked T-shirt. He leaned closer, resting the gun in his hand on the bar top.

Darby started to rush the man but stopped just as abruptly as he heard the man say, "You move again and I shoot the woman. Got it, hero?" Smiling, he reached over to fondle the necklace dangling freely so close to the cleavage above Mariah's breasts.

Heart in this throat, Darby saw her come up with the baseball bat so quickly, it completely took Lou off guard. If anything, the man had been expecting Darby to do something—not Mariah.

She swung the bat, catching Lou in the arm holding the gun, before the bat ricocheted off the man's shoulder.

Darby sprung forward as the man let out a curse of pain. The gun clattered across the smooth surface of the bar—right to Darby. Grabbing the weapon, he slammed the butt of it into the back of the Lou's head. The man dropped to the floor like a ton of bricks.

He and Mariah both quickly turned their attention to the back of the bar. Carl would be coming down any minute.

Darby motioned for Mariah to stay down and stepped to the side of the doorway at the sound of heavy footfalls descending the stairs.

"There's nothing much up there, Lou," Carl was

saying as he walked into the bar and saw his partner in crime sprawled on the floor.

Darby stepped out, jabbed the barrel of the gun into the man's ribs and took the man's weapon from him.

"I've called 9-1-1. The sheriff is on his way," Mariah said. There was a calmness to her that probably shouldn't have surprised him. But when she reached up to touch the pendant at her neck, he saw that her hand trembled.

He could hear sirens in the distance. "Looks like that necklace brought you some luck."

She met his gaze. "We make our own luck. Anyway, it's just a cheap piece of jewelry. He would have been disappointed when he found out that it wasn't worth anything. Still, I would have put a curse on it so he never forgot me for the rest of his life."

Was that what she'd done with the bracelet? Sure seemed that way because Darby knew he would never forget this woman. He felt confused and guilty. He'd thought all this was her doing. Until that moment, he hadn't been worried about her safety because of it. Now, though, he found his knees had gone weak as the realization of what could have happened here tonight hit him.

"Mariah, what you did…"

"Stupid, huh. I guess I wasn't thinking clearly."

Or she wasn't about to part with the pendant. In

which case, he now knew that she wasn't leaving without her bracelet.

Two sheriff's department cars pulled up out front. Mariah went to open the door.

DEPUTY HARPER "HARP" COLE transported the two men to jail. "Might want to have Doc have a look at that one," Flint told Harp. "I think he's just got a knock on his head and a nice bruise on his arm, but it won't hurt to make sure he's all right. And, Harp, straight to the jail. No side trips. Like to the diner to show off what you have in the back of the patrol car."

"Like I would do something like that," Harp snapped.

"He's got a girlfriend down at Sue's Diner. Vicki something or other," Flint said to his brother after Harp left. "I'm betting he was planning to do a little showing off." He shook his head. Harp would be the death of him. "Okay, let's get your statements." He turned to his brother, who looked sick to his stomach. "You all right?"

Darby nodded. "Mariah's the one who saved the day."

The sheriff looked over at her. "That was a smart, but dangerous move on your part. The man could have shot you."

She nodded and looked away. "In retrospect, I don't know what possessed me."

He had his doubts about that. The woman appeared awfully calm. He figured anyone who'd had a gun pointed at her like that should still be shaken. Unless it wasn't the first time she'd had a gun pointed at her.

He took their statements and then turned off the recorder. "Well, I think that's all I need. You've both had quite a night and there isn't that much left of it. Get some rest. If I have any more questions, I know where to find you."

After Mariah left, Flint turned to his brother again. "What do you know about her?"

"That's an odd question," Darby said as he stepped behind the bar to pour himself a cola. He looked like he could use something stronger, but he'd been going to AA for some time now and didn't seem to miss drinking. "Mariah saved the day, just as we told you."

He watched his brother, surprised by Darby's answer. "You sure she didn't know the two men?"

"Why would you ask that?" Darby demanded in a way that made him wonder if his brother hadn't suspected the same thing at least at some point.

"Because what did you have in the till? Not enough to get killed over," he pressed. "What she did was dangerous. And it wasn't even her money."

"What are you getting at?"

Flint shook his head. He hated being so suspicious of everything, everyone. "She took a hell of a chance. It just surprises me."

"It surprised me too," Darby admitted after taking a drink of cola. "She's a remarkable woman. I don't think there is anything she can't do. And, as it turns out, she's great at this job."

"Still, I'd keep an eye on her. In fact," Flint said moving around the bar to carefully pick up the glass Mariah had been using. "You don't mind if I run her prints do you? Just as a precaution."

MARIAH KNEW SHE wouldn't be able to sleep. She didn't even bother stopping at the cabin. Instead, she roared past it and kept going. All her instincts told her to get her things and move on. It was just a matter of time before Darby told his brother how they'd met. He was probably already suspicious. She'd overheard the brothers mention that the saloon had never had a robbery before.

Attempted robbery. She still couldn't believe the risk she'd taken. It wasn't even her money. She could have been killed. But the man had wanted her pendant and he would have taken it too if she hadn't stopped him.

Still, all he would have had to do was pull the trigger and she'd be dead.

What had she been thinking? Was her pendant—her bracelet—worth risking her life over?

She felt that old anger in her, that old need to fight. She'd fought her circumstances for so long that now all she had in her was retreat. Run and don't look back. That was what she needed to do. Keep running. It was the looking back that was causing the trouble.

Her thoughts went straight to Darby like an arrow. He'd shown her…kindness by hiring her and not calling his brother the sheriff. But it was so much more complicated than that. When she was around him, she felt…

That was just it, she *felt*. For so long, she'd turned all emotion off. It had been the only way she could survive. Run, don't look back and above all don't let yourself feel anything. There'd been no fight in her because she hadn't cared about anything but getting away.

Tonight she'd risked her life. She'd fought back. She'd felt something—for Darby, for his damned bar…for herself. She had drawn a line in the sand. She wasn't going to let that dumbass robber take her pendant. But mostly, she wasn't going to let Darby think that those men had been her idea.

She'd seen it in his expression when he'd looked at her after they'd come in and pulled a gun. He'd thought she was in on the robbery. Would she have let them take the money and leave if the man hadn't demanded her pendant?

Maybe. She didn't know. The money wasn't worth dying over. It wasn't as if she owed Darby anything. Soon she would be gone and she wouldn't look back. Couldn't.

But the disappointment she'd seen in his gray eyes

had been her undoing. She'd let herself care what he thought of her and had almost gotten herself killed.

Tears blurred the road ahead. She'd never felt more alone than she did right now. Alone and scared and so weary of running that she didn't care if she lived or died.

The two-lane highway was empty. Low clouds hid the stars and moon. A cool pine-scented breeze wafted down from the mountaintops.

It would have been so easy to keep going, to keep running and to let Darby believe the worst about her. Deep inside her she felt that small fire that had started tonight. That spark that had made her fight rather than give up.

She let up on the throttle and, slowing, turned around and headed back. She wouldn't run. But she also couldn't stay here any longer. She had to finish things here. No more putting it off.

ELY STOOD IN the moonlight staring at the eight-foot-high chain-link fence that enclosed the missile pad. No one believed him about the aliens or what he'd seen here just months ago.

His family thought that he was getting senile. Everyone else just thought he'd always had a screw loose. Lately he'd been feeling…old. More than old, strange. It worried him. He had to know what was going on at the missile silos. If he died before he did…

He glanced up as the silver moon burst from behind the clouds. It cast the entire valley in a bright white glow, glittering off the chain-link fence around the underground silo.

Flint had told him that what he saw three months ago wasn't aliens—but military personnel dressed in hazmat suits.

"And that doesn't scare you more than aliens?" he'd demanded.

"Dad, they do all kinds of emergency preparedness exercises out there. It probably wasn't anything."

Ely had looked at his son. "You don't believe that any more than I do."

"I called the commander."

"And didn't get anything out of him."

"It's military and over my paid grade," Flint had joked.

"I'm wondering if there is trouble at the other missile silos."

Flint hadn't known anything about them. "No one's reported a problem. Or seeing anything."

"Everyone's afraid of the military. Or worse, of looking like a fool. They won't report anything until it is too late."

Ely still believed that. He'd read about problems at other sites where there had been leaks of poisonous gases, mistakes where the missiles had been on alert but no one had touched the buttons.

"We don't even know if there is a missile in ours," Flint had said.

"Then why the guys in hazmat suits?"

He'd had his son there. Flint shook his head.

"I just wish you didn't worry about it so much, Dad."

"Someone has to." Ely had almost told him then about the notebook he'd been writing everything down in. But the moment passed. As long as he was kicking, he'd keep writing down what he saw and the dates. His sons were smart. They'd find the notebook when he was gone. They'd figure it out.

DARBY LAY IN his bed staring at the dark ceiling. After his brother left, he'd locked up, turned out the lights and stood in the empty bar alone. He'd known sleep was out given the mixture of emotions roiling through him. He still couldn't believe they'd almost been robbed.

Not that he hadn't known it was a possibility with the saloon outside of the town and no other businesses close by. But after all this time, he'd felt safe.

Now he could laugh at that. Safe? He'd hired a pickpocket to work for him. And Lillie was right. He hadn't been that careful with the other employees either. What did he really know about Billie Dee or Kendall Raines?

He reminded himself that the attempted robbery had nothing to do with any of his employees—including

Mariah. Flint had called a little while ago to tell him that the men had been on a crime spree through a half dozen states. Which meant the Stagecoach Saloon robbery had been random.

Random. Like seeing a woman in the crowd at the Chokecherry Festival and falling for her. That was what happened, wasn't it? Wasn't that why he hadn't thrown the bracelet away before he knew anything about it—or forgotten about the woman? Instead, he'd only gotten in deeper.

Tonight he'd thought for sure Mariah was behind the robbery, that she knew the men, that she'd set the whole thing up to get her bracelet back—and clean out his cash register in the process.

Instead, she'd risked her life. He still couldn't get his head around it. All his suspicions about her—

The throb of a motorcycle engine made him start. The sound was coming closer. He sat up in the bed, still fully dressed, and snapped on the lamp. Holding his breath, he listened.

The engine rumbled to a stop out back and then fell silent. A moment later, he heard her at the back door.

MARIAH KNOCKED, TELLING herself that he was probably sound asleep. She glanced out at the dark pines swaying in the breeze and felt a chill. Was she really doing this? She felt as if her life, which had been out of her control for so long, had finally gone off the rails. If she did what she was planning—

The door opened, startling her. She swung around to find Darby standing in the doorway, fully dressed. He seemed surprised to see her, but not displeased. Sometimes she forgot how handsome this cowboy was. Just seeing him standing there made her heart beat faster. How easy it would be to fall for this man.

"Couldn't sleep?" he asked, his voice as soft as his gray eyes.

She shook her head and hugged herself against the cool night. Could she go through with this? She'd done a lot of reckless things in her life—often because she'd been backed into a corner. But this...

"Come on in." He stepped back to let her into the small area outside the kitchen.

When he reached for a light in the kitchen, she said, "I didn't want to be alone. Could we..." She glanced upstairs toward the apartment where she knew he lived. He hadn't even let his sister up there.

Darby hesitated but only for a moment. "Sure. It's pretty basic. Not much to see." His gaze locked with hers. "I'm afraid you'll be disappointed."

She knew what he was telling her. The bracelet wasn't up there—or at least that's what he wanted her to believe. "Is there a bed?"

His gray eyes widened. "Mariah—"

"I don't want to be alone tonight," she blurted, then looked away embarrassed. She shouldn't have come here. Every instinct told her this was a mistake. And yet when she'd headed back, she'd driven right by her cabin and headed straight here.

She met his gaze again. "If you could just hold me tonight." She sounded close to tears. It was no act. She should be used to close calls. She should be used to someone wanting to hurt her. Even kill her. But it was one thing to run from your past. It was another to have complete strangers threaten to harm you.

His gaze was so compassionate that it made her heart ache. "I could do that. Do you want something to drink?"

She shook her head. "I just need..." She didn't know what she needed. Human contact? Somewhere she felt safe? A little tenderness. Just for tonight. And she knew there was only one place and that was in Darby's arms—the most dangerous place she could be tonight.

Without another word, he led her up the stairs.

A single light glowed in a corner of the room. She realized that until she'd arrived, he'd been lying up here on his bed, fully clothed with almost all the lights out. She could see by the quilt on the bed where he had been. She knew if she touched it, the spot would still be warm. Like her, he couldn't sleep.

She told herself it wasn't too late. She could leave. *Should* leave. And yet she didn't. She stood looking around the small sparsely furnished apartment. He was right about having only the basics. He'd done so little, she understood why he wouldn't let his sister up here. And yet, what was here felt like him.

Darby Cahill didn't need much to make him happy. It was one reason she liked him so much. She'd known men with fancy cars, expensive suits and shoes, fast-talking men who thought they could buy her. As her gaze came to rest on him, she knew that if she had the chance to choose, she'd pick this unassuming cowboy every time.

"Let me take your jacket," he said and held out his hand.

She slipped out of it. Exhaustion pulled at her, making her legs weak.

"Here, sit down," he said as if he saw how hard it was for her to stay on her feet. He started to lead her over to the old recliner, but she knew she'd never make it that far. She sat down on the edge of the bed and reached down to unlace her boots. To her surprise, her fingers trembled and suddenly she was all thumbs.

Darby knelt in front of her and, gently pushing her hands away, slowly unlaced her boots and pulled them off. Her hand went to his cheek, rough with a day's growth of beard. She felt tears blur her vision.

He lifted her hand to his mouth and kissed the palm. She told herself it was because she was exhausted from being on the run for so long. She couldn't remember ever being this drained. She wiped at the tears. This wasn't like her and that

scared her. She'd learned a long time ago how useless tears were. She shouldn't even be here. Especially with this man. Especially as vulnerable as she
was feeling right now.

"Here," he said. "Lie back. You'll be more comfortable without these." As she did as he said, she
felt his fingers on the buttons of her jeans and almost stopped him. He tugged them off, pulled her to
her feet and drew down the quilt on the bed. "You're
shivering. Get under the covers."

For a woman who no longer took orders from
men, she found herself doing whatever he told her.
She pulled up the sheet. It smelled like the out-
doors, reminding her of how her grandmother hung
clothes on the old line outside her house. He tucked
the heavy, thick quilt up to her chin.

"Could you just hold me?" Her teeth chattered.
She knew it wasn't from the cold. But she couldn't
have said exactly why she was feeling the way she
was. Everything was wrong about this in so many
ways. She knew the risk she was taking. That she
was throwing caution to the wind. If it had been any
other man but Darby…

He hesitated. She watched him begin to undress,
admiring his strong, lean body from his broad shoulders to his slim hips and long muscled legs. He met
her gaze as he got to the point of taking off his jeans.

Without a word, he left them on and climbed into
the bed. He pulled her to him. Again she felt hot tears

burn her eyes. She snuggled against him, needing his warmth, needing the feel of his strong body. She could feel his breath on her cheek. Then he reached over and turned out the lamp, pitching them into darkness.

"Are you all right?" he whispered.

She closed her eyes, soaking in his heat, his strength, his male scent, and let herself have this moment of weakness. "I am now."

CHAPTER SEVEN

LILLIE KNEW HER brother didn't want her help with his apartment. But she had some extra things that she thought would be nice up there. When she'd moved out, he'd insisted she take everything. Of course, she hadn't, but she'd only left things she thought he wouldn't complain about—practical things like a lamp, a television.

Men. Trask was just as bad. He'd been watching her furnish their new house with amusement.

"What?" she'd demanded one day when she caught him leaning against the doorjamb smiling and looking bemused.

"Nothing. Maybe I just like watching you do your thing."

"My thing?"

The strong, handsome cowboy looked a little flustered. "You know, arrange those pillows on the couch. You've moved them a dozen times and finally put them back exactly like they were to begin with."

She jammed her hands on her hips and looked indignant. "You think this is easy?" she'd demanded.

He'd instantly held up his hands in surrender. "No.

It looks damned hard to me." He was trying so hard to be supportive that finally she'd sighed.

"I want everything to be perfect."

Trask had stepped to her and taken her in his arms. "Everything *is* perfect, darlin'." She'd nodded against his chest. "We could live in the barn and I'd be happy."

That was exactly the problem with men, she thought this morning as she parked at the side of the saloon and got out. Especially cowboys. They *could* live in a barn and be perfectly happy—even sharing it with their horse.

As she turned the corner to the back of the building, she stopped abruptly. Mariah's motorcycle was parked next to her brother's pickup.

Lillie blinked. All this time she'd been trying to get them together, they'd already been together? She grinned, happy and excited for her brother, and yet, a little annoyed. This was so like him, keeping this from her. She'd just bet money this had started at the Chokecherry Festival. They'd both been there, even though they'd pretended they hadn't met. It also explained why he'd hired the woman the way he had.

Just then the back door opened and out came Mariah. She hurried to her bike, but she didn't start it. Instead, she rolled it toward the road, finally hopping on and coasting for a ways before she cranked up the engine and left.

Lillie couldn't help but laugh. Her brother's little

secret was out. Not that she was about to tell anyone. She could well imagine the fun Hawk and Cyrus would have razzing him about it. No, she'd keep his secret. She'd wanted someone for her brother for so long, she was smiling as she let herself into the back door of the saloon and raced up the stairs.

"HARP, I'M WARNING YOU," Flint said to his deputy. "One more complaint about you—"

"Ever since you became sheriff, you've had it out for me," Harper Cole complained. "I never hear you warning any of the other deputies."

"The other deputies just do their jobs and keep their noses clean," Flint said. "If you want to stay on this force—"

Harp scoffed at that. "You and I both know you can't fire me." His father was the mayor, as if Harp ever let him forget that.

"I wouldn't bet on that if I were you. One more complaint." He pointed to the door. "Now get out of here."

There were days when he couldn't stand the sight of the arrogant deputy who thought he was much better than he was. All he could hope was that Harp didn't mess up so badly that innocent people were hurt or killed. He felt as if it was only a matter of time before Harp did something so stupid, so irresponsible...

Flint shook his head and looked outside as Harp

left. It was a beautiful summer morning, the sun glistening off the mountains. Gilt Edge was surrounded by four mountain ranges—the Moccasins, Judiths, Snowies and Little Belts—often making it a snow hole in the winter. But in the summer, there was no place more pleasant.

He loved living in a small town in the middle of Montana most days. Gilt Edge was like a lot of small, Montana towns that weren't close to a larger city. It had the basics: a grocery store, a post office, a couple of gas stations, a clothing store, a hair salon and barbershop, a hardware store, a lumber yard and several restaurants and motels—a hospital too. It didn't have a stoplight. Its big box store was actually a small version of a big box store.

Anyone who needed more than that could either shop online or drive the two-hundred-and-fifty-mile round trip to Billings, the largest city in Montana.

What Gilt Edge didn't have was much crime, which made Sheriff Flint Cahill's job easy most days. Not that his office wasn't busy with all kinds of complaints. But most were minor disagreements that could be settled without incident.

So it worried him that the town was changing, given the rash of break-ins, the robbery at the Stagecoach Saloon and that one of the county residents was still missing. Jenna Holloway had gotten into an altercation with her husband, Anvil, on their farm outside of town and left. Anvil said that after twenty-four years of marriage she had confessed to an affair and left. When she didn't return by the next morning, he'd called Flint.

In the four months since she'd disappeared, her car had turned up in a tree-filled gully. It had also come out that she had been writing to male prisoners at Montana State Prison and she'd apparently taken up shoplifting and stealing money from her grocery budget.

What hadn't turned up was Jenna—or her body. Nor had Flint found her alleged lover. The state crime investigators hadn't had much luck either. But the case stayed on the books as a missing person case. And like the other crimes, it kept his mind off his love life. Or lack of one. At least while he was working. It was much harder at night. That's why he worked late most nights.

What he didn't like about living in a small town— and another reason he worked late—was that it was next to impossible not to run into your ex. Seeing Celeste the other day had left him in a funk. Somehow he often crossed paths with her while he never saw Maggie—not even in passing.

He thought about calling her, as he had so many other times. But the last time they'd seen each other, Maggie had made it clear that she didn't want to see him anymore because of Celeste. He really didn't know how to deal with that.

Unfortunately, Celeste still lived here and he

couldn't promise she wouldn't be a problem in the future. He'd never been able to do anything about the woman when they'd been married. What made him—or Maggie—think he had any sway with her now that they were divorced?

He spent the morning finishing up the paperwork on the two would-be robbers he had behind bars. Since they were wanted in so many states, it would be a nightmare to get everything processed.

Meanwhile, there'd been another break-in. He had the names of the three girls who'd purchased the expensive tennis shoes locally. That wasn't to say that there hadn't been someone else who'd bought them online. But since two of the three girls were best friends, he wanted to talk to them first.

He called and set up appointments with the parents, though he refused to tell them exactly why. Of course both parents were suspicious, saying "Whatever this is about, my daughter had nothing to do with it." Many parents were insistent like that even when the evidence was staring them in the face.

First thing this morning, he'd sent the glass Mariah Ayers had been drinking from to the lab to have the fingerprints run. Darby seemed sure that she wasn't involved in any way. Flint thought he was probably right, given what he'd learned about the two robbers and their history.

But he was curious about the woman. And it wouldn't hurt to check her out—and clear her, if possible, for his brother's sake. He got the feeling that there was more going on between the two of them.

He'd been about to check with the lab when his undersheriff Mark Ramirez knocked at his door.

"There's been another break-in."

DARBY CAME OUT of a deep, dark sleep as his door flew open. He sat up abruptly and blinked. First at his sister framed in the doorway and then at the empty spot next to him on his bed.

"So you heard," he said, lying back against the pillow as he watched his sister look around the apartment with both disbelief and horror before she finally settled her shocked gaze on him. "I should have called you, but it was so late."

She came into the room looking both surprised and strangely happy. "You were going to call me?" She sounded touched that he would do that.

He frowned. "I didn't want to upset you."

"*Upset me?* I'm not upset. *I'm delighted.*"

He looked at her smiling face, his frown deepening. "You're delighted the saloon was almost robbed last night?"

"*What?*" she cried, sitting down on the side of the bed that Mariah had apparently recently vacated because he could still feel her warmth.

"Do we really have to get into this now? What time it is anyway?" He rubbed a hand over his face.

"Wait a minute," he said, looking at his sister. "What were you delighted about?"

"*Mariah*. I just saw her leave. You thought you could keep that a secret from *me*?"

He groaned. "Sorry, sis, but it isn't what you think."

She rolled her eyes. "I think she spent the night here and probably has before."

Darby shook his head. It was too early in the morning after a very late, stressful and strange night. Mariah showing up at his apartment... "Call Flint. He'll fill you in on the attempted robbery. I'm going back to sleep." He rolled over and pulled the quilt up.

"Seriously?" she cried.

He felt her get up off the bed. He said nothing, hoping she would go away. He must have been dreaming.

"I'm going to go downstairs and make a pot of coffee," she said in a way that told him sleep was out of the question. "Then I am going to bring two mugs up here and you are going to tell me everything. *Everything.*"

THE CABIN WAS cold when Mariah got back to it. She'd gone for a long ride, needing to clear her head after she'd left Darby. Last night felt like a bad dream. The robbery and what she'd done was disturbing enough, but had she really gone to Darby's?

The thought of being curled up against him, warm

and secure, made her ache. Any other man would have tried to take advantage of the situation. Not Darby Cahill.

She pushed the memory of his tenderness away, telling herself she should be shocked at her own behavior. Her grandmother would have been mortified. Even more disappointed in her than she would have been for what she'd done before arriving on Darby's doorstep, she reminded herself.

As if she had to remind herself that her disgrace was already stalking her. If she'd gotten caught in Darby's bed...

Mariah shuddered now as she stepped into her cabin, glad it was her day off. She couldn't face Darby. Stumbling to the bed, she stripped off her jacket and boots and climbed in. But when she closed her eyes, she had a flash of Darby sleeping so peacefully. She hadn't wanted to leave him and that had made her get up and get out of there.

She'd awakened just before dawn and watched him sleep, fighting the urge to touch his handsome strong face. The cowboy drew her in ways she didn't understand. She didn't need anyone to tell her he was all wrong for her and yet...

He'd held her so gently last night, wrapping her in his arms. She'd known he wouldn't go any further than that. He'd known what she needed and it wasn't sex.

That alone made her soften again at the mere

thought of him. The cowboy understood her and yet he didn't even know her. Didn't know what she'd done—let alone who was after her or what they would have done to her—or him—if they'd found her in his bed last night.

This morning, with Darby sleeping so peacefully, she'd known that she couldn't let this go on. She'd planned to end it last night and look what had happened.

This morning, she'd thought about searching his apartment. But the second robber had looked and found nothing. She could assume that the bracelet wasn't there.

All her instincts told her that Darby wouldn't have gotten rid of it. The day she'd come to him asking for a job, he'd known what she was after. He would have told her if it was gone.

No, he still had it. What was he waiting for? For her to ask for it, she reminded herself. For her to open up to him. She shook her head at the thought, ashamed and scared. She'd stayed here too long.

DARBY LOOKED DOWN at the check in his hand. He could give it to Mariah when she came into work tomorrow. Or…

He folded the check and put it into his pocket as his sister refilled his coffee mug. Of course, she hadn't taken no for an answer after rudely awakening him earlier. Knowing that he had no choice, he'd gotten up, dressed and come downstairs.

"What do you have planned on your day off?" Lillie asked as she cupped her mug in her hands and grinned at him. "You know I have some things out in my pickup that I thought you could use in your apartment. Now that you and Mariah are together—"

"We aren't together. I told you. Nothing happened."

"Whatever. It's just some decorative pillows, a knit throw, some things to make your apartment more cozy."

"It's cozy enough. Anyway, I don't have time to play house. I'm going on a horseback ride. After last night, I really need it."

Though clearly disappointed, she nodded sympathetically. "I can't imagine how scary that was. But it ended okay, huh." She grinned again.

"Not the way you think it did, but… Why am I wasting my breath? You aren't going to believe me anyway." He took another drink of the coffee and then pushed his mug away. Getting to his feet, he headed for the door.

"I'll just leave the things I brought—"

He didn't catch the rest as the door slammed. Sometimes Lillie was so… Lillie. He really did need to be in the saddle, especially on such a beautiful summer day.

But once in his pickup, he didn't turn toward the

ranch. Instead, he drove down the road to the old cabin where he used to live—the same one Mariah was renting now.

He told himself she probably wouldn't be home. Hell, for all he knew she could have skipped town after leaving his bed so early this morning. He still wasn't exactly sure what that had been about last night. He wondered if he'd ever understand the woman. Last night was the most vulnerable he'd ever seen her.

Darby suspected it was one reason she'd left so early this morning without waking him. Sometimes he had to remind himself why she was even still around. It wasn't for the job at the saloon any more than it was because of him—at least not directly.

Her motorcycle was parked out front as he turned in. She must have heard his pickup engine. He wasn't even out of his rig before the door to the cabin opened.

"Darby?" Clearly she hadn't expected to see him today even this late in the morning. He thought he'd been right about her not wanting to face him. He got the impression that Mariah Ayers didn't allow herself to be vulnerable—at least not when anyone was around.

He couldn't tell if she was upset with him for stopping by like this or not. She stood leaning against the doorjamb, cupping a hand to shield her eyes from the bright morning sunlight.

"I hope I didn't catch you at a bad time."

"I just finished breakfast."

"How do you feel about horses?" Darby asked impulsively.

Mariah frowned. *"For breakfast?"*

He let out a nervous laugh. "Sorry, I meant to say, do you ride?"

"I have ridden. It's been a long time, but I like horses." She smiled.

"I thought maybe you'd like to go for a ride with me this morning. If you don't have anything planned."

She seemed to think about it for a moment. He could see that she was fighting it, trying to come up with a good excuse not to.

"I thought you might like to see the ranch."

She apparently couldn't come up with a good excuse to say no. "Okay."

"The horses are up at the family stables. You can go as you are unless you—"

"I'm good."

They climbed into his pickup and he drove them up to the ranch. She seemed to enjoy the ride and the country. The ranch sat in the foothills of the Judith Mountains. He was glad that neither of his brothers, Hawk and Cyrus, were around when they parked and walked down to the barn.

The moment Mariah saw the horses, she looked excited. When one of the mares came right over to her, she rubbed the horse's neck, leaning in as if enjoying the feel and scent of horseflesh. He couldn't help but smile since he was quite fond of it himself.

He didn't mention last night and neither did she. Instead, they busied themselves getting the tack out. When he started to saddle a horse for her, Mariah stopped him.

"I can do that." She took the saddle from him. "I used to help my uncle. He owned a kiddie horse corral. Three laps around the corral for a dollar." She shrugged. "They were just ponies, but I did most of the saddling and unsaddling."

Darby loved these glimpses into her life before he'd met her. It made him wonder though what she was running from. Certainly not a kiddie horse corral. Whatever was chasing her had her afraid. For a woman who didn't scare easily, it had to be a monster of a secret.

He watched her out of the corner of his eye, worried she might get the cinch too tight or too loose. But she knew what she was doing. He wondered if there was anything Mariah Ayers couldn't do.

Saddled up, they road from the foothills up Maiden Canyon. The breeze whispered in the ponderosa pines and made the tall grass undulate.

"So is that where you learned to ride?" Darby asked. "On ponies?" He knew so little about this woman, had no idea where she'd grown up or who or what she was running from now. So every little peek into her life felt like a gift.

She laughed. "My uncle taught me when I was young. He had an old mare I used to ride. She was a sweet horse."

"Where was this?" he asked, and for a moment, he thought she wasn't going to answer.

"Florida. That's where I grew up. My uncle took me in after my grandmother died."

"What did your uncle do for a living other than kiddie pony rides?"

"Odd jobs." She looked over at him, their gazes locking. "He taught me everything I know about surviving against the odds."

Darby raised a brow but didn't ask if her uncle taught her to pick pockets. He had a feeling from the look in her eye that this uncle had.

"Are you asking these questions as my boss or just out of idle curiosity?"

"I'm...interested. It has nothing to do with your work."

"Ah," she said and smiled. Then she spurred her horse and took off at a gallop across the field.

He went after her, catching up as they reached the creek. She swung down out of her saddle and walked to the edge of the creek. He watched her hop across the rocks to the middle of the stream with such grace that he wasn't about to join her. With his luck, he'd end up swimming.

Agilely she squatted down to dip her hands into the icy water pooling around the rock. She brought her cupped hands to her lips and drank heartily. She did everything that way, he thought as he watched her in a shaft of sunlight that made her black hair shine like a raven's wing. He envied her, sensing that she lived each day as if it was her last.

Slowly, she stood, stretching as she looked upstream. He thought again of the bracelet and the Roma queen's face carved into the gold. For a moment, he almost brought up the bracelet, but then she turned to look at him. He felt his heart do that thing it did from the first time he saw her. His throat tightened, his mouth suddenly dry.

He didn't want this to end any more than he knew how to keep it from happening. But he held his tongue. Mariah would leave soon enough. He'd let this play out—no matter how it ended. He knew the risk he was taking. To spend as much time as he could with this woman, he'd take the chance.

Riding back to the ranch as the sun burned off the last of the night's dampness, they talked about everything so long as it wasn't anything personal. She wanted to know what it was like growing up here, if he'd dated the senior class president or the prom queen or both.

They'd laughed companionably as he told her stories about growing up with a father who'd reportedly been probed by "aliens," what it was like having four brothers and Lillie for a sister, how he'd been restless until lately.

She'd met his gaze when he'd said that. "I've never stayed in one place except when I was young living with my grandmother. My uncle…moved a lot. I can't imagine living in one place long even if… even if I could."

"That's too bad," he'd said, pretending it didn't make his heart drop. "This is a pretty nice place to plant roots."

They rode the rest of the way in silence.

"Thank you," she said as they unsaddled the horses. "I hadn't realized how much I missed riding. I enjoyed seeing your family ranch and hearing your stories."

"Maybe we could do it again sometime," Darby said as they let the horses out into the pasture and the two of them walked back to his pickup.

He saw her look toward town, her earlier smile gone. "Maybe."

BORED DURING HIS dull shift, Deputy Harper Cole pulled into Sue's Diner. He knew he shouldn't, especially after that warning the sheriff had given him earlier. But screw him. Harp was sick of taking orders. He couldn't wait until he was sheriff and giving the orders. Anyway, it was a slow shift and if he was lucky, there would be pie and coffee and company.

The diner stayed open late so later it would have

a few drunks on the six stools at the counter and a couple of old farts in one of the four booths. But being right after dinnertime, it was nearly empty. The owner, Sue Pence, would be home with her teenage daughter, Rickie Sue. Now there was going to be a wild one.

As Harp got out of his patrol SUV, he spotted the object of his affection, the cute little new waitress, Vicki Welch. She looked fifteen and while that should have been a turnoff, it wasn't. She had big blue eyes like a doll and a mouth that turned him on just to think about it.

He pushed open the diner door and stepped in. "Got any of that apple pie left?" he called.

Vicki lit up at the sight of him, another reason he'd had to stop here this evening. With Sheriff Flint Cahill riding his ass again, he wasn't sure how much more he could take. He knew Flint would love for him to quit. It was the main reason he was determined not to. So seeing Vicki calmed him down, made him think about other things...

"I saved a piece just for you," Vicki said as he took an end stool.

"I like the sound of that," he said, lowering his voice and giving her a wink.

Fortunately, the diner was nearly empty. There were four old ladies at one of the booths. They'd looked up as he'd come in but quickly lost interest.

"What's up with the old biddies?" he whispered.

Vicki reddened and leaned closer so as not to be heard as she poured him a cup of coffee. "Bingo at the church."

He chuckled at that and grabbed her arm before she could get away. He liked touching her, loved seeing the way her wrist was swallowed up by his big hands. He couldn't wait to get her alone later.

"Your place?" he asked.

She pulled away. "My roommate's back from visiting her mother."

He didn't really care if the roommate heard everything later tonight, but apparently she did. "My place, then. You know how to get there?" It was a small town and he was betting she'd driven by his place after the first time they'd done it in the back of his patrol SUV. Wouldn't Flint lose his mind if he ever learned about that?

She nodded and looked shy. "I shouldn't stay all night, though," she whispered.

He shrugged. It wasn't like he was going to make her breakfast anyway. "Whatever you want, baby. Daddy's goin' to give it to ya."

She mugged a face at him, her pale skin reddening again. "I told you I don't like that."

She'd told him a lot of things, most of which he couldn't remember. "Sure, baby, whatever you say." He picked up the fork and dove into the pie she'd put in front of him, all the time watching her and getting excited. At times like this, he felt as if he ruled this town. Hell, he kind of did.

He was halfway through his pie when he got the call from dispatch.

CHAPTER EIGHT

MAGGIE WAS CLOSING up after her last client when she saw someone standing out front of the beauty shop.

Her heart rate quickened as the woman turned and she recognized Celeste Duma. She closed her hand over the keys in her hand, the sharp metal biting into her flesh as she moved to go around the front counter, wishing she'd locked up five minutes earlier.

Before she could reach the front door, just as she'd feared, Celeste stepped in.

"We're closed," Maggie said, stopping at the end of the counter. She could smell Celeste's expensive perfume.

"You're here later than usual," the woman said, glancing around as if checking to make sure Maggie was alone.

That sick, frightening feeling she'd had before around the woman washed over her. She looked toward the street. It was empty with all the businesses downtown closed and little traffic this time of the evening.

Normally, Maggie didn't stay here this late, but she'd been putting away boxes of product that had come earlier. Then she'd gotten busy doing a little paperwork that was getting behind.

Now she gripped the keys harder in her hand and glanced toward her purse in the back where she'd left it next to her shop chair—and her cell phone inside it.

"I won't keep you," Celeste said, smiling as if she saw how nervous she was making her.

"What do you want?" She knew she sounded impatient. Better that than afraid, which she was.

"I saw Flint earlier. He's so angry at me."

Maggie shook her head. "That has nothing to do with me."

Celeste narrowed her eyes. "I think it does."

"Well, you're wrong. I haven't seen Flint in weeks."

"Really?"

Maggie crossed her arms over her chest, the keys still clutched in her hand, anger making her feel less afraid. "What business is it of yours anyway?"

"You're not good enough for him."

Maggie blinked, then let out a laugh. "Talk about the kettle calling the skillet black."

"You need to leave him alone."

A chill raced up her spine. The threat in Celeste's words hung in the air between them. "*You* need to leave."

Celeste stood, her green eyes almost wide with innocence. "It's nothing personal. You're just all wrong for him."

"Compared to you."

The woman smiled. "I'm glad we understand each other." With that she turned and went out the door, closing it softly behind her.

Maggie stood for a few moments, so full of outrage that she could hardly think, let alone move. All the things she should have said flashed through her head.

For just an instant, she almost went after Celeste, ready to chase her down in the street to tell her what she thought of her.

But, her heart still pounding, she stopped herself long enough to remember something about Celeste Duma. The woman was crazy.

Celeste was a sick, rich, psychotic Narcissus who scared the hell out of her.

Not that it stilled her anger. Nor her desire to do just the opposite of what the woman had ordered her to—if she and Flint were still seeing each other.

So what had been the point? Maggie frowned. Why had Celeste come by to tell her to stay away from Flint? She hadn't seen Flint in weeks—just like she'd told the woman. What, she wondered, had set Celeste off again?

Something Flint had said?

She felt a shiver of excitement as she stepped to the door and locked it. Was it possible Flint still cared? Why else would Celeste feel threatened?

AFTER THE DAY he'd had, all Flint wanted to do was grab something to eat and go home and vegetate in front of the television. But as he was driving down the main street in town, he saw Celeste get into her huge SUV and pull away from the curb in front of Just Hair, Maggie's shop.

Seeing her always brought it all back. The ugliness of not just her affair, their fights, their subsequent divorce—but the stunts she'd pulled to keep him from getting serious with Maggie.

Worse, it brought back the memory of how he had stupidly defended Celeste to Maggie. It made him groan as he slowed along the main drag of Gilt Edge.

His sister, Lillie, had told him to do whatever he needed to fix it. "I like Maggie," she'd said. He hadn't needed to ask her what she thought of Celeste.

None of his family had been fans of his former wife. "She certainly makes no secret of the fact that she thinks she's better than us," Hawk had said once, and the others had quickly agreed.

It had been the truth and another reason why Celeste had left him for Wayne Duma. She'd wanted more than Flint could provide and had found it in Wayne. But Celeste was like a kid who wanted all of the marbles. He suspected it was the real reason she couldn't let go of him.

Or maybe she hoped to keep him in the wings in case her marriage to Duma didn't work out?

Either way, Flint had had enough. Celeste had thrown him for a loop, but he was finally over her. There would be no going back—although she didn't believe it. She seemed to think that all she had to do was snap her fingers and he would come running to her. He groaned, realizing he was the one who'd given her that idea since in the past he had gone running to her when she'd called needing help.

He slowed even more as he neared Maggie's beauty shop, surprised to see the lights still on. When he spotted movement inside, he swung into the parking space out front that Celeste had just vacated. Frowning, he wondered why Celeste had been parked here only moments before. Was there cause for concern?

With relief, he saw Maggie inside, although she looked as if she was about to leave.

On impulse he got out of his patrol SUV and started toward the front door. Through the window, he saw her look in his direction. Surprise registered on her face, but was quickly replaced with a smile.

He'd always loved the way she smiled. Only thing better was her laugh. He realized as he reached the shop door how much he'd missed both.

He tried the door. Locked. Their gazes met and for a moment, he thought she might wave him away. Instead, after only a slight hesitation, Maggie hurried to open the door.

"Sheriff," she said, sounding a little breathless.

"I was driving by and…" He met her gaze again and completely lost what he was about to say.

"I'm glad you stopped."

"You are?"

She nodded, her big brown eyes sparkling in the light of the single lamp burning in the shop.

"Would you like to go get a burger with me?" It was the first thing that came to his mind since he'd been heading to the drive-through for one when he saw her.

He couldn't believe how lovely she looked tonight. He realized with a start that she was wearing a pretty multicolored sundress with high heels and her long curly hair was down. It floated around her bare shoulders.

Normally at work, she wore low-heeled shoes, pants and a simple blouse. And usually her hair was just pulled back in a ponytail or some sort of knot at the nape of her neck.

"Oh, I'm sorry. You're all dressed up," he said. "You probably have other plans tonight."

She smiled again. "Nothing I can't change. I'd love to go have a burger with you."

He found himself smiling back at her like a fool. "I hope you don't mind riding in the patrol car." It would have everyone in town talking before midnight.

She met his gaze. They both knew who would find out. "I'm not worried, if you're not."

He shook his head, still smiling from ear to ear. Celeste was the last person on his mind right now.

DARBY WENT DOWNSTAIRS after he'd showered and changed from his horseback ride. He'd felt too antsy to hang out upstairs. There was nothing good on television even if he could keep his mind on a show. Also he remembered that he still had Mariah's check. He'd meant to give it to her earlier and had just forgotten.

He kept thinking about Mariah. At the end of their ride, he'd come close to telling her she could have her bracelet. No strings. No explanation required. But he knew that once she had it again, she'd be gone, and he wasn't ready for that and feared he might never be.

Lillie seemed delighted to see him as he walked into the bar. Kendall not so much. Was she worried that Mariah was going to replace her? She had nothing to worry about on that score.

"I just keep thinking about those two men who came in to rob you. Mariah's a hero," Lillie had exclaimed.

Darby figured if his sister had been going on like this to Kendall, it could explain the cold reception he'd noticed from her.

"No wonder you're so infatuated with her," Lillie said, leaning over the bar to grin at him as he took a stool. It was a slow night unfortunately so his sister had time on her hands. "So, come on, how long has this thing really been going on between the two of you?"

He groaned. "We spent the night together after the robbery because neither of us wanted to be alone. *Nothing* happened."

His sister first looked disbelieving, then disappointed, as if she was finally getting the message.

"Sorry, sis, I told you, Mariah and I don't have that kind of relationship."

"But I know you're interested in her and after what Flint told me about her risking her life to stop the robbers…"

"I'm grateful to her, okay?"

Lillie gave him a sulky look, but because she couldn't stay sad or mad long, she said, "Billie Dee made chili."

Darby realized he hadn't eaten all day and still he didn't feel all that hungry. "I think I might go for a drive."

"To check on Mariah."

He smiled at his sister. "To check on Dad. Didn't you say his Jeep wasn't in front of the house when you came by this morning?"

"He probably just went into town for supplies. Since none of us have seen him, I'm sure he's anxious to get back up into the mountains," Lillie said. "He's promised to be back for the wedding though. I want him to give me away, but I kind of wish you would be on the other side of me."

Darby couldn't help being touched. He gave his sister a hug. "I'll be right beside you, if that's what you want."

"Tell Mariah hi," she said, grinning after him.

Except when he drove by her cabin, her bike was gone and so was she. Same at his father's place. No Jeep parked out front. No Ely.

What was strange was that he couldn't shake off the feeling that both might be in trouble.

BEFORE FLINT COULD even drop Maggie off after their impromptu date, a call came in from the sheriff's department.

"We have a problem down here," Deputy Cole said.

For a moment, he thought that Celeste had already heard about his "date" with Maggie and the kiss.

He and Maggie had talked, catching up as they ate parked outside the fast food joint, which had no inside service. So when they finished eating and he hadn't been able to help himself, he'd kissed her.

Two cars honked as they passed, having seen the patrol SUV and them in the front seat kissing. They'd pulled apart, laughing. It had been the best date ever.

He had driven her back to her shop when he got the call that he was needed at the office. "What seems to be the problem, Harp?" He listened then sighed and turned to Maggie. "I'm needed down at the office."

Maggie's eyes widened in alarm.

"It's not the woman who shall not be named," Flint joked. "It's my father. Apparently, he's been arrested. Again. So he'll be spending the night in the slammer and tomorrow morning the wrath of my family will be on me. Again."

"I'm sorry. But I had a really nice time. Dinner was wonderful."

He laughed. It felt good since it had been a while. "You're a great date. Next time… Well, I'll surprise you, how would that be?"

"You're on." She started to get out of the patrol car, but he grabbed her arm and pulled her to him for another kiss—right there on the main street.

When he reached the sheriff's office, Harp was pacing the floor impatiently.

"Well, this time you're going to *have* to do something about your father," the deputy said with no small satisfaction. "He's gone and done it up good."

"Which cell did you put him in?" His now seventy-year-old father spent most of his time in the mountains, panning for gold and trapping. Fortunately, he only came down to town on occasion because he usually drank too much and ended up behind bars.

"Cell? He's still in the back of the patrol car. I couldn't lift him by myself and he sure isn't capable of walking."

Flint groaned. "Let's go get him."

"Don't you even want to know what he did?" Harp demanded as Flint headed back outside. "He drove his Jeep up over the curb, across the sidewalk and took out one of the city's trash cans!" The deputy often didn't agree with the way Flint did things—especially when it came to Ely. "So, you're going to just let him off with little more than a fine again, aren't you?"

Flint bit his tongue, reminding himself that when

he'd taken office he'd inherited Harper Cole because Harp's father was the mayor. But a few more complaints about the deputy's "methods" and Harp would be in the unemployment line. That's if Flint could keep from firing him before then.

"Anyone hurt?" the sheriff asked as he walked toward the deputy's patrol car.

"No, but—"

"Anyone file a complaint?"

"No, but—"

"I don't see him in the back of your car." Surely his father hadn't escaped. That would really set off Harp.

"He's passed out back there and if he throws up again like he did the last time—"

"Well, at least this time you don't have a black eye, so I'm assuming you cuffed him right away."

"He could hardly stand up and I couldn't understand a word he said."

Glancing in the back of the patrol car, Flint saw that his father was lying awkwardly in the back seat since he was still cuffed behind his back. "Open the door."

He leaned in, touched his father's shoulder. "Ely?" No answer. What took him a moment to realize was what he didn't smell—booze. "Dad?" He shook his father. Nothing. Hurriedly, he checked his pulse.

"Quick, get those cuffs off him and give me your car keys," Flint ordered.

"You're not going to let him go."

"He's not drunk, you damned fool. He's unconscious." No wonder his father hadn't put up a fight when Harp arrested him. He couldn't. Otherwise, the deputy *would* have another black eye just like the last time.

Harper unlocked the cuffs and stepped back as Flint grabbed the car keys and jumped behind the wheel. "Call the hospital and tell them I'm on my way!"

CHAPTER NINE

DARBY SAW THAT it was Flint calling and pulled over to take the call. He wasn't looking forward to going back to the bar and any more crazy speculation about him and Mariah from his sister. He couldn't explain why Mariah had come to him last night. Or why she went on the horseback ride with him earlier. It was just this cat-and-mouse game they were playing.

And he had no idea what the rules were. But he had a feeling they were about to change. That things had already changed between them.

Logically he knew that if Mariah had a motive for wanting to stay with him last night—other than not wanting to be alone—then she would probably have wanted a look at his apartment. He almost laughed. If that was the case, then she was disappointed. Still, she had seemed genuinely in need of comfort last night. And so had he, if he was being honest with himself.

"Good evening, sheriff," he said into the phone as he looked out at the mountains and thought about his horseback ride earlier with Mariah.

"I'm at the hospital with Dad," Flint said without preamble. "It appears he's had a heart attack."

The words took Darby by such surprise that he couldn't speak for a moment. His gaze shot to the Stagecoach Saloon just up the road.

When he finally found his voice, he said, "We'll be right there."

"We?"

"I'll pick up Lillie on my way. Do you want me to call—"

"No, I already called Cyrus and Hawk."

Darby disconnected and drove on down to the saloon. As he entered, his sister looked up.

"What's going on?"

"Flint called. Dad's in the hospital. He might have had a heart attack."

Her eyes widened in alarm.

From outside came the noisy clamor of Billie Dee's old car. For a moment he hadn't even given a thought to the saloon.

"I can cover for you," Kendall said to Lillie.

"Thank you. I'll tell Billie Dee," his sister said and hurried toward the kitchen as the cook came in.

"Kendall should be able to handle things by herself if it doesn't get crazy," Lillie said nervously. They were both anxious to get to the hospital.

He thought about Mariah. They would go right past her cabin. If her bike was out there... He and

Lillie climbed into his pickup. He reached over to squeeze her hand.

"Dad's going to be all right," he said. "He's strong as an ox and just as stubborn. Whatever has happened, he'll beat it."

She nodded, smiling at his attempt to reassure her, but worry was in her eyes. He was worried too. They'd known the time would come when Ely wouldn't be able to go back into the mountains, when he wouldn't be able to do whatever he wanted. They'd all been dreading that day. Their father would rather die.

For all they knew, he might be dying right now.

A few miles down the road, Darby slowed as he came around the corner and the cabin came into view. He caught the dull gleam of the motorcycle parked out front and felt a wave of relief. Had he thought she had taken off after their horseback ride? He always thought that it would be the last time he saw her. How could he go on like this?

Give her back the bracelet. Let her go. Don't do this to yourself. The thought made him sad and yet he knew it was the right thing to do. He told himself he would as soon as he found out how his father was doing.

"I'm going to see if Mariah can work with Kendall today." He pulled into the yard in front of the cabin and jumped out.

He reached the door before she could open it. She

stood just inside. Her hair was down, floating around her shoulders like a black cloak. The light from inside the cabin caught on it, making it shine. She was so striking that sometimes it took his breath away.

"I'm sorry to bother you, but—" The words were lost as he looked past her to her backpack on the bed. It appeared she'd been packing. To leave.

"What's wrong?" she asked as she looked from him to Lillie waiting in the pickup, then stepped to block his view of the bed.

"My father's in the hospital. My brother thinks it might have been a heart attack. Lillie and I are—"

"You need me to work." She shifted on her feet, her gaze darting over her shoulder toward the bed and her backpack before returning to him. "Don't worry. I'll cover the shift."

"Are you—"

"Go to the hospital. I'll take care of it. And I'm sorry about your father. I hope he's all right."

He nodded. "Thank you."

At the hospital he and Lillie rushed in. He was worried about his father and confused about how he'd gotten so involved with a woman who'd tried to steal his wallet the day they met. But Mariah had crowded his thoughts since the moment he'd first laid eyes on her.

Had she been packing to leave? Going without the bracelet? Or would she have paid him a visit before she left?

He promised himself that when he'd seen to his father, he would end this thing between the two of them. The thought almost made him laugh. He didn't even know what this "thing" was. He just knew that last night, with her in his arms, he'd slept better than he had in years. It had felt so...right.

They found Flint standing by the nurse's station as they came in.

"How is Dad?" he asked as he and Lillie rushed up to him.

"We don't know yet. The doctor is with him. He was unconscious when I found him."

"Found him?" Lillie cried.

They listened as Flint told them how their father had crashed his Jeep and Deputy Harper Cole had arrested him, thinking he was drunk.

"I'm going to punch Harp," Lillie said.

"Get in line," Flint said. "Let's just worry about Dad right now. I don't want to have to lock you up on an assault charge. Hawk and Cyrus are in the waiting room. The doctor said he'd tell us as soon as he knows something."

AFTER DARBY LEFT, Mariah turned to look back at her bed and the backpack lying on it. Earlier everything had seemed clear to her, what had to be done after last night. She couldn't stay here any longer.

She'd always had two choices. Leave without the bracelet. Or confront Darby. So what had the holdup been? She could have asked that first day for her bracelet. But she hadn't for whatever reasons had seemed logical—back then. Now, everything had changed. She cared about Darby. Which meant she couldn't stay here any longer.

She stared at the bed and groaned. She knew why she was dragging her feet. She didn't want to leave. She was content here, even happy sometimes. Today, horseback riding with him. Last night—

Mariah shook her head. She'd been here too long. It was getting more dangerous. For all she knew, her past was hot on her trail. It should have been easy to leave since running away was what she did. But she'd come to know Darby. Just as she knew now that if she asked him for her bracelet back, he would give it to her.

He probably wouldn't even ask for an explanation. But she felt she owed him one. The thought of telling him about herself and her past made her shudder. She couldn't bear looking into those beautiful gray eyes and seeing…revulsion.

What difference would one more night make? Before yesterday she would have said that her luck had run out. But the robber hadn't killed her. Nor had she let him take her pendant.

Yesterday she could have been killed. The thought was never far from her mind. She would have been killed if she hadn't brought the bat up as quickly as she had. If she hadn't knocked the gun out of the robber's hand.

What had her packing earlier was the realization that she was too close to the mark. She'd always liked to take her time with a mark, get to know his routine, get to know his likes and dislikes, get close enough that she knew what he was going to do next.

By then, though, she often didn't want to finish the job. She saw the mark's vulnerabilities—something she was supposed to exploit—but no longer wanted to follow through. It had gotten her in trouble a lot with her uncle since he was the one who'd taught her how to survive after her grandmother had died.

Before that, her fortune-teller grandmother had taken care of her. Once she was gone, Mariah had been forced to fend for herself—with the tools her uncle had forced on her. Later, she was glad that he had since she'd certainly needed them to survive. For her, there had been only one way out—something far worse—so she'd done what she had to.

Now as she stared at the backpack on the bed, she felt sad and afraid. She desperately needed to leave. It wasn't just that she could almost feel the past breathing down her neck. She'd gotten too close to Darby, too involved in these people's lives, too comfortable here.

With a sigh, she moved to the bed, picked up the backpack and dumped out its contents. She had told

Darby she would work today. Her word at least was still good.

But tonight…

She dug through the items on the bed until she found the knife. She had to end this so there was no chance of her ever coming back, or she would never leave. Tonight she would move on.

"YOUR FATHER HAS had a series of mini strokes," the doctor said, addressing the group gathered in the waiting room.

"Is he all right?" Flint asked.

"He's conscious. We can't be sure how much damage was done."

"When will you know?" Hawk asked.

"After we run more tests. For now, he's resting comfortably."

At the sound of yelling down the hall, the doctor turned and headed in that direction.

Flint and the rest of the Cahills followed the physician to their father's room.

Ely was sitting up in bed arguing with the nurse. "Good, glad to see my family is here. Tell this fool woman that I'm fine and to get my damned clothes."

"He seems to be his old self," Flint told the doctor. "Let me handle this," he said to the nurse. "I apologize for my father."

"Don't be apologizin' for me. All I did was ask her fer my clothes," Ely said.

"This might go better if Dad and I are alone," Flint said, turning to his siblings and his sister's fiancé, Trask Beaumont.

"If you need us, we'll be down the hall," Lillie said.

He waited until they'd cleared out of the room along with the nurse and doctor, before he closed the door and moved to his father's bed.

"If this is some kind of intervention…"

"Dad, you had series of small strokes."

His father frowned. "Who told you that?"

"The doctor. You were unconscious when I brought you to the hospital. What is the last thing you remember?"

Ely lay back against his pillows. Worry knitted his thick brows together. "I was feelin' real tired as I come out of the mountains. I went to my cabin."

"You don't remember taking your Jeep into town?"

Ely often drank too much after coming out of the mountains. But he'd always been smart enough not to take a chance driving when his cabin wasn't that much of a walk into town.

"Do you remember where you were going?" he asked.

His father shook his head. "I don't 'member goin' anywhere." Ely met his gaze. "Doctor said it was a stroke?"

"A series of small ones."

"But I'm all right now?"

"You appear to be, but they want to run some

more tests." Flint saw that his father was ready to argue and quickly cut him off. "You have to let them run the tests. I'll pull your driver's license if you don't."

Ely scowled at him but didn't put up a fight.

"Dad, the doctor wants you to rest now. I'm sure they will run the tests first thing in the morning and then we'll get you out of here."

Ely looked around the room like a lion waking up in a cage. "I'll stay, but only 'cuz you're not givin' me a choice. But come this time tomorrow—"

"You'll be out of here, I promise." Flint knew he shouldn't be making such a promise, but he also knew his father. Ely would be hard-pressed to stay here twenty-four hours.

Under the resignation, he saw fear. He could imagine what it would be like for a man like his father to lose his independence. He hoped to hell that day was still a ways off.

But for some time, he'd been telling his siblings that they needed to talk about their father. The day would come when he couldn't go into the mountains. And then what? Ely Cahill was cantankerous enough now when he got to do whatever he wanted. Try to tie him down and he would be unbearable.

WHEN MARIAH REACHED the saloon, Billie Dee was just leaving.

"I forgot something at the store. Kendall's here

and it's slow." the cook said. "Help yourself to some of my chili," she added with a wink.

"Thanks."

Billie Dee waved as she took off in her loud car, kicking up a huge cloud of dust.

Mariah stepped inside, stopping at the back door to just glance around. She could hear the jukebox playing and the sound of glassware being moved around in the bar. She hesitated. She thought she knew Darby pretty well. She'd been trained to read people. That was the basis of every con.

Now she stood looking around, trying to think like Darby. Where would he hide the bracelet? Not upstairs. He'd expect her to look there. No. Not in the kitchen or bar where someone might discover it and ask questions. Same with the ranch where his brothers lived.

She turned around and looked out at the stand of pines behind the place. His pickup was a possibility, though not here right now. He'd want to keep the bracelet close by. But the pickup was another obvious choice.

Stepping outside she noticed footsteps in the dirt. They led into the evergreen forest behind the saloon. She smiled, reminded of a story she'd heard Lillie tell about a secret hiding place she and Trask had used to pass notes when they were young. A hole in a pine tree.

She followed the footprints, feeling like someone

in a fairy tale following bread crumbs. It got tougher to see the tracks once she reached the pines. The forest floor was laden with dried pine needles.

Mariah looked around for a good hiding place for the bracelet. Somewhere that no one would think to look. She kept going, not even sure what she was looking for. She hadn't seen a tree with a hole in it and realized she might be wrong. But there could be something back here. A treehouse? An old shed?

She'd only gone a little farther when she saw it. A large old tree with a knothole in the side of it. Stepping to the tree, she tried to see into the darkness of the hole. Never know what else might be in there, she told herself. It looked deep.

At the sound of an approaching car engine, she couldn't wait any longer. She reached in. At first all she felt were pine needles. The hole went way back in, but it appeared to be empty. Could she be wrong about Darby?

She realized the hole also went down into the tree. Reaching down, she felt something. Cloth? She frowned. Something wrapped in the cloth?

The moment she lifted it, she knew it was her bracelet. Her heart soared. She hurriedly unwrapped the cloth to look at her prized piece of jewelry. Just the sight of it brought back wonderful memories of her grandmother.

She desperately wanted to put it on her wrist as she heard a patron drive up and park. It would be so easy to just take her bracelet and leave. What did she care about working the saloon tonight? If she left, it wasn't like she would ever see Darby again. Nor would it be the first time she'd broken her word to a man.

As she stared down at the bracelet, her heart began to ache. "Don't do it," she whispered to herself. "Please, you can't stay here, so why not just take it and leave now?" She closed her eyes for a moment as she heard Kendall in the kitchen at the back of the saloon.

With a sigh, she rewrapped the bracelet and put it back in the hole in the tree. She would come back for it later tonight. Before Darby knew the bracelet was gone, she'd be gone, as well. Better to leave without a goodbye. There was nothing keeping her here now, she told herself.

As she headed for the saloon, she should have been happy. She would soon have her bracelet back. She would have outfoxed her mark. She would have done what she'd set out to do—and she'd have money from her job to get her down the road.

"Don't look back," she said to herself as she walked into the kitchen to find Kendall rummaging around in one of the lockers.

The blonde jumped as she slammed the locker door. "I didn't see your bike parked outside."

"It's on the other side of the building," Mariah said, noticing how nervous the woman was.

"I didn't know anyone was here."

"Sorry, didn't mean to scare you."

"After those two men tried to rob the place, I guess I am jumpy," Kendall said.

"We all are," Mariah agreed. But it wasn't robbers who had her nervous. "I just heard someone drive up. I can handle it if you need to do something out here. Billie Dee should be back from the store in a few minutes."

Kendall nodded distractedly and looked toward the lockers. Mariah followed her gaze. The blonde hadn't quite gotten the door closed on the locker. With a start, she realized that the locker Kendall had been rummaging wasn't her own. It was *Lillie's*.

CHAPTER TEN

DARBY STAYED AT the hospital until Ely fell asleep. On the drive back to the saloon, he realized he didn't even know if Mariah had worked—or if she'd left for good. She'd definitely been packing when he'd stopped by her cabin.

His heart felt heavy in his chest as he pulled into his usual parking spot next to the bar. The bar was closed. Kendall's car was gone. So was Billie Dee's, not that he was surprised. She never stayed until the bar closed anyway.

As he got out and walked around to the back, he wasn't expecting to see Mariah's motorcycle. When he'd driven by her cabin on his way home, he'd seen that the lights were out, no motorcycle out front. He'd told himself she could still be at the saloon and had hated the hope he'd felt that it might be true.

He'd been so sure she had finished packing and hit the road. So when he saw her sitting at the kitchen table drinking a Mexican Coke out of the bottle, his heart did a little dip-dee-do, even though he warned it not to. Mariah looked up as he stopped in the doorway. He felt weak from all the emotions seeing her sitting there evoked in him.

"How is your father?" she asked, looking genuinely concerned.

"They're running tests but the doctor thinks he had a series of small strokes. It looks like he'll be all right. At least for a while."

"I'm so sorry," she said as she got to her feet. "You look exhausted." She stepped toward him as if anxious to tell him something.

Darby told himself that he couldn't do this. Not now. He'd been through too much since he'd met her. He held up his hand as if to ward off whatever she was about to say.

He looked into her beautiful face and felt something snap inside him. He'd played her game for weeks now, but he couldn't do it anymore. He couldn't take it anymore.

Just as he had at the Chokecherry Festival, he reached for her. Only this time, his fingers found purchase. His hands cupped her shoulders. He backed her against the nearest wall. She flattened her palms against his chest as if to push, but didn't.

He locked eyes with her as he took her hands from his chest, holding them above her head to cage her against the kitchen wall. Her eyes widened, but not in alarm. He could see that she was breathing as hard as he was.

"We have to stop this before it gets out of hand," he said, his voice rough with emotion.

"Stop?" she whispered.

"Stop this game we're playing."

"Is that what you want?" Her voice broke.

"You know what *I* want." He kissed her softly. She emitted a sigh, her fingers tightening over his as he pressed his body against hers.

He kissed her harder, unleashing the passion and desire he'd kept corralled since the day he first saw her. He wanted this woman—like nothing he'd ever yearned for—even fearing she was someone he could never have.

Her lips parted and he groaned as he plunged his tongue inside her, desperate to possess even a part of her. She was danger. Mystery. Excitement. Someone he should keep at a distance. This woman could do more than break his heart.

MARIAH HAD NEVER felt such fire. It raced along her veins, sending sparks of desire to her center. She felt the sudden heat between her legs and groaned against his mouth as his body pressed even harder against her own.

Never had she felt so weak from a kiss. But then she'd never been kissed like this. She wanted to lay herself bare to him. Surrender to this cowboy. Nothing else mattered. No matter the consequences—and they would be disastrous—but right now, she didn't care. She thought she would die if he stopped.

He pulled back from her lips to trail kisses down her throat. She arched against him, closing her eyes as his touch sent goose bumps skittering over her bare flesh. She bit her lip to keep from begging him not to stop as he dipped under the V-neck of her T-shirt to kiss the top of one breast.

She felt her nipple harden and press against the thin fabric of her bra. Having never felt this kind of desire, she told herself she couldn't take any more. She needed the release she knew he could give her.

Darby let go of her hands to grab the hem of her T-shirt. He jerked it off over her head, tossing it aside.

She met his eyes, no longer able to hold her tongue. "Please."

His fingers looped through the straps of her bra, pulling them off her shoulders and down until her bare breasts were exposed in the golden kitchen lights. She heard him let out a moan as he dropped his mouth to one aching nipple.

She cupped his face in her hands, drawing him to the other nipple as he flicked his tongue over the taut nub, then sucked. Her legs were so weak, she wasn't sure they would continue to hold her.

His hand moved down her flat stomach to the top of her jeans. She closed her eyes as his fingers slipped beneath the waist of her jeans, the waist of her panties.

"Please," she cried out again, her fingers digging into his shoulders as he sucked at one breast then the other while his fingers slipped between her legs.

He stopped. Her eyes widened in alarm as he looked at her. Surely he wasn't going to stop. Not now. "Please."

His fingers began to move again. She couldn't breathe. Couldn't think. She'd never felt anything like this before as his fingers began to glide over her expertly. She felt as if she would die if he stopped what he was doing again and yet her brain was screaming for her to stop him. She couldn't do this.

Suddenly her body began to jerk as she felt wave after wave of release. She threw back her head and cried out as he continued to touch her until her legs collapsed under her and they both slid down to the floor.

She was breathing hard, her body still trembling, the last of the wonderful waves slowing until she felt nothing but sweet exhaustion. She saw him through a fog of desire and shame. To her horror, she began to cry.

Darby drew her to him, holding her as she cried against his warm, strong chest. "Mariah," he whispered into her hair. "Whatever it is, you can tell me."

She lifted her head, shocked how much this cowboy had come to mean to her. Her gaze met his and she felt her heart break. What she had just done was bad enough, but if she had made love with him…

And yet even now, that was what she yearned to do—knowing that it would have meant a death warrant for both of them.

She shuddered and rose to her feet. Embarrassment and humiliation heated her cheeks as, with trembling fingers, she pulled up her bra and reached for her T-shirt where he'd tossed it. Turning her back to him, she pulled it on. She was still breathing hard, still fighting more tears.

"I'm so sorry."

"You have nothing to be sorry about," he said hoarsely. "That was all my doing. I shouldn't have… Mariah?" He touched her shoulder, turning her to face him. She saw surprise and puzzlement in his gray eyes. "Has no man ever done that to you before?"

Tears welled again. She shook her head as she said, "Darby, I can't—"

"You've never made love, have you?"

Her throat constricted. She made angry swipes at her tears as she shook her head and then saw his expression.

He looked so surprised, so confused. "It's all right," he whispered.

For a while, she'd forgotten who she was, why she was on the run, what she had to fear. This cowboy was her mark. He knew her as a thief who was only here to get her bracelet back. What she'd just done… What she was feeling…

"No, it's not," she cried. "Darby, I'm... I'm married."

He'd had a hand on her shoulder, but he withdrew it in surprise. She hurriedly slipped past him. Grabbing her backpack, she shot out the door. For an instant, she thought about going after her bracelet. But it was pitch-black in the stand of pines and without a flashlight, she'd never be able to find it.

Nor did she have time. She'd have to let it go. Right now, it was the least of her problems. She just needed to get away from here. From Darby. Her chest ached with a well of emotion at just the thought of him.

She ran to her motorcycle. Leaping on, she cranked up the engine and hit the throttle. The bike practically jumped out from under her.

Mariah hung on, taking off in a cloud of dust and gravel.

She didn't dare look back. Could never look back. Her bracelet was gone, but that was the least of her heartache. She kept remembering the way Darby had touched her, the way he looked at her, the way he'd held her. She shivered at the memory and felt racked with guilt and shame. She had let him touch her like that, knowing the cost.

The motorcycle's headlights cut through the darkness. Ahead the road was nothing but a black hole. She roared toward it.

CHAPTER ELEVEN

FLINT PUT DOWN the phone. The results weren't back on his father yet and Ely was giving everyone at the hospital trouble. Nothing new there.

But he didn't have time for this. He raked his fingers through his hair in frustration. There'd been another break-in. This time some jewelry was taken.

He sighed as he looked across his desk at his undersheriff. "I'm trying to figure out how they pick their targets. These kids are in school all day. How are they finding out who is going to be away from home and when?"

Mark shook his head. "Maybe they just stake out the house."

Flint couldn't imagine how they could have done that. "You see three girls like Tori Clark, Wendy Westbrook and Laralee Fraser standing outside your house, you're going to be suspicious. No, the homeowners would have noticed. This is small-town Montana where people keep an eye out for their neighbors. These girls have a method. They know what house they're going to hit and that no one is home."

Mark looked skeptical. "They're *kids*. I'm willing to bet they don't even get good grades in school. You really think they have thought this through to the extent that they have a way of knowing which houses are safe to hit?"

"I do. Otherwise they would have been caught by now. They're taunting us. These kids are smart. Also with technology they have easy access to each other."

"If we could get a warrant for one of their phones…"

Flint shook his head. "Even if the judge would allow it, I doubt they would keep anything incriminating on their phones."

"I don't get it. If you're right and Tori Clark and Wendy Westbrook are involved, I have to wonder why. These are kids from rich families by Gilt Edge standards. They don't need anything that they've taken."

"Exactly. It's sport for them. Which begs the question of why Laralee Fraser would be involved. She doesn't hang out with them at school. That much I do know. They're from completely different backgrounds."

Mark sighed. "You're thinking bullying."

"It's crossed my mind. It seems Tori and Wendy were with Laralee when she bought her sneakers. The clerk thought the other two might have been making her buy them since Laralee had to part with what appeared to be hard-earned cash. I need to talk to Laralee and her parents, but if I'm right, she isn't going to tell me what's going on if it's bullying. She'll be more afraid of Tori and Wendy than the law."

"If you're right, then they don't really want what they're stealing, so they won't be stupid enough to hang on to it either," Mark said.

"Anyway, getting a search warrant would be next to impossible with Wendy's grandfather being a judge. We need to catch them in the act."

He'd written down the houses that were hit, what time, what was taken. He pushed the paper across to Mark. "Do you see a pattern I'm missing?"

The undersheriff studied the sheet for few minutes before shaking his head. "It's so random. You would think they would have been caught by now. You have Harp watching out for them, right?"

Flint groaned. Deputy Harper Cole. The man was a thorn in his side. But not for much longer. "Who knows if Harper is paying attention to anything other than the new waitress down at Sue's Diner. These thieves should have been caught by now. We're missing something."

"If we just knew where they would hit next."

"Or how they're picking the houses to hit." His phone rang. It was the lab about the fingerprints he wanted run on Mariah Ayers.

DARBY HAD TOSSED and turned until the wee hours of the morning. *Married?* And yet the way she'd reacted to his touch… He couldn't make sense of it. If she was married, how was it possible that she'd never made love?

When he'd finally fallen asleep, it had been like dropping into a bottomless well. He'd come out of it with a start, not sure what had awakened him, until he'd heard someone banging on the door downstairs.

Bleary-eyed, he stumbled downstairs to find the sheriff at his door.

"Flint?" His mind raced. Was he here about Dad? Or someone else in the family? Or Mariah? His heart began to pound. "What is it?"

"One of the lab techs dropped that glass before we could get fingerprints off it," his brother said. "Mariah worked yesterday, right? Any chance…"

He swung the door open wider. "You can check in the bar."

"Didn't mean to wake you this early," Flint said, eyeing him standing there in his boxer shorts. "I didn't interrupt anything, did I?"

Darby groaned. Lillie and her big mouth. "No, you didn't. Just give me a minute to get dressed." He turned on his heel and raced back upstairs. Now his whole family would think that he and Mariah were an item. Just the thought of her and what had happened made him shake his head. He'd never felt so confused about his own feelings—let alone about what was going on with Mariah.

"Fortunately, I found a couple of dirty ones that

had been missed last night as if your waitresses had a drink last night after the bar closed," Flint said when he found him behind the bar. He was balancing a dirty glass. "If you don't mind I'll take both of these. Maybe we'll get a hit."

"You're still suspicious of Mariah?" Darby asked.

"Aren't you?"

He said nothing, hoping his brother was wrong about her—while fearing Flint was not. Just the thought that there might be something in Mariah's past worse than a pickpocketing charge—and a marriage—scared him.

Flint had packaged up two bar glasses when his cell phone rang. "It's the hospital." He took the call, listening and nodding. When he disconnected, he finally turned to Darby to say, "That was the doctor. He's releasing Dad. But he wants to talk to a couple of family members before he does. Want to come along?"

MAGGIE FELT AS if her feet hadn't touched the ground since her date with Flint. She found herself humming as she opened the beauty shop. It was her day off. The shop was closed, but she wanted to finish that paperwork she'd started last night.

If she could keep her mind on work. Flint had called her later last night and again this morning.

She wondered if they were still taking it slow?

Mostly she wondered if they would ever get around to making love?

"I want it to be special the first time," Flint had said. "No pressure."

She'd agreed, knowing then why he wanted to wait. The one time they'd tried to move to the next level in their budding relationship, Celeste had interfered and they'd broken up. Maggie blamed herself for overreacting, and yet Flint was the one who'd dropped everything—her included—when Celeste crooked her little finger.

But she felt that this time they might work through it. Where before Flint had refused to believe that Celeste was so manipulative that she'd purposely try to keep them apart, now he wasn't so naive. Still, Celeste was always on their minds. Maggie knew Flint must be like her, waiting for Celeste to find out they were together again, waiting for that other shoe to drop.

Not that she thought Celeste was going to be able to keep them apart this time. What could the woman do that she hadn't already done? She smiled as she unlocked her shop. Where they were now was so much better than before. It was as if they'd come through a storm and were stronger because of it. In fact, Flint had invited her to his sister and Trask Beaumont's wedding as his date.

"It's informal, mostly family," he'd said. "I want you there."

She'd readily agreed. She still hadn't worn that blue dress she'd bought. It was one that Celeste had caught her trying on. The woman had tried to talk her out of buying it, saying she had one just like it—in a smaller size of course.

Maggie laughed when she thought of it. She'd almost put the dress back. But Celeste had said something else that day. She'd said that she thought Flint would like it on her. Maggie thought at least that had been the truth. So she'd bought it—just hadn't had a chance to wear it for Flint. But she would now.

Flint asking her to his sister's wedding, well Maggie saw it as a commitment of sorts. They were a *couple*. Even though it was still weeks away, she wasn't worried. Before she would have been concerned about what Celeste might do to keep her from going.

After years of being in love with Flint and waiting for him to get over his ex-wife, Maggie had to pinch herself. Was it really happening this time?

She turned on the light and started back toward her station—and froze. A scream rose in her throat as she frantically dug for her phone.

"Good news," the doctor said when Darby and Flint walked into Ely's hospital room. They'd already heard that their father had been causing problems, certain he was fine and ready to go home.

"There appears to have been minimal damage done by the strokes."

Ely instantly looked relieved—just as Darby had been when the doctor told him. "But?" his father asked.

"But, there is a chance that next time it might be worse, more debilitating."

"If you're talking surgery—"

"Listen to what he has to say, Dad," Flint interrupted.

"Mr. Cahill, you're in great shape for your age."

"I get plenty of exercise."

The doctor nodded. "The concern is your diet. I understand you don't smoke but what about your alcohol intake?"

Ely chuckled and shot a glance at Flint. "Don't need to pussyfoot around me. I would imagine my son has mentioned that I've been known to go on benders."

The doctor smiled. "He did mention that. The problem is we don't know what caused your strokes. Or when they will hit again. If you're up in the mountains—"

"I'll be bear bait," Ely said. "And damned proud of it. The mountains are where I plan to die, doctor. Somethin' will get me sooner or later. If it's a stroke, well then so be it. Now please get my clothes because I'm leavin'."

LILLIE WAS WAITING for him at the kitchen table when Darby returned from the hospital. When he'd gone past Mariah's cabin both coming and going from the hospital, her motorcycle had been gone. He'd known that one day she would leave. After last night... She was married. He still couldn't get his head around it. Just as he couldn't bear the thought that he might not see her again. It left him feeling bereft and helpless.

He had a crazy urge to go after her. Track her down and... And then what? She was *married*. With all his thoughts on Mariah, it took him a moment to realize something was seriously wrong with his sister.

"What is it?" Not their dad. The wedding? Or something to do with the saloon? Had Mariah come by and quit? He remembered that he still had her check.

Billie Dee, he noticed, was cooking, but she wasn't singing, which in itself was unusual.

"What's wrong?" he demanded, suddenly scared.

"There's money missing," Lillie said.

His heart dropped. Mariah had worked last night. When he'd found her in this very room, she'd had something she wanted to tell him. "You mean from last night?"

"No, we've been short for a while," Lillie said looking miserable.

He stared at her. "Why didn't you say something?"

"Because at first it wasn't much. But lately..."

"How long has this been going on?" he finally

asked, afraid he already knew the answer. He'd thought he'd been watching Mariah closely enough…

Lillie started to answer but stopped as their brother Flint walked in the back door.

"Is it Dad?" Lillie cried, jumping to her feet.

"Dad's fine," Flint said quickly, looking to Darby as if to say, "Haven't you already told her?"

"I just got here. I haven't had time to talk to her about Dad."

"What about Dad?" she demanded.

"He's fine," Darby said. "The doctor released him. Flint took him home."

"He's as stubborn and irascible as ever," Flint told her. "I'm not here about that." Flint shifted his gaze to Darby. "Is there a place we could talk?"

Darby nodded, although he had no idea what this might be about. "We can talk later about the other thing," he told his sister.

"Shouldn't we tell Flint?" she asked as the two started out of the room.

"Tell me what?" their brother asked.

"Later. One thing at a time," Darby said as he led his brother upstairs to the apartment and closed the door half expecting Lillie to have her ear to it soon enough.

"Love what you've done with the place," Flint said sarcastically.

"What's going on?" He didn't have the time or

B.J. DANIELS   171

the patience for idle conversation. He realized that
he'd made up his mind. He was going after Mariah.

"I put a rush on the fingerprints from the bar
glasses I took," Flint said. "Didn't want to lose the
glasses or have them get broken again. The results
came back a lot quicker than I expected."

Darby sucked in a breath and held it as he braced
himself for the news. He was finally going to know
what Mariah might be running from. He was going
after her, but he didn't want the law after her too—
unless it already was.

"There were three sets of fingerprints on one
of the glasses. Two of them didn't bring up a hit,"
Flint was saying. "You said Mariah and Kendall were
working last night?"

He nodded, his stomach roiling.

"But the one set came right up because of a felony
theft conviction and a dozen other miscellaneous
charges, including fraud and embezzlement."

Darby told himself he shouldn't have been surprised. But he couldn't help feeling disappointed
nonetheless since against his better judgment he had
feelings for Mariah. Feelings he shouldn't have let
happen, but couldn't help.

"I guess it's good that Mariah doesn't work here
anymore," he said.

"*Mariah?* No. It wasn't her. It was Kendall Raines,
although that is just one of a half dozen different
aliases she has used. How is it you didn't know she

had a record? Didn't you run a check on her before you hired her?"

He stared at his brother. *"Kendall?"* He swore under his breath as the realization hit him. Not Mariah. Kendall. Mariah had no record at all.

Darby let out a relieved laugh as he opened the apartment door to call down to Lillie who quickly sprinted up the stairs. "How long did you say the money has been short?" he asked.

"Six months or so. Usually just a small enough amount that I didn't worry about it too much. I thought one of the regulars might have been dipping into the till when one of us turned our backs."

Darby shook his head. "It's Kendall."

His sister frowned. "What's Kendall?"

"She's the thief. That's what Flint came to tell me. She has a record."

Lillie looked from him to Flint and back again with wide eyes. *"Kendall is a thief?"*

Their perfect employee. Darby laughed again. "Who would have thought it?" All he could think about was Mariah—and going after her. It was a crazy thing to do. But for the first time in his life, his heart was running the show.

"Trouble is," Flint was saying, "you'll have a hard time proving it. I doubt you'll be able to get that money back."

From outside came the distinct sound of Mariah's motorcycle.

CHAPTER TWELVE

VICKI WELCH STOOD looking in the floor-length mirror at her naked body. Skinny white girl, she thought, was the best way to describe herself. Her breasts were small, nipples a dark pink against her pale skin. When she was in her teens, her father had called her boobs goose bumps and laughed, saying a boy wouldn't be able to find them.

But Harp had never complained. Her friends thought it was cool that she was dating a deputy. No one argued that he wasn't good-looking, even if a bit smug and condescending at times.

"Does he read you your rights first?" her friend Emma joked.

"Or has he used his stun gun on you?" Emma's boyfriend had wanted to know. "Imagine that right as you're about to—" Emma had elbowed him hard and told him to knock it off.

"Well, at least you shouldn't have to pay for any speeding or parking tickets," her boss, Sue Pence, had said. Sue was in her forties, a widow with teenager and the weight of the world on her shoulders.

She'd opened the diner with her husband's insurance money.

Vicki could tell that Sue didn't think much of Harp.

"Spoiled brat son of the mayor," she'd heard one of the older customers say once when Harp had stopped by for his usual—coffee, pie and flirting with her. Sometimes he would lower his voice and motion her close so he could tell her what he was going to do to her when they both got off work. Then he'd have to sit there for a while before he left so he didn't embarrass himself.

Harp definitely liked sex, anytime, anywhere and she was always accommodating even when she was dead on her feet from a long day at the diner.

She sighed and turned her attention to her body again. She didn't have much of a waist above her jutting narrow hips. With a critical eye, she decided her legs weren't bad, but she thought she looked strange without her reddish-blond pubic hair. Harp had talked her into shaving it all off. Said models did it. Said it was sexy.

Vicki didn't feel sexy as she turned sideways to consider her butt. It was small and fairly flat. Nothing to write home about. She glanced at the time, trying not to be overly nervous.

Turning back she stared into the mirror. Her eyes were her best asset, she thought, feeling a little kinder to herself. They were big and round and blue, and they went with her button nose. Still, she looked like a kid. No wonder she got carded every time she stepped into a bar.

Harp thought it was cute. He liked that she was quite a bit younger than him. He also liked that she'd let him do anything he wanted to her body, even if it hurt her sometimes because he was so much bigger than she.

The timer on her phone went off, making her jump. She took a final look in the mirror at her naked body before grabbing her robe and heading into the bathroom where she'd left the pregnancy test.

DARBY WAS SURPRISED and relieved when he'd heard Mariah's motorcycle. But she was too early for work. Maybe she'd just come by for her check. And her bracelet.

He left Flint and Lillie discussing what to do about Kendall and went downstairs. Mariah was in the kitchen, apparently busy helping Billie Dee.

"Aren't you a little early for your shift?" he asked Mariah, seeing the two of them with their heads together at the stove.

"Billie Dee is teaching me how to make tamales," she said over her shoulder.

"That should come in handy on your motorcycle," he muttered under his breath. They both turned to give him questioning looks. "It's just that I'm surprised to see you take an interest in learning to cook."

Mariah laughed and turned to look at him. Her

smile faded, her gaze intent. "Just shows how much you know about me. My grandmother taught me to cook. Every woman in our family had to learn because we were valued for our...culinary skills." With that she turned back to the stove and Billie Dee.

At the sound of his brothers Hawk and Cyrus arguing, he turned to see them come in the back door. His questioning look made them both stop.

"Flint called a family meeting before the saloon opens to talk about Dad," Cyrus said. "I hope you have a pot of coffee on."

"Or something stronger," Hawk joked. "This could get ugly."

Darby *had* forgotten about the family meeting. He'd had other things on his mind, he thought as he glanced over at Mariah.

Last night, he hadn't gotten any sleep. He'd lain in bed listening for the sound of her motorcycle. He had been so afraid that this time she really was gone. He couldn't get her response to his touch out of his mind. How was it possible that a woman her age hadn't—

He reminded himself how little he knew about Mariah—as she'd just pointed out—as Flint and Lillie came downstairs.

"Is everyone here?" Flint asked.

Darby motioned toward the bar. "Hawk and Cyrus just arrived." He watched Lillie and Flint go on into the bar. He wasn't in the mood for this, but didn't see any way out. Flint had suggested a family meeting—

after he'd done his best to talk their father into staying with him for a while at his house.

But Ely was having none of that so, giving up, Flint had dropped Ely off at his cabin near the mountains and called to ask his siblings to all meet at the Stagecoach Saloon before it opened.

As Darby walked into the bar, he heard his sister cry, "You're seeing Maggie again?" Lillie gave Flint a hug. "You must have taken my advice. It's about time."

"We aren't here to discuss my love life," his brother said quickly, no doubt hoping the others wouldn't join in. The man was kidding himself.

"He has a love life?" their brother Hawk asked and laughed.

"More than you do," Lillie shot back.

"Does Celeste know?" Cyrus asked. Cyrus and Hawk both worked the family ranch, living like two old bachelors.

"Everyone in town knows," Darby said as he stepped behind the bar. "I heard about the kiss at the drive-through." He could hear Mariah and Billie Dee's muted voices in the kitchen. He desperately wanted to talk to her. "Did everyone get something to drink?" He saw that Hawk and Cyrus had helped themselves to a beer, but Flint and Lillie hadn't gotten anything yet.

"What is this family meeting about anyway?" Hawk asked as if he didn't know.

"Dad," Flint said. "We need to decide what to do."

"I'm sorry, but at what point do we have the right to take over another person's life?" Hawk demanded. "That is what you're suggesting, isn't it?"

Flint sighed as he pulled up a bar stool next to his sister. "When that person is our father and he's in danger, yes, we should consider how we can help him."

Cyrus was shaking his head. "I don't see that much has changed. He is always in danger up there in the mountains by himself. It's what he lives for. You want to take that away from him?"

"No, but it's different now," Flint argued. "You didn't see him unconscious. Harp said he was disoriented, could barely stand and, stone-cold sober, he drove his Jeep onto the sidewalk, crashing into a trash can. He could have killed someone."

Everyone grew quiet for a few minutes.

"What do you suggest we do?" Lillie asked.

"I'm going to have to pull his license and make sure he doesn't drive anymore," Flint said. "He can't keep the Jeep."

They all shared a look as if debating who was going to take it away from him. Their gazes settled on Flint. No surprise there, Darby thought.

"I'll do it," he said and saw that everyone was relieved, including Flint.

"He doesn't hardly drive it anyway," Hawk said. "I'll volunteer to take him anywhere he needs to go."

They fell silent for a few long minutes until Lillie broke it. "Now every time he goes into the mountains, I'll wonder if it's the last time I'm going to see him." She sounded close to tears.

"He's promised to stay around until the wedding," Darby pointed out.

"Yeah, that will keep him in town for a while so he can recuperate. Let's not—" Cyrus was interrupted by the sound of Flint's cell phone.

Flint checked the screen. "I'm going to have to go," he said getting to his feet. "Stop looking like you're all at a funeral. If Dad sees you like that…"

"Flint's right," Lillie said. "I'm sure Dad's scared after this. If he hadn't realized he was getting old before, he has now."

"I agree. The thought of not being able to do what he wants has to have sent him into a tailspin," Hawk said.

"Don't kid yourself," Flint said as he pocketed his phone. "The old man is going to do exactly what he wants come hell or high water. Harp just texted me. He picked up Dad after a disturbance at the Old Town Bar."

"You have to be kidding," Cyrus said.

Hawk laughed. "Good for him."

Flint shook his head as he looked at his sister. Lillie was the one who always came to get their father out of jail after one of his rowdy nights had ended there. "See you in the morning, little sis."

"You aren't going to lock him up!" she cried.

"Like hell, I'm not. It's the safest place for him."

"I can't believe he'd pull this after just getting out of the hospital," Cyrus was saying.

They all turned to look at him in disbelief. "Have you ever met our father?" Flint demanded.

AFTER FLINT SAW that his father was safely behind bars, he realized he was late for his interview with Tori Clark and her mother.

"I don't understand why you want to talk to my daughter," Annette Clark said. She had been cordial enough, ushering him into their pristine expensively furnished living room and offering him a seat.

Tori had joined her mother on the couch, while Flint had taken a chair across from them. Mrs. Clark smoothed down her skirt and waited. Clearly she was a woman used to demanding and receiving answers.

Flint glanced at Tori. The girl didn't look concerned. Nor did she appear confused as to what this was about. She was waiting, ready to pretend to be surprised, hurt and upset at being falsely accused.

"Several young people have been breaking into local houses in town," Flint said. He was convinced he had his thieves. Now he just had to prove it.

"I saw that in the newspaper, but what does that have to do with Tori?" her mother demanded.

"The teens left footprints at some of the houses they burglarized," he said, watching Tori. She didn't look quite so smug. "We have been able to track down the shoes that made those prints."

Tori shifted a little.

"I'm going to need the tennis shoes your daughter is wearing to take to our lab, Mrs. Clark."

"What? You can't possibly think—"

"We need to run tests on them to confirm our suspicions," he said, figuring they wouldn't ask what tests. A forensic lab might be able to match dirt samples to select yards, but he wouldn't tie up the lab for underage criminals.

Annette Clark was sputtering. "I need to speak with my husband and he's at a business conference in Chicago—"

"I can get a warrant, but I thought the best way to rule out your daughter would be to keep this between us. The fewer people involved, you know."

"You aren't going to let him take my tennis shoes," Tori cried and jumped to her feet.

"Or I can take her down to the station and run the tests with them on her feet," Flint said also rising.

Tori looked as if she wanted to make a run for it. He was sure she did.

"It's the only way I can rule out your daughter since she was one of several people who bought this particular shoe locally."

The mother was wringling her hands, looking from him to Tori, clearly worried. "Tori, tell me you had nothing to do with any of this." The teen looked aghast that her mother would even ask but didn't deny it. "Fine, take off your tennis shoes."

Tori started to put up another fight but her mother silenced her, snapping, "Take them off *now*. I don't want to call your father, but I will." She turned to Flint. "I will expect a receipt. Those are very expensive tennis shoes."

"Of course," Flint said as he took out his notebook and wrote her a receipt while painfully slowly Tori took off her tennis shoes.

"Like I said, this should eliminate your daughter's involvement, but Tori, if you know anyone who might be responsible for these break-ins, please tell them that the first person who comes to me and confesses will get off easier than the others."

Tori finished taking off the tennis shoes and practically threw them at him. He carefully put them in the evidence bag he'd brought along.

"Why would you think she knew anything about it?" her mother demanded hotly.

"It's a small town. Kids hear things. Either way, we'll find them, and when we do I'm afraid they'll be looking at reform school. That's if the judge doesn't decide to treat them as adults and throw them in prison."

"You can't be serious?" Annette Clark cried. "They're just children."

"No, they're thieves and budding criminals. Better to try to reform them now than later."

He left Tori curled up on the couch, pouting. He figured she'd be on her phone to her accomplices the first chance she got.

DOWN THE STREET, Wendy Westbrook opened the door at Flint's knock. "My mother isn't here. She couldn't cancel her luncheon and she said she wanted grandfather here." He had figured Mrs. Westbrook would call her father the judge after Wendy had gotten Tori's call.

"That's all right, I was just stopping by to tell her I won't need to talk to her after all." He noticed right away that Wendy wasn't wearing the tennis shoes in question and smiled to himself. Tori had definitely called to warn her.

"You won't?" Wendy asked in surprise.

"No. I already got what I needed." He smiled, tipped his hat and left, leaving a stunned Wendy standing in the doorway.

When he got back to the office, his undersheriff was waiting for him. He told him how it had gone, tossing the evidence bag with the tennis shoes on the desk. He would return them once he'd caught these girls in the act.

"Aren't you worried that this will scare them off?" Mark asked. "I thought the idea was to try to catch them in the middle of a crime?"

"Since I didn't take Wendy's shoes or Laralee's, I'm hoping Tori will think she's the only one under suspicion."

"I don't get it."

"My hope is that when Tori hears that we didn't pick up Wendy's tennis shoes or Laralee's, she'll rat them both out. Or at least Laralee. So we wait and see if they turn on each other." His cell phone rang. He turned away to take it. "Maggie? What's wrong?"

MAGGIE STOOD HUGGING HERSELF, her body vibrating with fury. Flint hadn't said anything after she'd let him in the beauty shop and showed him what she'd found. She shot him an impatient look. "If you say you don't know who did this—"

"We both *suspect* who did this," Flint said carefully.

Maggie mugged a face. "*Suspect?* If you dare try to defend her—"

"I'm a lawman. I don't get to arrest someone, even if I know damned well who did it, unless I have a boatload of evidence to back it up, okay?"

Maggie felt tears of anger and frustration burn her eyes as she looked at the words scrawled across her station mirror. The person who'd written them in lipstick had been furious. The writing had started with the word *bitch*. But then the author had gotten more vulgar, the words more scrawled as the vandal lost control. Just before running out of space on the mirror the vandal had written *Die you stupid bitch!*

Apparently though, that hadn't been sufficient to satisfy the writer's crazy. The vandal had poured shampoo and conditioner all over the chair and floor before throwing the empty containers at the mirror and leaving.

Fortunately, the mirror hadn't been broken nor any real damage done. The place was just a mess. But the words on the mirror, still made her heart pound with fear and fury.

"You're saying you can't arrest her," Maggie said, without looking at Flint. "So what are you going to do about this?"

The sheriff sighed. "I'll try to get fingerprints, I'll look for any evidence, but we both know she's too smart to have left any."

Maggie hated how close she was to crying. She'd cried so much over Celeste, she didn't want to give the woman the satisfaction. "You realize that she'll do anything to keep us apart."

Flint grabbed her arm and turned her roughly to him. "But she won't succeed. This is childish, a tantrum. Once she sees it isn't going to work—"

"She'll do something more dangerous."

He let go of her as if he too feared she might. "I can go question her, but quite frankly, I think that's exactly what she wants."

"And what would be the point? Without evidence, she'll just deny it and pretend to be hurt that you would even think she would do such an immature thing—and to that sweet Maggie."

"You do know her, don't you?" he said.

She nodded, still spooked by this. "Unfortunately, I've run into her a few times—her doing. In fact, she stopped by the other night before our burger date. She told me to stay away from you."

"Why didn't you tell me?"

"And ruin our night?" She shook her head. "I knew she wanted me to tattle on her so you would go to her and tell her to stop. She's never going to stop trying to control you."

Flint said nothing. He looked as sick to his stomach as she felt. "I worry about how unstable she is, you know." Flint met her gaze and stepped to her to hold her in his arms. "I don't know how far she'll take it. I don't think she would purposely hurt you but…"

Maggie swallowed. "I'm sorry, Flint, but I think she is capable of much worse than vandalizing my salon." She stepped out of his arms to look again at the mayhem that had been done. She hugged herself imagining the mental state of the person who'd done this. "You've heard the expression *insanely jealous*?"

"Move in with me."

She turned to look at him. "What?"

"Look," he said as he stepped to her. "We've taken things slow. I think it's time to be reckless."

She didn't know what to say.

"Sorry, that wasn't very romantic."

Maggie put a hand on his arm. "Romantic was dinner the other night."

"At the drive-through?" He laughed.

"It was perfect and so was the kiss."

"Maggie—"

"I'd love to move in with you, but only if it is be-cause you want me there—not because you're wor-ried about me."

"I do want you there," he said drawing her close. "But I'd also feel better having you with me. How soon can you move in?"

DARBY DESPERATELY WANTED to talk to Mariah alone, but there hadn't been time once their shift started. The bar got crowded right away and both of them were too busy to do anything more than work.

When things finally began to slow down, it was late. He was thinking he would close early—as soon as a group of college-aged couples left. He could hear Billie Dee and Mariah talking in the kitchen. The last table had said they were through drinking. They were getting ready to leave so Mariah had gone back to the kitchen with some dirty dishes.

Billie Dee should have gone home hours ago. She'd been back there cooking most of the day. He knew she enjoyed visiting with Mariah. As for Mariah, he figured she was hoping to leave without the two of them talking about what had happened last night. Or about the bombshell she'd dropped.

He had decided he would give her the bracelet. If

that was all that was keeping her here, then it was time to let her go.

The front door swung open and a man walked in. Darby swore under his breath. He should have turned out the lights on the bar sign. Anxious to close now, he didn't have the patience to put up with a lone drinker who might want to stay until legal closing time.

With a start, Darby noticed something odd about the man. It was the way the dark-haired man was dressed. He wore brand-new jeans and a T-shirt with black dress shoes. If he was hoping to blend in with the locals, he should have gone with cowboy boots or at least tennis shoes.

The man glanced around as if looking for someone before he moved to the bar. As he took a stool at the end of the bar closest to the door, Darby called, "Sorry, but we're about to close."

"I'll drink fast," the man said.

He thought about refusing him service. It wasn't just the way the man was dressed. Something about him… Maybe the man was fine. Maybe he was anxious about the guy because of the attempted robbery. One drink. If the man didn't leave after that, he'd call Flint.

"Sounds like a deal. What'll you have?" he asked as he dropped a napkin on the bar. The couples at the last table were putting on their jackets and starting to leave.

"A beer. Whatever you have handy." The man turned away to look toward the back of the saloon—in the direction of the muted voices.

"How about a Moose Drool?"

The man's gaze slowly shifted back to him. "Just make it a Bud Light."

Darby nodded and turned. "I'll get that for you." He moved across the saloon and through the door into the kitchen.

"Both of you. Get out of here. Now," he said to the two women. "Go!"

"What—"

Mariah cut Billie Dee off. "Are we being robbed again?"

We. Surprising how one little word could make his heart soar even at a time like this. He kept his voice down. "There's a man at the bar. I don't like the looks of him. I want you both out of here. Mariah—"

Darby stopped because she had looked back toward the bar. All the color drained from her face. She stumbled, colliding with the kitchen table. She grabbed it as if needing the support. Who did she think was sitting in the bar?

Billie Dee was staring at her, as well.

"You should go out the back way," Darby said as he heard the scrape of a bar stool in the other room. Any minute the man could come back here. "I'll make sure he doesn't follow you."

Her gaze held his for a moment. What he saw in

those dark eyes wasn't just fear. He felt his heart break. She could have run last night and never come back. But she *had* come back. He touched her arm. "Go to the Creekside Cabins. We passed it the other day after our horseback ride. Remember? I know the owner. Stay there until I come for you. Okay?"

She opened her mouth, but then closed it and nodded.

"I'll meet you there as soon as I can." He locked eyes with her. "Wait for me." He turned quickly and went back into the saloon. The man was headed toward him. "There a problem?" Darby demanded.

The man tried to see past him. "Let's stop playing games. I'm looking for Mariah Ayers. I know she works here. I know she's back in the kitchen. If you don't want any trouble—"

He stepped in front of the man, blocking his way as the man tried to go around him. Darby saw that the college couples had left. "My brother's the local sheriff. He's on speed dial. If *you* don't want any trouble, you'll turn around and get out of here."

At the roar of Mariah's motorcycle, the man stopped trying to get past him. His steely gaze settled on Darby as she sped away. The man must have realized he'd never be able to catch her. "You have no idea what you're getting into. I just wanted to talk to Mariah and give her something that belongs to her."

"What's that?"

The man was right. He had no idea what he was

getting into. But this guy didn't look or act like a cop. He'd been around his brother enough to know that if the man had any jurisdiction here, he would have already pulled out his credentials.

"I have a package in my car. If you will be so kind as to see that she gets it?" He didn't wait for Darby to answer. He left.

A few moments later, the man came back in carrying a large box. He set it on the bar.

"I doubt she wants what's in that box," Darby said, believing it true.

"Well, it's hers and my employer wants her to have it."

"Who's your employer?"

The man didn't answer as he reached into his jacket pocket and took out a business card. He laid it on the bar. "Tell her to call me. It is the only way. It will save her and you a lot of…trouble."

DARBY CALLED HIS friend at Creekside Cabins and told him to give Mariah a cabin. He'd pay for it later. He waited until the man drove away in the opposite direction Mariah had gone before he locked the door, walked to the bar and finally looked at the business card. Albert Finch, Private Investigator.

He glanced at the large box. The flaps had been turned under—not taped. Whatever was inside…

Picking up the box, he carried it back to the kitchen. To his surprise, Billie Dee hadn't left.

"Everything all right?" she asked.

He figured she'd been listening, waiting to see if she needed to call the sheriff or not. He set the box on the table. "The man left this for Mariah."

She nodded, wiped her hands on her apron and walked over to look at the box. "You're going to open it, aren't you?"

"He left it for Mariah."

"Exactly. The same Mariah who just hightailed it out the back door. Somethin' tells me whatever is in that box isn't somethin' she's goin' to want to see or she would have hung around."

He hadn't thought that there might be anything dangerous in the box. Now he eyed it warily. It hadn't felt heavy enough for it to contain explosives. It seemed too large. Also wouldn't it have been all taped up if there was a bomb inside?

"You know you're going to look inside," Billie Dee said. "You don't want to take it to her if there is something…awful inside it."

Whatever the reason for the PI's visit, it had set Mariah on the run again. The PI had found her. He'd brought this box for her. He'd also known that his appearance would probably scare her off. So what were the chances that Mariah would want whatever was in this box?

He told himself he could be dead wrong. It could be a gift. Or maybe not. At least there might be some sort of explanation in the box. A letter or note. Some insight into who Mariah Ayers was and why she'd looked so scared when she'd lit out of here. Why she was on the run. Why she was married but apparently had never made love. Was there something important in the box that he should know about before he met her at Creekside Cabins?

He glanced at Billie Dee and then reached for the box. Opening it was as easy as lifting one of the flaps.

The contents seemed to explode as if they'd been stuffed into the box.

"What in the world?" he heard Billie Dee exclaim as she jumped back.

He stared at all the white, the gleam of rhinestones, thousands sewn onto the fabric. The dress tumbled out across the table, yards of lace and silk and bejeweled bodice and sleeves.

"It's a wedding dress," Billie Dee cried as he spread it out, the voluptuous fabric billowing.

The cook gasped at the same time Darby saw it. Billie Dee's hand went over her mouth. She took a step back and then crossed herself.

"Tell me that's not blood," Billie Dee said.

CHAPTER THIRTEEN

DARBY STARED AT the wedding dress, his heart pounding.

"You realize she's probably long gone," the cook said sounding sad about that. "Whatever that's all about…" She waved toward the bloody, torn wedding dress. "I'm betting she won't hang around to explain it."

Darby hoped she was wrong. Either way, he knew what he had to do. "I have to go."

"You taking that…dress?"

He shook his head as he quickly moved to it. Stuffing it back into the box wasn't easy. He ran it up to his apartment and shoved it into the back of the closet. He'd deal with it later.

Back downstairs, he hurried out the door into the darkness. From his pickup, he took out his flashlight and headed for the trees. It didn't take him long to find the tree deep in the pines.

The hole was dark. He shone his light into it and then reached inside. His fingers found the package he'd hidden there. His hand closed around the wrapping with the heavy gold bracelet inside.

He had thought of the bracelet as not just a way

of keeping her here, but a bargaining tool to find out more about her. From the moment he saw her, he'd been fascinated by the woman.

These weeks working together had only made him more intrigued by her. She was still a mystery he had yet to unravel. All he knew was that he couldn't keep the bracelet from her any longer. If that was all she was waiting for...

Shoving the package into his jacket pocket, he ran to his pickup. He couldn't let her leave without the bracelet. He'd been wrong to keep it. Wrong to keep her here. He feared he'd jeopardized her by doing so. If he got her hurt or worse...

That thought rattled him as he remembered the bloody, torn wedding dress. Was it a warning? Or a threat? Either way, the PI had found her. Which meant the person chasing her had also found her.

He knew she was running scared. He'd seen the look in her eyes. She'd been terrified that she'd been found. And after the attempted robbery, he knew firsthand what it took to scare Mariah.

The night was unusually dark. Low clouds obscured the mountains surrounding the town. Darby took the back way to the cabins because it was shorter. To his relief, he saw her motorcycle sitting out back behind the last cabin. He parked next to her bike and got out. Before he could knock, the door flew open. She was holding a gun. He had suspected she carried one in her backpack. Now he knew.

She quickly lowered the weapon as she recognized him. "Darby—"

He stepped past her into the cabin. Behind him, he heard her close the door and lock it. When he turned, he looked into her dark eyes and felt a piece of his heart break and drop like a stone. This was it. Once he gave her back the bracelet...

"I couldn't let you leave without this." He reached into his pocket and drew out the package. "It's your bracelet."

Her gaze went from the bundle in his hand to his face. Tears welled in her dark eyes. "Darby, I—"

"I'm sorry I didn't give it to you sooner." He held it out.

"Why didn't you?" she asked. She still hadn't reached for the bracelet.

He knew what she was asking. "I didn't want you to leave. Also I wanted to know more about you and thought you wouldn't tell me unless I had something to bargain with."

She smiled ruefully and he felt his heart ache. "But now you're willing to give it back to me, no strings attached."

"Yes." Unwrapping the bracelet, he took her hand and pressed the bracelet into it. "For luck."

She touched the gold filigree lovingly and then with trembling fingers, slipped on the bracelet.

He felt a sharp stab of guilt for keeping it from her. But he wasn't sorry he'd wound up with it. Otherwise, he would have had only those few seconds at the Chokecherry Festival and still the memory would have haunted him for years.

Whether she believed in Roma curses on not, she'd put one on him. Not only would he never forget her, he would spend the rest of his life comparing other women to her. In the end, no woman could ever make him feel the way he did right now.

"Here," he said. "Let me." She'd been fumbling with the clasp. He fastened the bracelet on her wrist. It fit like a second skin. His fingers brushed hers, sending sparks racing through him. Her gaze leaped to his as he finished latching the bracelet in place.

"I owe you an explanation."

He shook his head. "No strings, remember?"

MARIAH FELT HER heart break. Why couldn't she have met Darby in another life? She shook her head at the thought. She'd been born into this one, this life full of customs and culture, this life ruled by Roma law and family.

"I can't leave without telling you the truth about me."

"Or you could stay. Quit running. Let me help you."

She smiled even though it hurt to do so. "I can't stay. I would be jeopardizing you, your sister, your whole family."

"We're a pretty strong family and we pull together

when things get rough. Whatever you're running from—"

"Darby, I told you—I'm… I'm married."

He nodded. "So you said. But I gathered from the wedding dress that the private investigator left for you back at the saloon that the marriage didn't go well."

Rafael had sent her wedding dress? She closed her eyes and turned away, shame and humiliation making her face burn. "I never wanted you to know any of this."

She heard him behind her, felt his hand on her shoulder. He turned her around to face him. "Where is your husband?"

"I have no idea. He could be anywhere. Even on his way to Montana." And that alone should have terrified her enough to make her run as far as she could get from this place. From this man who she'd come to care for too deeply.

"He's what you're running from?"

She nodded, tears burning her eyes.

"Mariah?" He touched her arm above the bracelet. "You have to let me help you. Running isn't the answer. He'll eventually find you and then what? Talk to me."

She looked into his handsome face. She should have left this cowboy alone. Now she'd involved him in her trouble. Even if she left tonight and kept going, she'd already jeopardized him and his family. The private investigator who'd left the wedding dress would tell Rafael that she'd been working at the bar. Worse, that Darby had helped her get away.

"You don't understand how dangerous my husband is. I can't stay. If he finds me here, finds me with you…"

"I don't understand," he said. "Why run? You can get a divorce—"

She shook her head. "It isn't that simple."

"Clearly, or you wouldn't be running for your life," he said. "You don't have to tell me if you don't want to, but I wish you would."

She nodded slowly. She owed him at least this.

He took off his hat and coat, lowered himself onto the edge of the double bed.

Mariah swallowed the lump in her throat and sat down beside him. "It's all very complicated, bound up in years of culture, years of my ancestors being persecuted. It's why my people don't assimilate. There are more than a million of us living in this country, but few people know about us. We keep to ourselves. The elders believe it is the only way to retain the Roma culture."

"Your husband is…Roma? Surely if you don't want to be married to him—"

"In our culture, the husband rules the home. The wife submits to his rules. Her job is to take care of him and their children when they have them. She isn't allowed to work outside the home. Actually, the couple usually lives with his parents and the mother-in-law trains the wife until at least the first child is born, often longer."

Darby shook his head. "I'm sorry but, Mariah, I can't see you living like that. Why would you have agreed to this? Surely your culture doesn't force you to marry a man who would hurt you."

"Not all Roma families still believe in the old ways, but my grandmother did. Under Roma law, the parents of the boy select the bride when both are very young. It is the responsibility of the parents to find their son an appropriate girl. They judge her value based on strength, stamina, health, disposition, manners and, above all, domestic skills. But they also look at the girl's family. Usually they want one with a good reputation. In my case, the family looked at my grandmother who was a Loveridge, a strong, influential and respected family. Not my uncle who taught me how to pick pockets."

"Wait, are you telling me you had an arranged marriage?" He sounded shocked. "They still do that in America?"

"Many Roma still do. They hold great value in their culture because for many that is all they have since they have no homeland. Customs, traditions, the laws that they have lived by since the thirteenth century are all they have after having been forced out of country after country."

"How old were you when this happened?"

"Fifteen."

"Fifteen?"

"I was promised to my husband's family. A *darro* or dowry was paid to my uncle for me, so the deal was made."

"That's crazy. A bride price? Surely it can't be legally binding."

"My family believes that any woman who rejects a formal proposal is considered tarnished, an outcast. She brings disgrace not just to herself but to both families."

Darby shook his head. "Dowries, arranged marriages, this is so archaic. You were sold to this man."

"The money is to compensate the father for the loss of his daughter. It's not to purchase a bride."

"Really? Sure sounds that way to me. So what happened?"

She looked away. "I refused to marry him. I ran away. My future husband was having fun so he didn't bother looking for me for a while even though most Romas marry in their teens or early twenties. My uncle pleaded with my intended to give me time. I was still young, 'foolish…' 'Strong willed,' he said. But because of that I would make a bride worth waiting for, he assured the family." She swallowed. "Rafael wasn't worried. He said he would beat that strong-willed foolishness out of me when the time came."

Darby swore.

"I stayed away, hoping he would give up and find someone else. Then one day he and his cousins caught up with me. He made sure I didn't get away. I was held in captivity right up until the wedding and then guarded by his cousins afterward. Some Roma still demand purity—and ultimately proof of it."

Darby rose from the bed and began to pace. "Your wedding dress was torn and bloody." He stopped pacing to look at her. "Whose blood was on it?"

Tears welled in her eyes. As one broke loose and started down her cheek, Darby stepped to her and caught it with his thumb. The rough feel of it sent a shiver through her. She reached up to take his hand. She placed a kiss in the center of his palm and held it to her cheek for a moment.

"The blood on the dress?" Darby asked again.

"His. Mine. After the wedding, he tried to…" Her voice broke. "I fought back. I couldn't bear the thought of him…" She swallowed. "Now you understand what I've done. I've shamed him, his family and my own. But worse, I've put Rafael's manhood in question. He can't let that go."

"What will he do when he finds you?" Darby asked as he knelt down in front of her and took both of her hands in his.

She looked down at their hands entwined together. "I am legally bound to Rafael under Roma law. Even though he is hated and feared in his Roma community, none of them will help me. He is a violent, hard, uncaring man and I fear him, but he is still my husband. He will force me to go back and be his wife. He will make me pay for the humiliation I put him through. If he doesn't kill me, he'll make me pay for the rest of my life. I can't go to the police. For them, it is a domestic dispute. And in reality a restraining order is all but meaningless." Mariah looked up. "Do you understand now why I have to keep running?"

Darby rose and pulled her up with him and into his arms. "You aren't going anywhere, especially back with him. I won't let you." He drew back to look at her. What she saw in his gaze made her heart expand to near bursting. "Tell me you want to stay with me and fight."

RAFAEL VALE LISTENED impatiently to the report from the private investigator.

"Just tell me where she is."

The PI sighed. "She *was* in Gilt Edge, Montana. She'd apparently been there for some time working as a barmaid at a place called the Stagecoach Saloon. It's a bar and café."

Rafael cursed under his breath with disgust. It was against their culture for her to work. Could she dishonor him any more than she already had? Apparently so. Which was another reason she had to be stopped. He was sure she didn't keep her head covered either, as a proper married woman should have done.

"I'm sorry, but one of the owners of the place, a cowboy by the name of Darby Cahill, helped her get away."

"A *cowboy*?" He shook his head. As the elder of the family, his father had wanted to handle this. Vernon Vale was old-school, old *country*. His idea of rectifying this was to drag Mariah back, force her to obey her wedding vows and see that the marriage was consummated. Once her purity was lost to Rafael, they would be bound together, for better or worse.

And it would be for worse—at least for her. But even that was too good for Mariah. She had disgraced him, disgraced her family and his. He would not forgive. She deserved the most severe punishment.

Once she was dealt with, he could remarry. His father would take care of the details, but he already had someone in mind, someone better than Mariah, someone who would submit to him without bloodshed.

But before he could remarry, he had to annul his marriage in a way that appeased the humiliation she'd caused.

So he'd gone outside the family and hired a private investigator. He'd been right to do it. Finch had been tracking her for weeks. He'd finally caught up to her. Which told him that she was getting tired of running. Or that she thought enough time had gone by and she was safe. Why else would she stay this long in one place unless…

"Tell me about this cowboy," Rafael said through gritted teeth. "Do you think she confided in him?"

"Possibly. He was very protective of her. I suspect he knew someone was looking for her before I arrived. The moment he saw me, he was suspicious and got her out of there. I hope it was all right—I gave him the…package you sent. Unfortunately, I was unable to serve her with the annulment papers."

As if that had ever been Rafael's intent. But he'd had to tell the PI something. "You did a good job. If you hear anything else from her, let me know. Otherwise, just send me your bill." He hung up. Where the hell was Gilt Edge, Montana?

Just the thought of seeing Mariah again made him hard and furious. She'd gotten away from him before he could consummate the marriage. Not this time. He'd have her, force her to sign the annulment papers and then he'd kill her. It should be easy to get rid of her body in a place like Montana. Only then would he be free of her.

But it sounded as if he might have to get rid of the cowboy, as well.

CHAPTER FOURTEEN

"YOU DON'T UNDERSTAND," Mariah said, getting up to pace the two-room cabin. "If Rafael even thought that I cared about you…" She stopped to look at him.

"You mean if he saw you looking at me like that?"

She nodded.

"Or if he saw me looking at you the way I do?"

Again she nodded. "If he thought for a moment that we'd…"

"Made love? Mariah, we didn't make love."

She shook her head. "Even if he knew that you… touched me down there." She closed her eyes, remembering what he'd done to her and how badly she'd wanted more. Opening her eyes, she locked gazes with him. "He'd kill us both."

"Mariah, I'm not afraid of him."

"You should be."

"I want to do more than touch you. I want to make love to you."

A moan escaped her lips as he stepped to her and took her in his arms.

"I'm a married woman."

"No, you were forced into something you didn't

want. No law in this land would allow that contract to stand."

"But Roma law would and does."

He looked into her eyes. "Doesn't Roma law require you to be with a Roma man?"

Tears filled her eyes. "Yes."

"Then how many laws are you willing to break with me right now?"

From the beginning, she told herself that she would never marry Rafael. That she would prefer to die before that. And yet he'd caught her, dragged her back, forced her into the marriage. But she refused to let him rape her on their wedding night. He'd told her that he liked it rough, and that because he'd been forced to chase her down to get her to marry him, he was going to hurt her bad.

He'd grabbed her, telling her that once he had her he was going to use a wine bottle on her and anything else he could find in every orifice he wanted. That she was his now and he could do anything he wanted to her at any time. She'd fought back with everything she had in her—and had managed to get away after breaking that wine bottle over his head.

Was she ready to give up now? The private investigator had found her. By now he would have told Rafael. For all she knew, Rafael was on his way to Gilt Edge. He wouldn't stop looking for her. He couldn't remarry until he'd dealt with her.

She looked into Darby's handsome face. She'd

fallen for this cowboy. Under Roma law, she couldn't be with him even if she wasn't married. Her grandmother had begged her to live her life as a Roma and keep their heritage alive.

Her fingers went to the bracelet. Just the touch of it had always grounded her. She was Roma but she could no longer live by the ancient laws.

I'm sorry, Grandmother.

Stepping into Darby's arms, she said, "You are willing to risk everything?"

"For you? Absolutely."

"DARBY, I'M SCARED."

He pulled Mariah closer. "Don't be. I won't let him hurt you, let alone take you."

She shook her head. "Not for me. I can't bear the thought that Rafael will try to hurt you, perhaps even kill you because of me."

Darby knew the danger. He didn't doubt that Mariah had every reason to be terrified of this man tracking her. He refused to think of Rafael as her husband.

"Don't you realize that I would die before I'd let anyone hurt you?"

"I know." Her eyes filled again with tears as she reached over and cupped his cheek. "That's what terrifies me." She pulled back. "I shouldn't have involved you in this."

He grabbed her hand and pulled her back to the

bed beside him. "I was involved the moment I saw you out in the crowd at the Chokecherry Festival. I was up on the bandstand throwing Stagecoach Saloon T-shirts into the crowd, when I saw you. I felt as if I'd been hit by lightning."

She shook her head as if thinking he wasn't being serious.

"Nothing like that had ever happened to me before. As soon as I was done on the bandstand, I came looking for you."

Mariah shook her head. "You were looking for me and I was looking for a mark. Not exactly the kind of romantic story you want to tell your children." She turned to look at him. "I needed gas money and I was afraid to stay long enough to get a job."

"Someone bumped into me…"

"Me," she said with a laugh.

"I saw you as you went past me. I grabbed your scarf, determined to talk to you, and ended up pulling off your bracelet."

"Making me drop your wallet."

He laughed. "And the rest is history. I fell for you in spite of everything."

Her eyes grew darker. "How is that possible? A woman like me? Weren't you afraid I would come for my bracelet in the middle of the night?"

He chuckled. "I was waiting that first night. I even left open the door to my apartment and the back door of the saloon."

"If only I had known." She smiled at him. "I couldn't believe you gave me the job."

"I wanted to see how far you would go."

Their gazes locked.

"Last night," she began looking embarrassed. "I wanted you more than I have wanted anything. But I've broken so many rules in my life. I couldn't."

"And now?" Darby asked.

"It will only make things more dangerous."

It was dangerous enough right now for her, he thought.

"If you and I were to make love…" Her voice broke. "And if Rafael thought for a minute that we had…" She shook her head. He could see the fear in her eyes. "He would kill me and then come after you."

"Mariah, I fell for you right then and there at the festival. I know it sounds crazy. Believe me, I'm never telling a member of my family. Love at first sight? I'm not even sure Lillie believes in that." He pulled her closer. "Over the past few weeks, I've only fallen harder. I didn't care about your past. I still don't. Mariah, I'm in love with you."

Her dark eyes shone with tears. "Oh, Darby, I love you too. I found where you hid my bracelet." She laughed at his surprise. "I didn't take it because… because I didn't want to leave you. As dangerous as I knew it was, I kept making excuses not to leave."

"The other day you were packing," he said.

She nodded. "I realized that I loved you too much to stay and put you in danger. That's why you have to let me go."

He shook his head. "We're in this together now."

CHAPTER FIFTEEN

AFTER A SLEEPLESS NIGHT, Darby dropped Mariah off at his apartment. He asked his brothers Hawk and Cyrus to stay there until he got back. Since Billie Dee was already there cooking, they were glad to stick around and have breakfast with her.

Even if the private investigator had told Rafael Vale that he'd found Mariah, there was no way the man could have reached Montana yet. But still, he wasn't taking any chances.

Retrieving the box from his closet, he took the wedding dress and drove to sheriff's department.

"I need your help," he told Flint after he'd closed the door behind him and taken a seat in front of his brother's desk. He told him everything from the moment he'd seen Mariah at the Chokecherry Festival right up to last night and how he and Mariah had stayed up until dawn talking.

Flint made no comment, his expression staying lawman-like throughout. But as he finished, his brother looked worried.

"Did she go to the police?" his brother asked.

"No, she was led to believe she couldn't trust the police to help her."

"And the marriage ceremony happened? The marriage just wasn't consummated?"

Darby nodded. "Can you find out if she is legally married? I'm thinking he might not have filed the paperwork after she left."

"Even if the marriage isn't legal, you think he'll come after her?"

Darby nodded. "He hired a private investigator to track her down and bring her this box."

Flint glanced at the large box warily.

"It's her wedding dress. It's torn and there is blood on it. Mariah says the blood belongs to the two of them. Apparently she put up a good fight. He'd told her in detail how he planned to rape her numerous times on their wedding night before she got away."

His brother sighed as he leaned back in his chair. "How exactly are you involved?"

"I'm in love with her." The words were out. No truer words had been spoken, but he hadn't wanted to tell his family yet.

Flint raised an eyebrow. "That was quick."

"Quicker than you think. I know you don't believe in love at first sight, but that's what it was. Like a lightning bolt, and if you tell our brothers or Lillie, so help me I'll—"

Flint held up his hand. "I'll stop you right there before you threaten an officer of the law. I won't say anything to Hawk or Cyrus. But I would imagine your sister already knows. I'm just not sure how finding out whether or not she is legally married will solve the problem, but," he said, picking up the phone, "I'll be happy to see what I can find out."

He made a quick call and hung up. "I have someone checking into the marriage. But that aside, it sounds like her...*intended* is determined to consummate the marriage. So what is your plan?"

"Mariah's been on the run for weeks. He's going to catch up to her. I've talked her into staying here and fighting."

"Staying with you at the saloon?"

He nodded.

"I can have a deputy drive by. Leave that front light on, the security one out front of the saloon. If it's out, the deputy will know there's trouble and call in for backup."

"Thanks. It is probably going to get ugly. This man is apparently violent in all his dealings, not just with women."

"Give me his name and I'll see what I can find out about him."

"Rafael Vale. He might be bringing reinforcements."

"It would help if I know when he's headed this way."

"I suspect he's already on his way," Darby said. "But I'll let you know if I hear anything. And thanks."

"That's what I'm here for," Flint said. "As sheriff. And as your brother." But Darby could tell he was worried.

RAFAEL VALE PICKED up the knife and went to work on his sunny-side-up eggs. Across the table, his cousin Angel watched with disgust.

"You have a problem?" Rafael demanded.

Angel shook his head and looked away.

Diving into his breakfast, Rafael talked while he ate. "You really need to eat something. We still have a long way to go." They'd driven all night, taking turns at the wheel. Rafael hadn't realized what a big country this was. Driving from Florida to Montana was going to take at least another day of solid driving.

"My stomach's bothering me."

Rafael laughed. "You're just spoiled by your mother's cooking. Wait until you get married. You'll have to get used to your wife's cooking."

Angel mugged a face. "I'm never getting married, then."

His cousin was six years younger, a mama's boy. No woman would be good enough for his mother.

Rafael thought of his so-called wife. His mother had urged him to forget Mariah. "She has shamed us enough. A woman like that…" His mother didn't understand that his honor was at stake. Also Mariah had denied him what was his on their wedding night.

He would have her. He would hurt her in ways he hadn't even imagined yet. That made him smile.

"I'm thinking I should go back. I could catch a flight or even a bus—"

"You're not going anywhere but Montana with me so forget going back. You'll be eating your mother's cooking soon enough."

Rafael finished his breakfast and shoved the plate away. "We need to pick up a few things. I saw a store across the street that should have everything we need."

Angel looked worried as he glanced past him to the store. "A hardware store?"

"What did you think I was going to buy? Flowers for her?"

Angel hadn't wanted to come along. He was timid, but he was family. When the time came, he would do whatever Rafael told him to do and he would keep his mouth shut about it.

"Come on. I want this finished by tomorrow night." He rose, tossed some money on the table and headed for the door.

Across the street, he loaded the items he would need into the cart. Duct tape, rope, a tarp and a large container of bleach.

Angel looked a little sick to his stomach as they walked out to the van he'd rented. "Are you sure about this?" he asked as they climbed in.

Rafael laughed. "She's my wife." The laugh died

on his lips as he thought of Mariah and what he'd suffered at her hands. She would pay for the rest of her life. He just hoped her life wasn't cut too short. Sometimes he lost his temper…

Just the thought of what he would do with her made him hard as he started the van's engine and drove north toward Gilt Edge, Montana.

FLINT PULLED TO the curb to wait. Maggie still had a client in her chair. He glanced at his watch and thought about her moving in with him. Was it too soon? Had he only asked because he was scared that Celeste was crazy enough to hurt her? Was he still letting Celeste run his life?

The door of the salon opened and he looked up expectantly. Betty Arnold came out and waved at him before driving away. A minute later, Tori Clark came out with the ends of her blond hair dyed green. He didn't get the weird hair colors, which his sister would have told him meant he was starting to sound like their father. He groaned at the thought.

Tori didn't see him. She was looking in the direction of the retreating Betty Arnold and smiling as she began to quickly text.

Flint watched, frowning as Tori hurried down the street. She was practically skipping in her joy. Seeing that only Maggie and Daisy were left inside the shop, he got out and went in.

Maggie looked surprised to see him, at first smiling until she saw his expression. "What's wrong?"

"I need to see your appointment book."

"All right." Maggie shot Daisy a look and shrugged.

"How long has Tori Clark been a client?" he asked as she picked up the book on the counter by the door and handed it to him.

"Not long," she said. "Flint, what is this about?"

"I'm not sure. Just a theory." He flipped through the appointment book, pulled out his notebook and pen, and began jotting down when Tori had come in—and who had been in Daisy's adjacent chair at the time. Almost at once he saw a pattern.

Then he found a discrepancy—and just when he thought his theory wasn't going to pan out. Then, another name leaped out at him. *Wendy Westbrook.* He looked across the page to see who was in Daisy's chair on the day Wendy had an appointment with Maggie.

"This book," he said to Maggie as he glanced to the back of the shop to see the sight angle. "It sits out here all the time?"

She nodded. "What are you getting at?"

When Maggie and Daisy were working, they often couldn't see the counter—and the appointment book.

"If someone had been in the waiting area, they could have had access to the book without your noticing," he said. "They could have known who was coming in on a regular basis and when."

Maggie frowned. "Why would they care?"

He glanced out the front window. "If I'm right…
I'm going to have to test out my theory." Flint glanced
over at her. "I just saw Betty Arnold leaving. Did she
mention where she might be going tonight or some
other night?"

Maggie and Daisy exchanged a look.

"She said she and Jack were going to take the dinner train tonight with friends. The Charlie Russell
Chew Choo." Daisy rolled her eyes. "But I've heard
that the prime rib is really good."

The three-and-a-half-hour trip followed the route
of the Chicago, Milwaukee, St. Paul and Pacific Rail-
road for fifty-six miles over breathtaking trestles
and one half-mile-long tunnel, and it included dinner. Plenty of time for some local teens to break into
a person's house while they were gone. If he was
right, his teenage burglars would be hitting the Arnolds' tonight.

"I'm going to have to work tonight," Flint said,
hoping this was the breakthrough they needed. "Are
you going to be all right?" he asked Maggie.

"I'll be fine. I have a lot of packing to do and I'll
get more done without you around." She smiled. He
loved her smiles.

Stepping up to her, he cupped his hand around
the back of her neck and pulled her to him for a kiss.
"I'll come by after I'm done."

"Be careful."

"Always."

WHEN DARBY RETURNED, Mariah was sitting in the kitchen visiting with Billie Dee. The cook grabbed a large butcher knife and turned in his direction as he walked in.

"I see you told Billie Dee," Darby said.

Mariah nodded. "I just sent Hawk and Cyrus home. Rafael isn't stupid enough to strike during the day." She felt safe in the kitchen with Billie Dee and she'd needed the female company. Otherwise, when she was feeling like this, she usually got on her bike and rode. But she'd promised Darby that she would stay put.

"Did you talk to your brother?" she asked as he joined her at the kitchen table. He reached over and took her hand, smiling reassuringly at her.

"Flint is going to see if Rafael filed the paperwork. We'll know whether or not you're legally married soon."

"Like that is going to make a difference to Rafael," Mariah said, lowering her voice even though she'd told Billie Dee everything. "You don't know Rafael. He's—"

"I know he planned to rape you on your wedding night. That tells me everything I need to know," Darby said.

"He will bring help. You don't know the extremes he went to just to get me to the altar. He plans to win this fight, as well."

"He's never come up against a Montana cowboy before."

"He's never even seen one before. But I'm serious. Rafael is dangerous. He has no honor. He—"

"He doesn't fight fair."

Mariah smiled sadly. "No. Whatever he has planned—"

"Flint has a deputy watching the place at night." He explained about the front light. "Even if Rafael gets past the deputy, he'll have to get past me to take you. If he does anything, he'll be arrested."

She nodded but wasn't convinced. She knew that nothing would stop Rafael. She still thought it would be better if they both ran, but Rafael would hurt anyone they left behind. She looked over at Billie Dee and thought of Darby's sister, Lillie. She couldn't do that to them. Darby was right. They had to stay and fight.

His cell phone rang. "It's Flint," he said, getting up and heading upstairs to the apartment.

Mariah said goodbye to Billie Dee and followed him. When she entered the apartment, she saw that Flint seemed to be doing most of the talking. When Darby finally disconnected, she saw his expression.

"According to Flint, Rafael never filed the papers. You aren't legally married. Except under Roma law," he added before she could.

She nodded, surprised how much this news pleased

her. But under Roma law… She thought of her grandmother.

*Keep the old ways. Promise me you will live by
the culture we have fought so hard to keep for you,*
her grandmother had said on her deathbed.

She'd promised.

Now she touched the bracelet and shivered. Rafael was not what her grandmother would have ever
wanted for her. If the woman had still been alive…
Instead, her side of the family was mostly gone. Even
her uncle wouldn't have wanted this.

Anyway, she'd already broken so many Roma
laws by continuing her education, getting a job, refusing the man she was supposed to marry.

She looked at Darby. "I need you to do something
for me. We have so little time before Rafael gets here.
I would have only one regret in life if things don't
go as we hope."

He met her gaze. "Name it. If I can give it to you…"

She stepped toward him. Oh, he was the only one
who could. "Make love to me."

He met her gaze with a questioning one of his
own. "Are you sure?" She'd told him what a sin it
was in her culture.

She nodded. "I have tried to keep my promise to
my grandmother in this, but I no longer can. If Rafael gets his hands on me…" She put her finger to
Darby's lips as he started to argue that he wouldn't

let that happen. "I can take whatever happens as long as I have known a tender man's touch."

He pulled her to him and kissed her softly on the mouth. Drawing back, he met her gaze again. "I want you, Mariah. I have from the first moment I saw you. But—"

She touched his lips again and then pulled away to go to the door and lock it.

MARIAH TURNED AND looked back at him with such longing that he felt fire race along his veins. He could see that her mind was made up. He wanted her more than his next breath, but he also remembered what she'd told him.

If Rafael found out, he wouldn't just rape her if he got his hands on her. He'd kill her.

"Mariah—"

She stepped up to him and slowly began to un-button her blouse. He stopped her and, moving her fingers away, freed the remaining buttons.

Smoothing back the fabric, he brushed his fingers across the warm skin at her waist, making her shiver. Slowly he slipped the blouse off her shoulders. It fluttered to the floor. His hands cupped her strong shoulders and, hooking onto the straps of her bra, slid them down her arms.

Under the thin lace of her bra, her nipples hardened. He pulled down one bra cup to free her breast and bent his head to it. His tongue flicked over the hard nub. He heard her moan. As he sucked the nipple into his mouth, she arched against him.

Pulling her into his arms, he carried her over to the bed and gently lay down next to her. He couldn't wait to have her naked in his arms. But he knew he had to take this slow. He would be the tender, gentle touch she needed.

Unbuttoning her jeans, he slipped his hand under the waistband and found her center. She was wet and warm. He looked into her face. Her eyes were bright with need.

She smiled up at him and then lifted her head to kiss him. He wanted desperately to lose himself in her, but he would take it slow. Given what this could cost her—cost them both—he wasn't about to rush it.

MARIAH HAD NEVER known such pleasure. What Darby did to her, with his mouth, his tongue, his fingers and finally his entire body… She'd thought that her heart would stop, it was beating so hard. She'd gasped, her breathing ragged, as he'd filled her and stopped.

"Please. Don't. Stop," she'd pleaded, her fingers digging into his back. If he stopped, she thought she would die.

He began to move slowly. She'd always heard that there would be pain. She felt only pleasure as he moved with sure strokes, as he caressed her breasts, kissed her and finally took her to such heights that she cried out again and again—and finally she heard his own groan as he stroked even deeper in her. He shuddered and settled on her for a moment. His gaze met hers. She smiled up at him through a haze of pleasure before he rolled off, drawing her to him as he did.

They lay, both spent. The cool air coming through the window rippled over her bare skin to dry the perspiration. She felt sated. Fulfilled. At peace. She'd waited all these years, fearing her first time…and with good reason given who she was to marry.

Darby pulled her closer. She laid her head on his chest and listened to the steady beat of his heart. As her breathing slowed, her heartbeat did, as well. She waited to feel guilty. Or at least scared. What they'd just done…

But she couldn't feel either right now. She had wanted this too deeply. She leaned back a little to look into the cowboy's face.

He smiled. "You all right?"

"I don't think I've ever been better." She touched the bracelet at her wrist, her eyes welling with tears. "Years ago, my grandmother read my fortune. She said I would have a long life, would fall in love with only one man and spend my life with him. When my uncle agreed to my marriage to Rafael…"

Darby pulled her to him. "You knew it was wrong so you fought it and fate brought you here, to me."

She looked into his beautiful eyes and burrowed deeper against him.

"This was meant to be," he said softly. His smile broadened but she saw worry in his gray eyes. What they'd just done could get them both killed, and by now Rafael would be on his way with blood in his eye.

She touched the pendant, warm between her breasts. They would need all the luck they could get.

CHAPTER SIXTEEN

"I NEED TO know what you're planning," Angel said as they neared the small Western town of Gilt Edge.

"I'm planning on taking my wife home." He could feel his cousin's gaze on him. He tried to keep his face straight, but figured Angel knew he was lying.

"I don't want any trouble."

"Trouble." Rafael scoffed at that. "Why would there be trouble?"

"Because she doesn't want to go back."

"Are you saying the woman doesn't want to be married to me?"

Angel seemed to flinch at the edge in his voice. "She won't come without a fight."

"You don't know that."

"You also said that there was a cowboy where she was working who'd helped her get away from the private investigator."

"What are you getting at?"

"She won't be alone."

Rafael gritted his teeth. "She'd better be alone," he said under his breath. "The man is her boss. Once he realizes that she is married to me…" He shrugged.

"No one is stupid enough to come between a Roma man and his wife."

Angel looked skeptical. "This cowboy isn't one of us. He might not give a damn about Roma law."

Rafael shot his cousin a look. Angel had never been this argumentative. He was regretting forcing him to come along. He'd asked some of his other cousins, but they'd grown tired of his wife problems.

We got her to the altar. If you can't handle her, then that is your problem, his cousin Damien had told him.

"Stop borrowing trouble. I'll talk to her. I'll ask her to come back. I'm sure by now she's ready to come to her senses."

Angel said nothing, merely turned to look out the side window. His silence was clear enough. No one believed Mariah was coming back to him willingly.

WHEN THE THUNDERSTORM hit that evening, Flint thought about calling off the stakeout. He was worried about Darby and Mariah, especially since the only deputy on duty tonight in the area was Harp. The other two deputies had already been called to a far corner of the county on a truck rollover. So it would have to be Harp watching the saloon tonight until Flint was free.

He had to stop these teens from burglarizing any more houses and if his hunch was right… He spoke into his headset. "See anything?" he asked into it.

"Nothing," his undersheriff answered.

They'd been staking out the Arnold house since it had gotten dark—before the storm had hit. Now it was pitch-black out with pouring rain punctuated by blinding flashes of lightning and deafening bursts of thunder. The girls weren't going to come out into a storm like this. Not to break into a house for some items they didn't need or want. Even for some bullying initiation, if that's what this was about.

He checked the time. The Arnolds would be coming home from their dinner train trip in an hour or so. How much longer was he going to stay out here in the storm? And worse, keep Mark out here too?

Flint just hoped he and Mark hadn't been spotted earlier. He'd taken position behind the tall wooden fence that ran across the side of the yard. Mark had climbed a tree on the other side of the house.

If the teens didn't hit this house soon…then he'd have to admit that he was wrong. But he'd been so sure when he'd seen Tori Clark come out of Maggie's beauty shop behind Betty Arnold. Once he'd seen the appointment book…

But if the teens didn't try to rob the Arnold house, then it would blow his theory all to hell. Worse, they needed to catch the teens in the act. If his theory was wrong…

He started as he spotted movement in the alley. He couldn't believe what he was seeing. Three small figures all dressed in black. Were they wearing large black garbage bags?

"Here they come," he said to Mark as the three figures moved through the drowning rain headed his way.

They disappeared from view as they entered the back gate of the Arnold house. He waited. He couldn't hear anything but the storm. The hard part now would be keeping their positions until the three actually broke into the house.

He had to move closer. He edged along the fence, pretty sure one girl would be the lookout while the other two did the burglarizing.

At the faint sound of breaking glass, Flint stopped next to the side of the house. He'd been right. In a flash of lightning, he saw one of them standing guard by the back fence. The other two had disappeared around the side where Mark was.

"Tori Clark and Laralee Fraser have entered the house," Flint heard in his earpiece.

He waited for his undersheriff to alert him that they had caught them in the act. While they'd set up video surveillance equipment earlier with the Arnolds' permission, they wanted to make sure they caught all three of the girls involved.

A light came on inside the house. He could hear the teens moving around in there.

"Are we getting video?" he asked quietly.

"Affirmative."

The one guarding the back looked at her phone. She appeared to be getting a text. A minute later, the other two came out. One of them had what looked like a laptop computer tucked under one arm.

As they reached the one at the back of the house, Flint stepped out. "Sheriff, hands up," he said, turning on his flashlight.

For a moment, the three were blinded by the light, but then they tried to scatter. But Mark had come up behind them. He grabbed Laralee's arm before she could get away and got a hold on Wendy, as well.

Flint chased down Tori, who dropped the computer. He was glad he'd warned the Arnolds not to leave out anything they valued. The laptop was old and didn't work and was a perfect prop.

"We didn't do anything," Tori was saying. "There's no law against walking in the rain."

"But there are laws about breaking and entering," Flint said as he cuffed the girl and went to help Mark.

"You are going to be in so much trouble when my parents hear about this," Tori said as the other two were restrained.

Flint got on the radio and Deputy Christopher Hanson came roaring up the alley in a patrol SUV. All three teens were put in the back. "Take them down to the office and put them in a cell. I won't be long."

He was glad he'd chosen Chris for this job tonight instead of Harp. He couldn't trust what Harper might have done with the three teens—or what they might have done to him—before they reached the sheriff's office.

"Let's get that surveillance video. I'll call the parents. This will get ugly before the night's over," he told Mark.

"We got them. I suspect they'll all walk with little more than a slap on the wrist," Mark said with a shake of his head. "You know the judge isn't going to send any of them to reform school."

Flint nodded. "But they won't be breaking into anyone's house for a while once it runs in the newspaper that three teens were arrested for the break-ins. You know this town. Everyone will be speculating. It should shame the parents enough that they will keep the girls in line for a while."

RAFAEL WIPED HIS hand across his face and looked out at the mountains as the bruised sky seemed to open up and rain began to fall in sheets. He couldn't believe that he'd just spent so many hours in this damned van driving straight-through from Florida all the way to godforsaken Montana to chase down his wife.

What made it all so ridiculous was that he hadn't wanted to marry Mariah Loveridge Ayers. He'd had no choice since the marriage had been arranged by his father and her uncle. Even if he wasn't Roma, he couldn't go against his father since he held the purse strings.

Mariah was beautiful, which didn't hurt, and spirited. If he had to marry her, then he looked forward to breaking her like a wild horse. That had been the draw, not lust, not interest on any level and certainly no chance for love. When she'd refused to marry him and had taken off, it had become a battle of wills. He'd been determined to have her. To soil her so no man would ever want her.

He hadn't planned to actually marry her after she'd dishonored him. But with his father ill and his mother in tears, he'd had no choice but to find her, drag her back and marry her. He'd just never filed the legal papers. According to Roma law, they were married as soon as he consummated the marriage.

But according to the laws of this country, they were not. That pleased him to no end. With his father teetering, one foot in the grave, the man would never know the truth and Rafael would have what he wanted—Mariah's virtue—and still get to walk away. His mother would understand and Mariah would have no recourse against him even with Roma law since she was the one who'd broken her vows.

But first he had to find her. Once he had her tied up in the back of this van... He felt himself grow hard again. He would take her as roughly as possible. She would pay for his humiliation. She would pay dearly. The thought of keeping her alive appealed to him. He could take her back to Florida, heap abuse on her, both in and out of the bedroom. She would be his slave. He could do anything he wanted with her.

But killing her also appealed to him. He could take what he wanted from her, bury her out here in this wilderness and then he could go back home and live the life he had desperately wanted for so long. With his father gone, he could leave the Roma community. He'd had enough of its rules, its outdated culture. He would be a free man.

He glanced over at his cousin. He'd been on his cell phone. How he'd managed to get coverage out here in the middle of nowhere, Rafael couldn't imagine.

"Well?" he demanded when his cousin hung up.

"Your father is very ill, but he said he can't die until you are married to the woman he chose for you," Angel said.

Rafael swore. Why didn't the man die? He looked again toward the mountains. "Then we'd better get this taken care of, don't you think?" He tossed the map over onto his cousin's lap. "How far are we from Gilt Edge and this Stagecoach Saloon?"

Angel studied the map for a moment. "About thirty minutes. But you know you can't just walk in there and take her—even if she is still around."

"She's still around," he said through gritted teeth. "I got an email earlier from the investigator I hired along with his bill. He said, if I was still interested, she is at the saloon."

Angel looked surprised. "I thought the private investigator said she took off?"

Rafael smiled. "Apparently, she came back. You know what that means, don't you? She's just asking for what she's about to get."

SINCE THE ATTEMPTED robbery and finding out about Rafael Vale, Darby couldn't help being nervous as closing time approached. They had one table of customers who hadn't left yet. He moved to the front door to turn out the Open sign, but was careful to leave the security light on at the front of the building.

As the neon *Open* blinked off, he looked past it to the empty road and the grove of pine trees on the other side. The night was unusually dark. No moon. No stars to be seen through the low cloud cover that hung over Gilt Edge.

He'd heard there was a storm coming. So far it hadn't reached them, but as he opened the door and looked out, he could smell rain on the wind. It appeared to be pouring rain in the mountains and even in town.

The pine trees swayed and whispered in the wind. He could barely make out the lights of town through the storm. The first few drops of rain slashed down to splash at his feet. He closed the door, turning to see the last table starting to put on their jackets to leave.

All he could think about was closing up and going upstairs with Mariah. He glanced to where she was washing glasses behind the bar. She looked as nervous as he felt.

It was the storm, he told himself as the last table headed for the door. He could feel the electricity in the air. It seemed to spike the hairs at the back of his neck as he opened the door for the stragglers.

"Have a good night," he said, closing and locking the door behind them with a sense of relief. Turning, he smiled at Mariah.

"There's a thunderstorm headed this way," he said as he moved toward her. "I don't know about you, but I'd like to spend it in bed."

She laughed. "You must have read my mind." She glanced toward the closest window. The branches of a pine tree scraped against the glass, throwing shadows across that end of the bar.

"The wind has really come up," she said, and she jumped as a bolt of lightning lit the room. Thunder rumbled, low and deep, seeming to make the building vibrate.

"Don't worry about this stone stagecoach stop," he told her. "It's survived many a storm over the years." It would survive this one too. But he was glad to be locking up for the night. Another bolt of lightning splintered the sky outside. The thunder was much closer this time.

"Leave those," he said. "Let's get upstairs. You

aren't afraid of thunderstorms, are you?" His voice was drowned out by the loud crack of lightning, followed instantly by a drum of thunder that seemed to go on and on for several minutes. The wind howled along the eaves, making the glass rattle in the windows.

He reached for Mariah just as the back door blew open.

CHAPTER SEVENTEEN

FLINT GATHERED THE parents in the conference room at the sheriff's department. They couldn't have been more different. Tori's and Wendy's moms wore velour-jogging suits, their hair recently done with nails gleaming from their recent manicures.

Laralee's mother, Tammy, was still in her uniform from her night cleaning job he'd heard she'd picked up at a dozen local businesses. Her hair was pulled back into a ponytail. Her nails were bare and short, her hands red and chapped from cleaning supplies.

None of the fathers were in attendance. Wendy's pilot father was on a run from Billings to Amsterdam, Holland. Tori's was in Chicago on business. Laralee's was on the road.

"As you know, we are holding your daughters until the judge can see them in the morning," Flint said as he entered the room. Both Tori's and Wendy's mothers had instantly gotten to their feet at the sight of him, both beginning to argue that they would be talking to their lawyers. Their husband's lawyers.

He silenced them as he said, "I have a video I'd like you all to see." He turned it on and the room grew quiet as Tori and Laralee appeared on the screen. From their conversation, it became clear that Flint had been right. Tori was bullying Laralee into taking something.

"I think you should break something," Tori said.

"No." Laralee shook her head. "I'll just take something but this is the last time."

"Wendy and I will tell you when it is the last time. Now find something to take."

When the video ended, the conference room was deathly quiet. Laralee's mother appeared angry with her daughter. Tori's and Wendy's were subdued.

"We will be keeping them overnight. Tomorrow I will show the judge the video and let him decide what should be done," Flint said.

Tammy Fraser got to her feet, ready to leave. She had said nothing since being brought down here. "I'll come back in the morning."

"I've been trying to reach my father, *Judge* Harmon. I'm sure once I talk to him that the girls won't have to stay in jail—"

Flint cut off Wendy's mother. He didn't need to be reminded that her father was a judge. "They stay overnight. Maybe it will give them time to think about the consequences of their actions. Bullying is against the law as is breaking and entering, theft... I'm sure you'll all be getting a call in the morning from Judge McDonald." McDonald was called the hanging judge around the county.

In a huff, the other two rose to leave.

"Mrs. Fraser," Flint said. "If you'd like to file bullying charges, you can meet with the judge in the morning at nine."

The woman lifted her gaze to meet his. "Mostly I want to talk to my daughter. But thank you, Sheriff."

Flint watched them leave, hoping that this experience would change the girls. For some reason he thought of his ex, Celeste. Her childhood had been like Tori's and Wendy's and look how she'd turned out.

DEPUTY HARPER COLE drove past the Stagecoach Saloon, glanced to see if the light was still on and kept going. This was such a waste of time.

"So basically we're providing sheriff department protection to your brother and his girlfriend," Harp had said when Flint told him what he wanted him to do.

"We provide protection to all the residents of this county."

"Right, but in this case you want me to drive by when I'm on duty and make sure a light is still shining out front. Otherwise, I'm to get on the horn to you. Sounds like we're providing special treatment for your family to me."

"Harp, if you can't handle this, then maybe you'd better turn in your badge and gun now. Since you'll be driving around on your shift anyway, I don't think going by the saloon will be that difficult for you. Unless you want to revisit those complaints I received from residents saying that on the night you were supposed to be checking local businesses, you were sitting in Sue's Diner drinking coffee, eating doughnuts and hitting on one of the waitresses."

"It was pie."

The deputy swore now as he drove east into the foothills. Flint had had it out for him from the beginning. It was because he was the mayor's son. One of these days he was going to be sheriff of this county and when he was, he wouldn't give the Cahills the time of day—let alone let them get away with what they did now.

The first thing he would do was lock up the old coot for good. Then he would wait around for the rest of them to mess up. There would finally be justice in Gilt Edge.

As the road forked, Harp considered taking the long way back to town. But his stomach growled at the thought of one of Sue's cinnamon rolls or a piece of her apple pie. He could get it to go since apparently someone had complained he spent too much time parked there. That's if Flint was even telling the truth about that.

Turning around in the road, he saw lightning flicker as the violent thunderstorm the weather bureau had predicted moved into the valley. Harp welcomed it. He hated the night shift. Driving around bored him. He couldn't see why sitting in Sue's visit-

ing with Vicki Welch was so bad. If something happened, he'd hear about it on his radio—if he didn't
have it turned down too low—and he could take
care of it then.

DARBY QUICKLY PUSHED Mariah down and, flipping
off the outside light, he grabbed the shotgun he'd
only recently added behind the bar. He had firearms
all over the place, afraid he was going to need them
when Rafael showed up.

Wind and rain blew into the kitchen. A curtain
snapped in the strong gale. It sounded like one of
the pans hanging over the stove banged against the
one next to it.

Darby didn't move. Neither did Mariah, who had
earlier risen to pick up the baseball bat from behind
the bar. She stood next to him, a determined terrified look on her face.

The wind howled, rain splashed onto the kitchen
floor, but no one came down the hallway. Darby
motioned for Mariah to stay where she was as he
eased out from behind the bar and started toward the
kitchen. He could see the door was wide open—only
rain and darkness beyond it.

If someone was hiding in the kitchen, they were
getting soaked, Darby thought. Rafael? Had he
brought reinforcements, just as Mariah had suspected?
Were they waiting outside for his signal to enter?

He trained the shotgun on the open doorway as he

moved slowly down the hallway toward the kitchen.
Billie Dee had left only a small light burning back
there. The pans clanked together harder as a gust
rushed in. He caught it in the face, the wind, the
chill of it.

Darby was almost to the kitchen. Someone could
be hiding on either side of the door. On the kitchen
table side. Or on the stove side. He would have only
a second to choose which side to swing the shotgun
toward. If he chose wrong—

The back door slammed shut with a thunderous
bang making him jump. His trigger finger jumped,
as well, leaving him shocked that he hadn't fired the
shotgun at the slamming door.

He swung the shotgun to the right. No one by the
kitchen table. And quickly to the left. No one by the
stove. He stood trying to catch his breath, to still his
pounding heart, to will strength back into his limbs.

Slowly he lowered the shotgun and turned to find
Mariah directly behind him. She was gripping the
baseball bat with white knuckles. Her dark eyes were
wide and wild.

He stepped to her, pushing the baseball bat aside
to pull her into his arms. "False alarm." At least this
time. "I need to turn the light back on. Otherwise,
we're going to have a deputy come busting in next."

HARP DROVE BACK down the road toward the saloon.
It pissed him off all the more, thinking about how

he could be at the diner having a cup of hot coffee and a piece of Sue's homemade pie. He thought of Vicki. She'd said she wanted to "talk" tonight. That had him a little worried. It was never good when a woman wanted to "talk."

After he checked the saloon this time, the hell if he wasn't going to the diner. He'd make it quick, but he wanted to make sure that he and Vicki were still on for later tonight. On these kinds of nights, there was nothing he liked better than making love. He just hoped Vicki would be up for it. He'd found that women were willing until they got their hooks into you and then they started having a lot of headaches. That better not be what she wanted to talk about.

He was almost to the saloon when he realized that the damned light was out. Harp blinked and slowed his patrol SUV. "What the hell?" he muttered. He glanced at the time. Probably one of the hired help forgot about the so-called signal and turned it out. As he drew closer, he could see Darby Cahill's pickup parked outside. Next to it was a motorcycle.

He grinned to himself, thinking about the owner of the bike. That was one good-looking woman, but there was something about her that said hands-off. He remembered the contemptuous look she'd given him when he'd flirted with her one night at the bar. The warning look in her eyes told him she was stuck up. He wanted nothing to do with that.

There were too many women like Vicki who came

willingly. He didn't even need to make much effort. He wasn't about to put in a lot of work for a woman like Mariah. But apparently Darby didn't feel the same way since Harp had noticed that the motorcycle never left anymore. Maybe Mariah liked cowboys better than deputies, though he certainly couldn't understand why.

There were no other vehicles around. As he drove past, he tried to see inside. Too dark. He glanced toward the upstairs apartment. Dark. There seemed to be only one light on—a small one back in the kitchen. He kept driving, debating what to do.

The sheriff had been very specific. Light out, call him. Do nothing.

Flint treated him like he was a child instead of a full-fledged sheriff's department deputy and Harp was damned sick of it. If there was trouble back at the saloon, he could handle it. Might make the sheriff finally realize just how valuable he was.

Around the next corner, he pulled over in front of an old cabin and sat for a minute deciding what to do. Lightning splintered the sky around him, followed by a teeth-rattling boom of thunder. Huge raindrops pelted the hood of the patrol SUV. Did he really want to get out in this deluge for a damned Cahill?

MARIAH WAS STILL shaking as she stared at the kitchen floor by the back door. "The floor is soaked."

"I'll turn the light back on in front," Darby said. "Bolt that back door. It must not have been closed all

the way before. I don't want it coming open again.
I've had enough excitement for one night."

Mariah nodded, her heart still trying to beat its
way out of her chest. She'd thought for sure it was
Rafael and a half dozen of his cousins. She started
toward the back door but there was water everywhere. Retracing her steps, she went down the hall
to the storage cabinet and got the mop.

As she began mopping her way toward the back
door, the lights flickered and went out, pitching her
into blackness.

"Darby?" She hated the way her voice cracked.
"Darby?" She dropped the mop handle, trying to
remember what she'd done with the baseball bat.
Her mind was whirling. Why hadn't he answered
her? "Darby!" She practically screamed it over the
thunder and lightning and rain that hammered at the
kitchen windows.

"I'm looking for the flashlight," he called back.
Relief washed over her. She stumbled into the table
hitting her hip hard. She heard the bat roll away from
her and reached for it.

"There are candles in the cupboard by the kitchen
table," Darby called. "I'll be there in a minute."

Her fingers closed over the bat. She took a step
toward the back door. A fluttering bolt of lightning
lit the kitchen. Something moved outside the window, a dark hulking figure.

Mariah screamed as the window suddenly shat-

tered, glass going everywhere. She rushed toward the
back door. The floor was still slick with rainwater.
She slipped in her hurry and fell to one knee, dropping the bat. Pulling herself up, she managed to grab
the knob. Fingers trembling from fear and cold, she
frantically turned the lock. Collapsing on the floor in
a puddle of cold water, she leaned against the door.

Rain lashed through the broken kitchen window.
Even in the dark, she could now see what had burst
through the window. The leaves on the limb from the
old cottonwood tree next to the building fluttered in
the open window.

Darby came racing into the kitchen, the shotgun
in one hand, a flashlight beam bobbing in the other.
His face was white in the ambient light. He looked
from her on the floor to the limb now partway into
the kitchen and slowly lowered the shotgun.

"Apparently it is going to be one of those nights,"
he said with a humorous chuckle. "Are you all right?"

She nodded and, picking up the baseball bat, let
him help her to her feet. "I just want to go to bed, but
I guess that's out of the question until we do something about this window."

Darby nodded. "You can go on up. I'll pull the
limb out and cover the window as best I can for tonight. We'll deal with it tomorrow."

She hugged herself, unwilling to let go of the bat
just yet. The storm roared, the wind whipping her
hair, raindrops drenching her even more. She shiv-

ered from the cold and the scare. "I'm not going anywhere without you. I'll help. The way the wind is blowing, it is going to take both of us anyway."

HARP SAT, WATCHING the storm intensify. Rain thundered on the roof of the patrol SUV. Lightning lit the western landscape. The explosion of thunder was so close it made the hair stand up on the back of his neck.

He swore. Call Flint? Or go back and see if there was even a problem?

Cursing the weather, he shifted the SUV into gear and headed back toward the Stagecoach Saloon.

He'd been in a snit all evening. Feeling anxious, he thought about Vicki at Sue's Diner. She would be getting off her shift about now. He'd promised to stop by so they could "talk."

Well, that wasn't going to happen now. Not that he had been looking forward to it. She probably wanted some kind of commitment. Didn't all women?

He'd managed not to get caught, barely skating by on more than one occasion. As much as he liked doing it with Vicki, he wasn't interested in taking it any further.

So he supposed he didn't mind putting off the talk for another time as he came around the corner and the Stagecoach Saloon came into view.

He had been hoping the light would be back on. That would solve at least one of his problems. But even through the driving rain, he could see that the damned light was still out.

He slowed and then sped up. If there was trouble at the bar, he couldn't very well just pull up out front in a patrol car. He'd have to go on up the road, park and walk back.

In this weather? He cursed the Cahills as he found a place to pull off and turned in. It would be a good quarter mile walk unless he cut across the pasture and dropped in the back way. That would be the wisest—if there were trouble.

And there damned well better be. If some fool had forgotten and turned off the light, making him have to trek through this storm... He didn't know what he would do. Punch something.

He reached in the back for his rain jacket, checked his weapons and sat again for a moment, trying to talk himself out of doing this. If there was trouble, he could use his shotgun. If not...

The shotgun was heavy and it would be a good walk uphill for a while before he could drop into the back of the saloon.

Shrugging into his rain jacket, he pulled up the hood. He opted to just take his service revolver, stun gun, handcuffs and baton. He doubted he'd even need those as he braced himself and shoved open the patrol SUV door. It took all his strength against the wind.

Rain beat down on him as he turned his back to the wind to zip his jacket up higher and then started up the hillside toward a stand of pines.

CHAPTER EIGHTEEN

HARP HAD JUST topped the hill, when he saw a set of headlights blink out down the road behind the saloon. He stared in that direction for a moment, figuring it was probably some teenagers back there in the pines making out.

If he didn't have to check on the Cahills, he'd go have a look. He'd love to catch a couple of teens going hot and heavy. He loved the looks on their faces when he snuck up to their vehicle, popped up and shone the flashlight over them. Talk about scrambling to cover up. He smiled now at the thought. At least it would perk up his night because so far this sucked.

Rain ran off the brim of his raincoat. He could barely see the saloon at times as he started down the hill toward the backside of the building. Still no light burning out front. But with a curse, he noticed that there was no light burning in the back now either. Glancing toward town, he saw that there were no lights for about a mile or so from here.

The power must have gone off. Swearing, he stopped halfway down the hillside. What was the point of going the rest of the way? He'd just have

251

251251251251

to climb this hill again. Or get Darby Cahill to give him a ride back to his patrol SUV.

He glanced behind the saloon to where he'd seen the headlights blink out. The opportunity to fool with some half-naked teens—or even naked by the time he reached them—was too tempting. Anyway, he'd come this far.

Dropping off the hill, slipping and sliding in the mud and wet grass, he finally reached the side of the saloon. As he started to step around to the back, he saw the limb that had broken off the nearest cottonwood. A nearby window had been boarded up with a sheet of plywood. That, he thought, could be why he couldn't see the light that had been burning in the back of the saloon.

The thought stopped him for a moment. He looked behind him, not all that sure what he might be stepping into. But it still appeared that the power was out. As he reached the corner of the building, he heard voices coming from a small storage building off to one side in the pines.

"Deputy Cole here!" he called as he snapped on his flashlight. At the sound of his voice, two figures started. He pointed the flashlight at them. Darby Cahill and Mariah Ayers, owner of the motorcycle. He smiled to himself. Damn, she looked good soaked to the skin. "What's going on?"

"Had to fix a window. A tree limb took it out,"

Cahill called, shielding his eyes from the glare of the flashlight.

Harp lowered the flashlight as he moved toward them. "Saw the outside light off. Thought there might be trouble."

"No power," Cahill said. "Hadn't planned on that."

"Well, glad it's nothing too serious." He was anxious to check on the teenagers parked a quarter-mile behind the saloon. "I'll move on, then."

"Thanks for stopping," Cahill said.

"All part of the job." Harp turned and started back toward his patrol SUV. He thought about driving closer to where he'd seen the vehicle park. But he was already wet, his boots caked with mud, the walk would do him good.

He went only as far as needed to disappear from view of the saloon and then turned north. The rain wasn't so bad in the dense pines. Vicki kept interrupting his thoughts. What the hell did she want to talk about? Conversation wasn't her best skill. Neither was waitressing for that matter. He chuckled as he thought of her.

A van seemed to materialize out of the storm only yards ahead of him. With a start, he realized he'd been so lost in his thoughts that he'd almost walked right into it. He slowed to listen. If there was hanky-panky going on inside the van, it wasn't much. He'd hoped to catch it rockin'.

Crouching down, he began to sneak toward the

vehicle. It only had a window in the door, the rest of the back was a panel van. He was almost to the door when he heard a sound. Only it didn't come from inside. It had come from directly behind him.

VICKI COULDN'T BELIEVE Harp wasn't going to show. She stared out the diner window through the pounding rain, her heart in her throat.

"He isn't coming," Sue said as she bagged the last of the day's receipts. "You need a ride home?"

Vicki shook her head, her hand going to her stomach. She'd felt nauseated and had all day.

Sue leaned a hip against the counter. "You told him you needed to talk to him, right?"

Vicki shot a look of surprise at her boss. "How did you—"

"Let me guess. You're pregnant."

Her stomach roiled. She swallowed back the lump that rose in her throat and tried to hold down the club soda, the only thing she'd been able to keep down all day.

Sue waved a dismissive hand through the air. "Don't even bother to deny it." She shook her head. "I should have foreseen this. Didn't you use any kind of protection?"

"I can't take the pill and Harp doesn't like—"

"I get the picture. Now what are you going to do?"

Vicki looked outside again. It was raining harder than before, lightning flashing, thunder rattling the

diner windows. Huge puddles had formed just outside with water running like a river down the street.

"Maybe he can't make it tonight but he'll—"

"He isn't going to marry you, honey. He's going to
break your heart and leave you with a baby to raise
by yourself. You picked the wrong guy if you were
looking for happy-ever-after. It isn't Harper Cole."

The words hurt even though Sue had said them
kindly enough.

"I need to close up. Sure I can't give you a ride?"
Sue asked.

Vicki shook her head. "I have my car." She took
off her apron and got her jacket, still looking for
Harp's patrol SUV as she pushed open the door.
Water poured off the overhang in a drenching wa-
terfall. She had no choice. She pulled her thin jacket
up over her head and made a run for it, splashing
through puddles that were almost up to her knees
before she reached her car.

Once inside, she sat behind the wheel, shivering.
Harp hadn't shown. But Sue was wrong. He loved
her. He hadn't said as much, but she knew he did.
He wouldn't desert her and their baby. He'd step up,
they'd get married, maybe buy a little house. Like
Harp always said, one day he would be sheriff and
then they'd be on the gravy train.

She reached to put the key into the ignition. Soaking wet and cold and disappointed and scared, she
turned the key. The older model car's engine made

a whirring sound. She tried it again. It often did this when it was cold or wet. She told herself that the third time was the charm. It wasn't. She laid her head on the steering wheel, surprised how quickly she was in tears. The sobs racked her thin body and made her stomach roil again.

At the tap on the window, she jerked upward, thinking it would be Harp's handsome face looking in.

It was Sue holding an umbrella. She motioned for Vicki to get out and follow her to her car.

MAGGIE STOOD AT the window, watching the storm. Since the vandalism at her beauty shop, she'd had trouble sleeping. She hadn't told Flint and since they hadn't moved in together yet, he didn't know just how spooked she was.

The problem was that she knew Celeste would strike again. Now she felt as if she was waiting, not sure when or where or how, but knowing the woman wasn't through with her.

Flint seemed to think that Celeste's attack on the beauty shop was just a childish tantrum. Maggie knew better. It had been to show her that she could get to her. That time, it had been through a back window that had been pried open. Celeste had made it look enough like kids could have done it, but Maggie hadn't been fooled.

Neither had Flint. The only station vandalized

was hers. Kids would have torn up the whole place. No, Celeste had been sending her a message, one she had gotten loud and clear. It was a warning of what would come if she continued to see Flint.

All Maggie could think about was what would happen if she actually moved in with the sheriff. Flint seemed to think that Celeste would be forced to back off. Maggie scoffed at that as she stared out at the rain. Wind rocked the pines outside her house, sending dark shadows scurrying across her yard.

When she'd come home, she'd locked all the doors and windows and searched the house to make sure Celeste wasn't hiding in one of the closets. Maggie knew it sounded ludicrous. What woman in her right mind would spend the day hiding in your closet? But she wouldn't put anything past Celeste.

This morning at the shop, she'd heard that Wayne Duma had flown to Denver on business. That meant that Celeste would be at loose ends. Was the woman afraid of thunderstorms? Maggie could only hope so. The storm at least might keep her in tonight.

Or maybe not. At a sound at the back of the house, Maggie froze.

DARBY COULD SEE that Mariah was relieved that the deputy had stopped by. When he'd told her that Flint said he'd have a deputy drive by during the night and that they were to leave the front light on as a signal that everything was all right, she'd looked skeptical.

"Rafael will check out the area before he makes his move. He's…smart. He won't want to get caught. He'll be very careful. And very deadly."

He'd realized that for Mariah, Rafael had become a monster. A monster she feared she couldn't best. That worried him more for her sake than his own. But once Rafael was caught and jailed, he wouldn't look so scary. At least that's what Darby hoped.

"Let's go up and change. I'll bolt the door," he said. He saw her glance toward the plywood over the window as if to say "like that will keep him out."

As he watched her go upstairs, he picked up the shotgun he'd taken with them when they'd gone out to fix the window. He thought of the other guns hidden around the place. Other than what he'd done so far, he didn't know what more he could do to protect them from this man.

Knowing Harp was out there had given Mariah a little comfort. Unfortunately Darby knew the deputy. If trouble was coming, he'd much rather have Deputy Christopher Hanson or Undersheriff Mark Ramirez looking out for them. Even better his brother Flint. The thought surprised him a little.

The family thought of Flint as being a pain most of the time since his brother had never met a rule he didn't like. But when the chips were down, Darby realized he'd rather bet on Flint than anyone else.

He listened to the sound of the storm raging outside. The lightning and thunder had moved off some, but the wind and rain still pounded the old building. He shivered a little and thought about checking the other windows and doors but stopped himself.

If Rafael Vale wanted to get in bad enough, he'd find a way. Darby just hoped they'd be ready for him when he did.

MAGGIE SCREAMED AS a face appeared on the other side of the glass. She jerked back, stumbling and almost going down before she caught herself. The face standing at her back porch wasn't Celeste's. It was Flint's.

His gray eyes were wide with both guilt and worry. He hadn't meant to scare her—let alone terrify her.

She moved to the door and hurriedly unlocked it. He shook rain off his hat and removed his raincoat before stepping in on the enclosed back porch rug. Flint was always so thoughtful. Her heart ached at the sight of him. She had loved this man for far too long to be afraid of what his ex-wife would do. And yet, she couldn't quit shaking.

"It's all right," Flint said, taking hold of her trembling shoulders. "This storm has everyone on edge tonight. That's why I stopped by to check on you. I knocked at the front door. You must not have heard me."

She shook her head. She could tell by the way he was looking at her that he thought she was a raving maniac. He had no idea.

"I heard something and when I looked out…" She shuddered.

"I scared you," he said pulling her into a hug. "I'm so sorry. When you didn't answer the back door either, I looked in."

They were quiet for a few moments. She could imagine what was going on in his head.

"I'm sorry, but I have to go back out," Flint said, sounding apologetic. She could tell he was worried about her given how easily he'd terrified her. "A fallen tree limb is blocking the main road out to the east and the power is out in some areas. I need to go help. But I can come back later if—"

She pulled free. "No, I'm fine. Go do whatever you have to do. I'm…fine." She smiled but she could see that he wasn't so sure she was fine. In truth, she hated being alone tonight. It wasn't the storm. It was a foreboding feeling she'd had all day.

"If you need me—"

"I know. I can call." She nodded, still smiling like a fool. Like he said, wasn't that what Celeste was hoping for? That a scared Maggie would call Flint, who would confront Celeste, who would weasel her way out of it. Celeste wanted the attention from Flint. Maggie wouldn't play into her hands no matter what, she promised herself. She'd handle it herself.

"Go," she said, pushing him toward the door. "I'll be fine." She followed him to the back door. He hesitated as if wishing there was something more he could say. "Flint, I can take care of myself."

He couldn't have looked more skeptical, but he smiled, leaned in to kiss her and pushed open the door to step out. She locked it behind him, smiling and waving as he disappeared into the rain and darkness.

The moment he was out of sight, her smile disappeared. She doubled-checked the door, making sure it was locked and bolted, and then she turned back into the house.

In the kitchen, she stood hugging herself, thinking that the house seemed much colder without Flint. She moved to a drawer by the sink and opened it. Taking out a large butcher knife, she stared at it. The blade caught the light. The thing looked lethal. She put it back and took out a smaller knife.

"Lethal enough," she told herself. Turning off the kitchen light, she headed for the living room. The blinds were open. She couldn't see much in the darkness and rain. A car passed going slow. She moved to the window and closed the drapes.

Then she glanced up the stairs. Holding the knife in front of her, she climbed the steps, all the time listening to the old house moan and groan. She knew its complaints after living here for years. Hearing nothing new, she headed for her bedroom, fearing she would never be able to get to sleep. Not with the storm. Not with the feeling that Celeste was out there watching her house.

Watching and waiting for what, though?

HARP'S HAND FELL to the weapon on his hip as he started to turn. He managed to get the Glock unsnapped and partway out of his holster before he took the first blow in the face. The fist had been big, the power behind it enough to knock him off his feet. As he fell, he'd tried to get the gun up, but it was wrenched out of his hand before he could.

"What the hell?" said a male voice as the deputy hit the wet ground. "He's wearing a *uniform*. He's some kind of cop."

"Not a real cop," a different male voice said from above him as a flashlight beam bobbed over him.

Harp fumbled for his stun gun. The boot that kicked his arm was steel toed. He screamed in pain. Then the sole of that boot was on his chest.

"Reach for a weapon again and I'll kick your brains out," said the male standing over him.

Blinded by the flashlight beam, the rain and his pain, Harp couldn't see the man's face. He lay in the wet grass and soil trying to breathe and trying hard not to think about dying.

"So who are we protecting your brother and his girlfriend from?" he had asked the sheriff when he'd been given his orders.

"Are you familiar with the Roma?"

Harp had stared at Flint. "Like spaghetti?"

"Many people still know the Roma as Gypsies."

He'd laughed. "Gypsies, in wagons, singing, dancing, stealing children and chickens?"

Flint had given him one of his distasteful looks. "Mariah is Roma. There is a man after her who claims to be her husband. Apparently he is very violent and plans to kidnap her. If so, it wouldn't be the first time."

Harp had been surprised and fascinated. "No kidding?"

"The man's name is Rafael Vale. He probably won't come alone," Flint had said. "And I wouldn't describe them the way you just did to me. At least not to this man's face."

Harp hadn't been worried. Until now.

"So what are you doing out here?" the man with his boot resting on Harp's chest asked.

He opened his mouth. Nothing came out.

The man leaned over him, putting more pressure on the boot—and Harp's chest. "I asked what you're doing out here."

"Looking for teenagers."

A laugh escaped the man who turned to the second man. Harp couldn't see him at all—just a large hulk of a shape in the trees. "He's out looking for teenagers."

"What are you going to do?" The man in the woods sounded nervous.

"You thought there were teenagers in our van?" the man over him asked, laughing. "Surprise!"

"Rafael, I don't think you should—"

"Don't think, Angel. I didn't bring you along for your brain power. You're here for the heavy lifting."

Angel made a sound as if in pain himself. "I thought we were just here for Mariah."

"What kind of cop are you?" the man called Rafael asked him.

Harp licked his lips. He was shaking so hard from the cold and the fear that he could barely get the words out. "Deputy sheriff."

"Deputy sheriff?" This cracked up Rafael. "We really are in the Wild West. Where is the sheriff?"

Harp shook his head. Probably asleep in his warm bed while Harp was out here about to… He couldn't bear to think about what this man planned to do to him as he heard Rafael say, "Hand me his gun."

Harp hadn't realized that the man had tossed it aside. He turned his head and watched Angel come out of the trees to pick up the gun with two fingers as if it was a dirty diaper.

Rafael snatched it from his hand and almost backhanded Angel with it before leveling the gun at Harp's head. "Any last requests?"

"You can't kill a cop."

"He's not a cop. He's a *sheriff's deputy*," Rafael said with scorn.

"Think about this. What if someone hears the

shot?" Angel said as thunder rumbled in the distance as that part of the storm headed east.

The next sound like thunder reverberated through Harp's chest. Only this one was definitely a gunshot. His body jumped. He blinked, trying to assess how badly he'd been shot and realized the shot had hit next to him.

Angel swore. "If you're determined then get it over with," he snapped. "You don't have to torture everyone who crosses your path."

Rafael laughed. "My cousin knows me so well." He pointed the gun at Harp's head.

Harp took a breath, his last, and held it as he waited for the bullet to pierce his skull.

"Hey!" he heard Rafael say. "Look, he pissed his pants."

The laughter made Harp open his eyes. He felt the warmth and looked down to see steam rising from his crouch.

"Help me get him in the van. He's given me an idea."

"You know someone's going to be looking for him," Angel said.

"I wonder where he left his patrol car." Rafael looked down at him. "Where is it?"

Harp motioned with his good arm.

"You wouldn't lie to me, would you?" Rafael was digging in the deputy's rain jacket pocket for the keys.

He shook his head vigorously. Right now he'd tell the man anything he wanted to hear.

"What are you going to do?" Angel asked.

"You'll see."

Harp snaked his hand down to his Taser again. If he could just get it out.

He didn't see the kick to his head coming. As darkness closed in, he heard Angel say, "Did you have to do that?"

"Yah, I did. Now help me get his Sheriff's Deputy raincoat off. It's time I pay my wife a visit."

CHAPTER NINETEEN

"DID YOU HEAR THAT?" Mariah asked Darby as they entered the upstairs apartment. They both froze and listened.

"Sorry, I didn't."

"It sounded like a gunshot."

"Not thunder?"

She couldn't be sure. She listened but heard nothing but the storm and shook her head. "I guess it wasn't anything."

The wind slammed one of the shutters hard against the side of the building making her jump. Darby moved to her, holding her. "It's going to be all right."

Mariah nodded again. The storm had her on edge. Darby too, she thought. She wanted to think that Rafael wouldn't do anything on such a night—if he was even in Montana. But she'd learned not to underestimate him.

"Why are you still in your wet clothes?" he asked. "Mariah, you'll catch your death of cold. Change."

She'd come upstairs, trying not to jump at every sound. But it was impossible. Hugging herself against the chill that snaked around her neck, she watched Darby shuck his wet clothing. At a loud crash downstairs, he swore and hurriedly pulled on jeans, a shirt and his boots again.

"Stay here. I'm sure it's nothing. I'm going downstairs to check the window and make sure the plywood is holding," Darby said. "When I get back, we're going to climb into that bed and snuggle up and shut out the storm."

She hugged herself, yearning to have his arms around her but still spooked by the storm, by the thought that Rafael might hit tonight. She started to take off her wet jeans when Darby stopped in the doorway.

"Remember, Deputy Cole is out there," he said. "He'll be checking on the place. If he sees anything, he's to call my brother, and Flint will send the cavalry." He came back into the apartment to lean in to kiss her. "Try to relax. You remember where we hid all the weapons?"

"Yes and my knife is under the mattress on my side of the bed."

"Now that is a comforting thought," he said, clearly trying to lighten the mood. "You don't have nightmares do you?"

"Only one." She met his gaze. "Be careful down there and hurry back."

"Will do. Can I get you anything while I'm downstairs? Something to drink. A snack?"

She shook her head. She couldn't eat a bite and, while tempted to drink herself into oblivion, she wasn't about to. All her instincts told her to be on alert from now until Rafael showed up. He would show up. By now the private investigator would have told him enough to send her so-called husband on the rampage. She'd seen him like that before—on their wedding night.

"I'll be right back," Darby said, and still she reached for him, pulling him into a hug and holding him tightly. He kissed her hair, smoothing it out of her face as he looked into her eyes. "I love you."

She felt the full weight of her love for him. He was as worried as she was. She swallowed the lump in her throat. "I love you, Darby Cahill." They hugged tightly, tears blurring her eyes.

She hastily wiped them away so he didn't see that she was crying as they parted and he headed out. At the doorway, he turned back to look at her again as if he didn't want to leave her any more than she wanted him to. She smiled through her fear, afraid that when he disappeared through that doorway, she might never see him again.

The feeling was so strong that she almost called him back. Better he think she was crazy than let him go if this feeling pressing down on her chest was a warning. Her grandmother had been psychic—at least that's what people believed. Mariah had loved the woman to death but never really believed in her fortune telling. That was for the *gadjos*. Then again, Mariah had been a preteen, skeptical about everything, when her grandmother had died.

Darby disappeared from the doorway. She felt a tug at her heart, her mouth opening to call him back and then closing as she hurriedly changed her clothes. She thought about just climbing into the bed naked, but her fear tonight kept her clothed. At least until Darby returned.

She moved to the bed and checked to make sure her knife was where she'd left it. Her gun was loaded and sitting on the windowsill above the bed. There was a shotgun by the door, loaded, as well, and a gun in the bathroom.

"I know it's overkill," Darby had said when he'd brought back the arsenal. "But better safe than sorry, right?"

So why did she feel as if it wasn't enough? That Rafael Vale was invincible? That no one could stop him?

Because he'd caught her before. She had no doubt he could do it again.

VICKI SAT ON the floor in the bathroom and tried not to throw up again. After Sue had dropped her off, she'd gone right up, planning to go straight to bed.

Instead, what little she'd consumed today came back up. So this was morning sickness? But it wasn't even morning yet.

Vicki knew some of it was anxiety. She'd been worried about telling Harp. She liked to think that he might be okay with it, even a little excited.

But there was that fear that he would be furious with her, blame her, think she was trying to trick him into marriage.

Not that she didn't like the idea of a baby, a husband, a little house in town where she could take the baby for walks in its stroller. She'd already gone online and picked out a stroller. A bassinet too and even a crib. They made such cute things for babies.

Not that she and Harp would be able to afford many of them. Neither of them made much, but if they saved their money…

She felt her stomach roil again but didn't have the energy to stand. She scooted across the floor to the toilet and hung on. The one thing she didn't want was for Harp to ever see her like this.

She hoped he wouldn't stop by when he got off his shift. Vicki knew what she must look like. She was glad she had tomorrow off. Maybe she and Harp—

Curling around the toilet bowl, she threw up. Except there was nothing to come up. She heaved and heaved until her whole body was shaking.

No, she definitely didn't want Harp to see her like this, she thought as she managed to get to her feet, wash her face and, cupping her hands, rinse out her mouth.

The one time she'd had the flu, she'd found out

what a weak stomach he had. She doubted he would even be able to handle changing a diaper. Harp really was a big baby himself.

That thought made her smile as she walked into her bedroom. She felt exhausted after the day she'd had. Now maybe she would be able to get some sleep. With luck, Harp would wake her up later to have that talk.

Climbing into bed naked, she pulled the covers around her and, closing her eyes, dreamed about the life she and Harp would have.

DARBY TURNED ON the flashlight as he tromped down the stairs. He stopped to check the back door's lock before he entered the kitchen. The flashlight beam skittered over the wet floor to the broken glass scattered over the kitchen table and finally to the plywood he'd tacked up on the outside to keep the rain from coming in.

He stopped to listen. The thunder and lightning had moved on, leaving only the driving rain. It had almost a peaceful feeling after the noise of the storm. Even the wind had died down some. He couldn't wait to get back upstairs and into bed with Mariah. She was more frightened than he'd ever seen her. He'd be glad when daylight came and hopefully the rain stopped. Once the sun came out, everything would at least feel better.

Not that he thought Rafael Vale would give up.

From everything Mariah had told him, there would be no stopping the man from coming after her. Darby had taken every precaution. Now he just hoped it would be enough. That *he* would be enough. He couldn't let the man take Mariah. He would die trying to save her if that was what it came to.

"You have it bad," his brother Flint had said. "Are you sure you're up for this? We could hide Mariah somewhere safe and—"

"He would eventually find her." He'd shaken his head. "We need to end this."

Now as he moved through the dark of the saloon, the flashlight beam bobbing ahead of him, he hoped he hadn't done wrong by having the two of them stay here to fight. But hiding out would do no good. Rafael wanted a showdown. Putting it off would only leave Mariah living in this constant fear. Or worse, continuing to run. Darby couldn't stand to see her like this. He'd do whatever he had to in order to free her.

The empty dark bar felt strange. He stood for a moment, listening to the rain. Outside the window, he saw the flash of headlights cutting through the downpour and quickly turned off his flashlight as he moved closer to the front window.

His heart took off like a gunshot as the vehicle slowed. Was this it? Was this the showdown he'd been expecting?

As the vehicle turned in, Darby saw that it was

a sheriff's department patrol SUV, the emblem on the side, the light bar on top. He only got a glimpse of Deputy Harper Cole behind the wheel in his raincoat, the hood up.

Through the side window, he saw the deputy park, get out and head for the back door of the saloon.

CHAPTER TWENTY

DARBY STEPPED TO the door, unlocked it and reached for the knob. Before his hand touched it, the wind caught the door, swung it open and banged it hard against the side of the building like earlier.

He looked through the doorway out into the darkness, wondering why Harp had returned. The deputy stood just outside, his back turned as he looked toward the stand of pines. The rain still fell hard, Darby noticed as he glanced past Harp to the trees. Had the deputy heard something back there? Seen something?

"Did you see something?" Darby asked and started to reach for the shotgun beside the door.

Harp didn't answer, but slowly began to turn toward him. He felt a chill on the wind, a shiver that ran the length of his spine. The night seemed to have gone too quiet suddenly as Harp turned and Darby saw the gun in his hand.

It surprised him that the deputy had drawn his weapon. He glanced past him to the pine trees, black against the night and the pouring rain. His hand closed over the shotgun by the door. The deputy was half turned, his head down, raindrops cascading off the hood in a dark shower. Only the gun in Harp's hand caught any light.

As Darby lifted the shotgun, a voice came from under the hood.

"I wouldn't do that if I were you."

Not Harp's voice. Not Harp. The thoughts raced from his brain, but not quickly enough. He glanced up to find the weapon in the man's hand pointed at his heart. The man lifted his head—and Darby knew he was looking at Rafael Vale.

HARP CAME TO with a start. For a moment, he didn't know where he was. It sounded as if he was in a tin can. Rain drummed on a metal roof overhead.

It took him a few moments. He was in a van. That brought everything back in a rush. He tried to sit up, knowing he had to get out of here and fast, but he was bound and his head felt too heavy for his neck.

He shivered, remembering why he was wet. He'd been lying on the ground in the rain earlier. But he'd been wearing his sheriff's department raincoat then. He wasn't now.

In the dark of the vehicle, he tried to assess how bad his situation was. His head ached where he'd been kicked in the temple as did his arm. Had the blow to his head knocked him unconscious? Or had he been shot and passed out? He remembered Rafael pointing a gun at his head at some point.

He hurt all over so it was impossible to tell how badly he'd been attacked. His wrists were bound with duct tape behind his back. His ankles were also bound and there was a piece of tape across his mouth. But he didn't think he'd been shot.

Where were the two men who'd put him in here? With a start, he remembered enough of the conversation before he'd been knocked out to know. The Stagecoach Saloon. They were the men after Mariah Ayers.

He closed his eyes, sick to his stomach. He'd really fucked up this time. If this didn't cost him his job, he didn't know what would. And as crazy as that Rafael one was... He swallowed back the bile that rose in his throat. Mariah was screwed. But that meant so was Darby Cahill.

He listened to the rain, fighting panic. What if they came back? They couldn't let him go.

His eyes had adjusted to the darkness inside the van enough that he could make out a couple of duffel bags as well as some plastic shopping bags with rope and duct tape.

Maybe there was something he could use to free himself. And then what?

All he could think about was getting out of this van and as far away as he could before the men returned.

Anything was better than waiting here in the dark for those two men to come back. He was no hero.

Using his feet, he pushed his way toward the bags at the front of the van, praying he could find something to cut the tape and free himself.

He tried not to listen to what was beyond the rain pounding on the van's roof. He probably wouldn't hear them come back until they slid open the side door on the van. And by then, it would be too late.

Harp realized he didn't even know how long they'd been gone. He could have been out for an hour, even longer. Or it could have been only minutes.

He reached the bags, rolled onto his side and began to go through them. It was slow and painful work since his hands were bound behind him, and his arm, while not broken apparently, was so badly bruised that it hurt like hell.

Nothing in the first bag. He groped for the second bag and froze. Was that a gunshot he'd just heard?

DARBY KNEW HE'D never get the shotgun up and fired in time. He brought it up quickly, lunging at the man in the doorway. He'd known before he acted the chance he was taking. Rafael was a big man. More than that, he'd been ready for Darby to react.

Suddenly the sound of the pouring rain seemed amplified as he shoved the shotgun at the man in the doorway. Rafael took the glancing blow off one shoulder and knocked the gun aside. Darby heard the report of the shot as the man fired. The bullet tore into his side, forcing him to let go of the shotgun.

The shotgun was wrenched from his hands and, bleeding, he was forced back into the building. Darby grabbed his side, his fingers coming away wet with blood as he saw a second man follow the first into the entry just outside the kitchen and the stairs to the apartment.

Mariah had never described the man who she'd been promised to at fifteen. Darby was only a little surprised to see that Rafael was a large handsome man. One look in the man's dead dark eyes and he knew why Rafael was so dangerous.

"Where is my wife?" the man asked as he handed Darby's shotgun to the other man.

Darby could understand why he'd made the mistake he had. Rafael was wearing Harp's raincoat. He'd also been driving the deputy's patrol car. Was Harp dead? He thought he probably was since he'd apparently crossed paths with these two men.

"Darby?"

His blood ran cold as Mariah called down.

"Mariah, don't—!" he yelled as he lunged for Rafael. The blow with the butt of the gun knocked him to the floor. The second one turned the lights out.

MAGGIE REALIZED THAT she must have fallen asleep because she woke with a start to the smell of smoke.

Sitting straight up in bed, she assured herself it wasn't a dream. She definitely smelled smoke.

Swinging her legs over the side, she slipped her feet into her slippers as she turned on a light.

Grabbing her robe, she hurried downstairs, turning on lights as she went. As she reached the kitchen, she saw the blaze on the back porch. Nothing seemed to be on fire and yet she could still smell smoke.

She grabbed the landline phone on the wall and dialed 911. Someone had set her back porch on fire!

That's when she saw a small figure standing in the rain wearing a blue and white striped raincoat and what appeared to be black designer boots.

Maggie stared. Leave it to Celeste to commit arson dressed fit to kill. The 911 operator answered.

"What is your emergency?"

Maggie couldn't speak as Celeste pushed back the hood of her raincoat exposing her blond bob that shone even in the rain, even in the dark night.

Celeste was looking right at her.

"Hello? What is your emergency?"

Maggie glanced at the back porch, surprised to see that the blaze had burned out. She couldn't see what had been burning, but whatever it had been had gone out.

The smell of smoke still lingered in the air, though, along with the bad taste in her mouth. This was just another threat. Another promise of what would come if Maggie moved in with Flint.

The 911 operator was trying to get her attention.

"There was a fire, but it appears to have gone out," Maggie said into the phone. "I'm sorry for the call."

"Are you sure you don't need help? I can call the fire department—"

"No. There's no need." She hung up and looked out into the darkness. Celeste was gone.

FLINT WATCHED THE city maintenance men move the large cottonwood limb from the street, then signal the utility company crew that they could go to work on the downed power line.

He'd gotten a call earlier that part of town was without electricity and still the storm raged on. He knew what would be next and wasn't surprised when he heard from dispatch.

"Flooding along Main and out by the overpass. One car stalled."

"I'm on it," Flint said. "Have you heard from Harp?"

"Not since earlier."

"Let me know when he checks in." He planned to go by the saloon as soon as he took care of getting the road blocked until the flooding subsided. First he had to get the stranded car out of the middle of the street.

He got on the horn to the city boys to ask for some help, figuring they were probably already inundated with calls.

As he drove, he thought about Maggie. Maybe he should run by, just to make sure everything looked all right at her house. Her fear of Celeste seemed overblown compared to what his ex had done—if she had vandalized the beauty shop, which he suspected but couldn't prove. He was still a lawman, biased as he was.

Maggie was so sure that Celeste's antics would escalate if she moved in with him. Was that why she was dragging her feet?

Maybe it was too soon. Maybe they should wait. But wasn't that what Celeste hoped to accomplish with her childish tantrum at the beauty shop?

Flint told himself he couldn't think about it now. He stared out through the rain, his windshield wipers flapping. No lights were on at Maggie's house. No cause for alarm. He tried to relax, wishing Maggie would do the same.

He made sure the city had the flooded street blocked off and was about to make a run out to the Stagecoach Saloon to check on his brother and Mariah, when he got a call from dispatch.

"You asked to be notified if there were any problems at this number?" the dispatcher said.

He recognized the number at once. Maggie's landline. "What is it?"

"She called earlier to report a fire but then said it was out."

Flint tried not to panic. "Like a kitchen fire?"

"She didn't say. Seemed…disoriented," the operator said. "Called us to see about sending someone over there. I recognized the number."

"Thank you. I'll run by and check." He was already headed there as he disconnected. A fire?

HARP DUG FRANTICALLY through the second bag, his hopes evaporating. What had he hoped to find? Something sharp that he could—

He almost missed it in his hurry. His fingers returned to the object he'd tossed aside in the bag. He latched onto it, telling himself it couldn't be a sheathed knife. That would make things too easy.

Hurriedly, he pulled off the cover and felt the sharp bite of a blade. He closed his eyes for a moment. This felt almost like a trick. Too easy. Were they standing outside just waiting for him to think he was going to get away before they dashed his hopes to death?

His head hurt so bad he just wanted to go to sleep and not wake up until this was all over.

A sound outside the van made his eyes fly open. Holding his breath, he listened. Just the rain? He slipped the knife blade between his wrists and felt a sharp pain as it bit again into his flesh.

More careful, he positioned it and then began to move his wrists up and down, up and down. When he cut through the tape, he almost stabbed himself in the back. But he was so relieved to have his hands free, that he let out a sob as he ripped the tape off his mouth.

Sitting up, he groped around in the dark for the

knife, found it again and went to work on the tape around his ankles. He was so close to getting away now, they couldn't come back. Not now. Just a few more minutes.

The tape gave. He ripped it off and, still holding the knife, reached for the door handle. It took him a moment to find it. He hesitated, knowing it would be loud when he opened the side door.

But he didn't want to take the time to climb into the front of the van and use one of those doors.

A thought struck him. Could he get even more lucky? He pushed the bags aside and slipped between the seats to reach for the ignition, saying a prayer as he did.

When he found the keys gone, he told himself he should have known his prayers weren't going to be answered. He was a sinner. Maybe this was his payback for the life he'd led so far. He hadn't been that bad, he told himself.

He started to draw back, when he figured he should check one more place. He pushed himself farther forward and felt on the floorboard. No keys.

Then his fingers brushed something that jiggled. A key ring. He couldn't believe it and he closed his fingers around it. Four keys.

Scrambling he slid into the driver seat and started trying keys. He found the right one on his second try. Stepping on the clutch he turned the key. The motor started right up. He turned on the headlights and threw the van into gear. His heart was pounding so hard he thought he might have a heart attack. He expected the side door to bang open at any moment and the two men to kill him before he could get away.

As he pulled back onto the muddy road, the blinding headache making him see double, he couldn't remember a time he'd felt better. He roared up the road, his headlights cutting through the rain and night.

"WHAT WAS IT?" Maggie asked as Flint inspected the small area that had been scorched black by whatever had burned there. Angry, sick and near tears, she hugged herself as she watched him. She wasn't sure how much more of this she could take.

"I'm not sure," he said. "Something that burned up but miraculously didn't catch your back porch on fire. If it hadn't landed on the tile…"

He rose to look at her. "Maggie, what were you doing on the back porch in the middle of the night?"

"I wasn't." She had answered the door in her robe and slippers, having given up any chance of a good night's sleep after that. When Flint had arrived, she'd been sitting in the dark living room. She'd seen his headlights and had answered the door even before he'd knocked.

She felt in shock. Like a sleepwalker, she seemed in a fugue state. But a part of her roiled in fury. Celeste had to be stopped. And who was going to do it?

When she'd opened the door to Flint, all she'd

done was point at the back porch. Now she felt his intent gaze. She saw the worry. Unfortunately, she suspected he was more worried about her mental state than that of his dangerous ex-wife.

"Did you notice the window on the porch? It has been pried open—just like the one down at the shop. That's how whatever was burning was dropped onto the porch floor."

She could tell that he hadn't noticed. He'd just assumed she had started the fire. Her patience felt as if it was wearing thin with him.

"So how did you—"

"I woke up and smelled smoke. When I came downstairs I saw it burning and called 911."

"But it burned out and you cancelled the call."

"That's because I saw who did it."

He looked only mildly surprised and seemed to brace himself.

She felt anger bubble up inside her. He'd said he agreed that it had "probably" been Celeste at the beauty shop. But she could see him already wanting to find a reason it couldn't have been Celeste tonight.

"She was wearing a blue and white striped raincoat and black boots and standing in my back yard. She had the hood up until the fire was almost out and then she pushed the hood back exposing her blond hair. She was looking right at me, daring me to..." That was just it, she wasn't sure what Celeste was hoping she would do. Probably exactly what she was doing right now.

Flint cleared his throat. "I'm not saying it wasn't Celeste."

"That's big of you," she said and started to step past him.

He grabbed her arm. "I'll check the window for fingerprints—"

"She was wearing gloves. Flint, we've been here before. She's taunting me. She's knows we're back together. She's warning me what will happen if I move in with you."

He sighed and let go of her arm. "How could she know about that?"

"I told my landlord. You know how news travels in this town." She rubbed the spot where his fingers had been, feeling close to tears.

"I'll go over and talk to her, but again, I need proof to arrest her." His gaze met hers and in it she saw him pleading with her to understand. She did understand.

"I *saw* her. How much more do you need to arrest her?" she demanded.

"You saw her standing out in your yard. You didn't see her pry open your window, throw in a burning object, you didn't catch her in the act."

"I was *asleep*! That's what normal people do this time of the night!"

"I know." He stepped to her and drew her into his

arms. She came reluctantly. She knew she shouldn't be blaming him for this, but she couldn't help it. He'd married the damned woman.

"What can we do?" Her voice broke. "What if she burns down the house with me in it next?"

He shook his head.

"I know you don't believe she'd go that far, but unlike you, I do believe she will go as far as her demented mind tells her to. She can't stand us being together."

He let go of her to walk to the window again. He raked a hand through his thick dark hair. She could see from the slump of his shoulders that he was as frustrated as she was by all this.

"She wants attention, no doubt about that," he said. "She's probably sitting at home right now waiting for me to stop over and ask her if she was out tonight, if she—"

"I heard at the shop today that Wayne is out of town. I had this feeling that she would do something tonight." Maggie was trembling again. She hugged herself wishing she was still in Flint's arms.

"Once you move in with me—"

"You really think she will stop?"

He turned to meet her gaze. "What choice will she have? So why are you dragging your feet?"

Mariah heard what sounded like a gunshot just moments before Darby called up to her. But she didn't catch what he said over the rain drumming on the roof overhead—and the pounding of her heart. "Darby?"

No answer. She rushed to the side window, thinking earlier that she'd heard what sounded like a vehicle. With a wave of relief, she saw the patrol SUV parked beside the building.

Was that why Darby had called? Had they gotten Rafael? She didn't dare hope. She'd been on edge all night. Darby had tried to reassure her, but she still felt anxious.

Now she grabbed the shotgun by the door and looked downstairs. It was still dark down there. "Darby?" she called again.

A flashlight came on in the kitchen. In the ambient light, she saw a large figure standing with his back to her at the bottom of the stairs. He wore a sheriff's department raincoat with the hood up, the back to her. What had Darby called the man? Harp?

The light went out. She could hear movement down there. She craned her ears. It almost sounded as if they were dragging something. Someone? Rafael? Had they caught him? Was it possible he'd come alone?

She started to put the shotgun back by the door before heading downstairs, but stopped. Darby had yelled her name and something else. "Don't." Don't what? Don't come down because they'd caught Rafael and he was wounded? Dead?

"Darby?"

"Down here!" The voice was muffled since it appeared to be coming from the bar area. She hesitated, then put down the shotgun, but returned to the bed where she reached under the mattress and pulled out the knife in its leather sheath. She tucked it into the top of her right boot. She felt a little foolish, but even if they had caught Rafael, she didn't trust him. Better to be armed.

Still, as she started down the stairs, something stopped her. The deputy she'd seen earlier was no longer standing down there. No one was, which in itself felt wrong. Very wrong. The feeling was so strong, she couldn't ignore it.

She retraced her steps as quietly as she could, feeling as if someone was standing just around the corner at the bottom of the stairs listening. Waiting.

The feeling became even stronger. When she reached the top of the stairs, she turned and saw something move fast in the darkness. "Darby?" she called, but she knew it wasn't Darby. Oh God, where was he?

At the pounding of boots on the stairs, she frantically closed the door, locked it and looked around for something to push against the door. She spotted the chest of drawers and rushed to it, jumping when a body slammed into the door behind her. The door shuddered, but the lock held. For the moment.

She shoved the chest of drawers over against the

door, knowing it wasn't going to hold once the wood around the lock splintered. Unfortunately, there wasn't anything heavy enough to keep out whoever was on the other side of that door.

As if she didn't know who it was.

But where was Darby? Her heart broke. For all she knew, he was already dead. And she was next, she thought as the door shuddered again.

Mariah reached for her cell phone but before she could key in 911, the door shuddered again—this time wood splintered. She picked up the shotgun and moved away from the door.

The door shattered around the lock and was flung open. The chest of drawers tipped over on its side and slid toward her a few feet before coming to a stop. She caught only a glimpse of Rafael's face before she fired the shotgun.

He managed to get the apartment door closed so the buckshot lodged in the wooden door.

Rafael swore on the other side of the door. "Put the gun down, Mariah. You are only making things worse. If you ever want to see your friend alive again, you won't do anything stupid, like call for help."

She felt a hitch in her chest. "What did you do to him?" she asked through the door.

Silence and then, *"Darby?"* There was a mocking tone that did little to hide his contempt. "He's still alive. But if you call 911 I'll kill him before anyone can get here. Same with the shotgun. Put it down and come out. I'm going to count to three."

Could she believe him that Darby was still alive? Probably not, but she held out hope that Rafael wasn't lying. Why would he when he could kill Darby at any time?

The 911 call operator answered. Mariah started to speak but knew that Rafael would be able to hear her. She quickly turned off her phone.

"One. Two. Three," Rafael said just on the other side of the door. "Angel? Are you down there with Darby?"

She heard a muffled answer.

"So should I tell him to kill your friend, Mariah? Or are you ready to talk?"

"Talk? You mean the way we did on our wedding night?" She could almost hear him grit his teeth.

"You are my *wife*. I can do whatever I want with you."

Mariah shook her head. Anger bubbled up. She wanted to tell him that she wasn't his, would never be his, that she had given herself to another.

But if he hadn't already killed Darby, she feared he would if he flew into a temper. So she held her tongue.

"I'm not going back with you," she called through the door. The shotgun was getting heavy in her hands. Her arms had begun to ache. She rested the butt of it on her thigh for a moment.

"You'd rather stay here?" he asked through the partially open door.

"I'd rather be anywhere but with you." She waited.

"I don't believe you," he finally said. "I think you've fallen for this cowboy."

She held her breath for a moment. If she denied it— She heard what sounded like a commotion downstairs and lifted the shotgun.

"Your cowboy is waking up," Rafael called from the other side of the door. "It's time you came out of there. Without the shotgun or I'll kill him myself.

"Entirely up to you, Mariah. You know I don't care one way or the other. Actually, that's not true. I want to cut him up in chunks and feed him to hogs because if I find out he's touched you…"

CHAPTER TWENTY-ONE

MARIAH KNEW THAT if she put down the shotgun and let Rafael in, she was dead. But if she didn't, he'd kill Darby. If Darby wasn't already dead. She couldn't assume that Rafael was telling the truth and that the cowboy was still alive, especially given that she'd heard what sounded like a commotion in the bar.

Which meant she had to be ready to fight for her life. Again.

She had managed to best him on their wedding night, but it had been just the two of them. At least one of his cousins was downstairs right now. For all she knew there could be a half dozen of them.

But still, she had no choice. If there was any way to save Darby, she had to take it.

"Okay." She started toward the door when the lights suddenly came on, flickered, almost went out again, and then remained lit. It caught her off guard for a moment. She blinked, unaccustomed to the brightness after getting used to the subtle differences in the darkness.

She looked at the splintered door. This shotgun was the only thing keeping Rafael out now. She felt more vulnerable than she had before as if there really was no place to hide now.

Hadn't she known Rafael would show up tonight? Hadn't she felt it? She and Darby thought they'd been ready for it. But Rafael had shown up in a sheriff's department patrol SUV wearing the deputy's raincoat. She thought of Harp. Dead somewhere? Probably. Just like she and Darby were going to be if she didn't do something.

Mariah moved to the door. She didn't put down the shotgun. Not yet. She stepped around the fallen chest of drawers, leaned the shotgun against the wall by the door and reached for the doorknob.

She hadn't seen Rafael in the weeks since the wedding night. All the time she'd been on the run, she'd been watching for him, expecting to see his face suddenly appear in a crowd or next to her at a gas station. How many times had she awakened in the middle of the night terrified he was standing next to her bed?

Now, as the door swung open, she saw him standing on the top step, a shotgun in his hands. She looked into the black hole of the barrel, then at him. He moved it to the side, holding it across his chest.

"Well, if it isn't my loving wife," he said, his lips twisting into a sneer.

A shiver scaled the length of her spine as she stared at him and was struck by how different he was from the mental picture in her head. The man was handsome as the Devil. That wasn't the only thing he and the Devil had in common. In her mind, he'd become so ugly that she'd actually forgotten what he looked like.

But the eyes couldn't hide the real him. Cold as a grave and as hard as the stone towering over it. Hate hunkered in those dark depths and a meanness that boiled just under the surface.

He cut her a smile, one full of promise and pain as he leaned back against the wall, looking smug.

Mariah saw that he thought he'd won. He had her where he wanted her. He believed she would do anything to save Darby—including offering herself up to his punishment.

Surely he didn't think she'd changed that much. That she would give in so easily. And yet from the smirk on his face, that seemed to be exactly what he thought.

The stairs were steep and Rafael wasn't ready for it, which made her next move easier than she'd hoped. She grabbed the shotgun he held across his chest and pulled as if to take it away from him. He came off the wall, facing her on the second step from the top as they struggled for the shotgun.

He was much stronger than her, so it wasn't much of a struggle. She knew when to quit. Suddenly instead of pulling on the shotgun, she shoved, knocking Rafael off balance. He flailed, letting go with one hand to try to grab the railing. But he couldn't hold on and went over backward.

She watched him tumble down the steep steps, banging his way down as he continued to try to hold on to the shotgun—and save himself.

Mariah knew that the fall probably wouldn't keep him down long—let alone kill him. She grabbed the shotgun she'd set by the door and hurried down the stairs after him to find him lying on his side, his back to her.

She stopped four stairs up and pointed the shotgun at his back. All she had to do was pull the trigger and end this. Just shoot him in his back. Her hands were trembling from the weight of the shotgun and what she needed to do.

With a start, she saw Angel Vale suddenly fill the space just beyond Rafael. She raised the shotgun. She'd always liked Angel. He looked like a man who wished he was anywhere but here. He glanced at Rafael who was groaning and trying to get up. Angel blinked, looking confused and scared.

"Where is Darby?" she asked, her voice breaking.

"He's…" Angel made a motion toward the bar area. She remembered hearing what sounded like a body being dragged into the saloon.

"Is he still alive?"

Angel's eyes widened some in the ambient light from the kitchen. "I think so. I had to hit him again. But I think he's still breathing."

Rafael had pulled himself up into a sitting position at the bottom of the stairs. He started to reach for the shotgun that had landed next to him after he'd finally dropped it.

"Don't!" she ordered.

He turned his head to look back up the stairs at her as if it hurt to do so. An angry scowl marked his handsome features. "You won't shoot me."

"I will."

"No," he said. "Or you already would have." He started to get up.

She knew she had to stop him now. She closed her eyes and pulled the trigger.

HARP HADN'T GONE far when he was forced to stop the van, open his door and throw up. His head was killing him and he was sick to his stomach. His blurred and often double vision told him that he was hurt badly. Probably a concussion. He was having trouble thinking clearly.

But even through the fog of his brain, he knew he was in serious trouble. He'd screwed up going to check what he'd thought was teenagers. For all he knew Darby Cahill and Mariah Ayers were dead by now. This was going to get him fired. Worse, he'd be a pariah in town. He'd have to move. He wouldn't be able to get another law officer job—not with this hanging over him.

But more to the point, what was he going to do

right now? He was driving the would-be killers' van. He'd lost his weapon, stun gun, his raincoat and his patrol SUV. He couldn't very well storm the saloon without a weapon. Nor could he radio in for backup.

As he came around a corner, he saw the Stage-coach Saloon through the diminishing rainstorm. The lights were on—and his patrol car was parked along the side.

IN THAT INSTANT before the boom of the shotgun re-verberated in the stairwell making Mariah's ears ring, Rafael lunged—not for the shotgun at his feet—but for her.

Her eyes flew open as he grabbed the end of her shotgun and shoved it aside. The blast of buckshot went off to the side, peppering the wall and sending up a cloud of sheetrock dust.

Before she could fire again, he grabbed the barrel, jerking her off her feet. Off balance, she fell down the last of the stairs and into him.

Rafael caught her, wrenched the shotgun out of her hands and threw it onto the floor. It skittered across the tile to come to rest at Angel's feet, with Rafael barking at his cousin to pick it up. Then his hands were on her, his face twisted in fury. She noticed that some of the shot had hit his right arm, cutting through the deputy's raincoat.

He slammed her against the wall. If he was wounded, he didn't show it. He'd always been strong and violent. Neither the fall down the stairs nor the spray from the shotgun had changed that.

"You slept with him, didn't you?" he demanded.

She didn't have to ask who he meant. Rafael was no fool. She could have stayed upstairs with the shotgun and tried to wait him out. She could have called 911 and waited for help. But then he would have killed Darby.

Mariah looked him in the eye, refusing to be cowed by him. "Yes."

"You lousy—"

The slap knocked her head back against the wall with a loud smack. "But he is only one of a dozen men I have slept with since I left you."

He stared at her, his eyes bulging with fury. "You're lying."

"Am I? I would sleep with anyone but you and now I am…damaged, no longer pure, and if you touch me, you will be tainted, as well."

He grabbed her by the throat, his fingers digging into her flesh. "I'll kill you."

Stars danced before her eyes and her head ached. Darkness began to close in around the edges of her vision. He *would* kill her. She'd known that, but this way was better than being raped by him first.

Her vision narrowed to a pinpoint. She couldn't breathe. She clawed at his hands, but it was useless. All his fury was in his hands. He wanted to squeeze the life out of her and now he was.

She kneed him hard in the groin, as hard as she could. His hands released her neck, but only for a moment. She tried to get away from him, her vision fading in and out.

He grabbed a handful of her hair and jerked her back into him before slamming her against the wall again. She fought, clawing at his face, his arms.

He slapped her with his free hand, then closed his fist and swung. She ducked most of the blow, but still he grazed her cheekbone, knocking her back with a smack into the wall. Stars glittered brightly and, for a moment, she thought she was going to pass out.

"Just get it over with," she spat, glaring at him as he raised his fist again.

"Let go of her," Darby ordered as he motioned Angel aside with the gun he held before turning it on Rafael.

HARP SLOWED THE VAN. If he could get to his patrol car's radio… He turned off the van's headlights and coasted down the hill, stopping a hundred yards out. Killing the engine, he sat for a moment trying to stop the spinning in his head. He was majorly messed up and that scared him—just not as much as the chance of running into those two men again.

But he needed medical attention and, unless he missed his guess, so did Mariah and Darby—if it wasn't too late for them.

He pushed open the van's door. It groaned open.

He closed it gently not sure what was waiting for him out there in the darkness. The rain had pretty much stopped. He pointed himself toward the patrol car and put one foot in front of the other, weaving on trembling legs. He stumbled and almost fell just a few yards from the van.

He could see that the lights were on in the back of the saloon. But the signal light was still out. Harp would have thought that the sheriff might have driven out this way to double-check on his brother. Flint must have thought Harp could handle it. That almost made him laugh, but he hurt too bad and didn't have the energy.

Stumbling along through the open field like a drunk on a runner, he was almost to the patrol SUV when he heard the sound of a gunshot. He tripped and fell face-first in the wet, soggy earth. His heart was pounding so hard that he couldn't hear anything else. Had they come out? Were they about to get into the patrol car? They would see him.

He kept his head down, gasping for breath, his head a bass drum that wouldn't quit pounding.

After a few moments, he raised his chin. He could see the patrol SUV sitting only yards from him. There was no sound from inside the saloon.

Dropping to all fours, he crawled to the passenger side door of the patrol car, reached up and grabbed the door handle. For a moment, he thought it was locked. To his relief, it opened. The interior light came on.

He hurriedly closed the door, leaned against the side of the car and waited, half expecting someone inside would have seen it and come to investigate. He still had no weapon, didn't even know if he could fire accurately enough to stop anyone if he had been carrying.

Again, no one came out. This time, he pushed to his feet and, keeping low, opened the door and quickly slid inside and closed it again. *Hurry.* He had a bad feeling that whatever was going on in the saloon was almost over. *Hurry.*

He grabbed the radio.

FLINT DROVE BY his ex-wife's house. All the lights were out. He parked a few houses up the street, got out and walked back. He wanted to believe she'd been in the house all night and was now sound asleep. The last thing he wanted to believe was that she was targeting Maggie. Stalking her. Tormenting her.

When he reached her house, he walked along the side until he reached the garage and could peer into the window. Her SUV was parked inside. It was wet, just as he'd feared. She'd driven it tonight. He feared that if he checked the hood, he would find it still warm.

Swearing under his breath, he headed for the front door. After ringing the doorbell, he glanced around at the other houses on the block. No one was up at this hour. No one should be, he thought. He hadn't realized how tired he was until that moment. It had been a long night. Daylight wasn't that far off. All he wanted to do was go home and go to bed.

But first he had to check on Darby and Mariah—as soon as he dealt with Celeste. He tried to reassure himself that they were fine. Harp would have radioed if there was trouble out there.

Celeste's porch light came on. He turned back to the door as Celeste peered out before feigning surprise at seeing him at this hour. As she opened the door, he saw that she wore a large velour robe. She cinched it tighter at the waist and played with the wide collar as she said, "Flint? Is something wrong?"

He didn't bother to answer as he pushed his way in. "Wayne home?" He knew he wasn't but he guessed he wanted to see if she would lie.

"No, he's in Denver. What is it?"

He turned to look at her. Damn but she was a fine actress. "Where have you been tonight?"

"I beg your pardon?"

"Celeste, I know you went out tonight." Behind her he could see a blue and white striped raincoat that was still dripping on a hook by the door. There were a pair of black leather boots parked under it.

"Just to the gas station and the grocery. I needed a few things. Why are you asking me this?"

He sighed, removed his Stetson and looked at her.

He was too tired for this. Too angry. He didn't feel like the law right now. He felt like the ex-husband she'd left for another man. "Damn it, Celeste, I know you were over at Maggie's tonight."

Her green eyes widened as if surprised. "What? I just told you—"

"I know what you told me. Gas and groceries." He met her gaze. "I know about the beauty shop, I know about the fire tonight." He shook his head. "You need help. When Wayne gets back, I'm going to tell him what you've been up to."

"He won't believe you." At least she was no longer pretending she didn't know what he was talking about.

"I think he just might." He put his hat back on. "You want to end up in prison? If that fire had spread tonight… Or are you headed for the nut house?"

She looked at him with condescension. "Unless you can prove that I've done something…" She smiled. "I didn't think so."

"Maggie saw you."

"So it's my word against hers?" She chuckled. "On a dark, rainy night? How can she be sure of what she saw? I've heard she hasn't been herself since someone broke into her beauty shop and wrote awful things about her."

Flint closed his eyes, his anger so intense that it scared him. "We both know who wrote those things."

Celeste quirked one finely honed eyebrow. "Oh?

You've found some evidence? Thrown someone in jail?" Her smile was all teeth. "I guess not. That would explain why you aren't here with a warrant for my arrest, wouldn't it?"

"The next time I have to stop by, I'm going to take you in—evidence or no evidence. I'm also going to have a talk with your…husband. He needs to know what you've been up to." He saw that it was a threat that wiped the smile off her face.

"I'd be careful making false accusations against me. Same with your girlfriend. Wayne has a high-powered lawyer who will take you both for everything you're worth—and let's face it, neither of you are worth much."

"You're lucky I'm not a violent man, Celeste." He tipped his hat and left, his blood pressure through the roof. He feared that if he ever got his hands around her throat… The thought shocked him. As he'd said, he wasn't a violent man. Or at least he'd always thought he wasn't.

His radio crackled to life.

CHAPTER TWENTY-TWO

AT THE SOUND of Darby's voice, Rafael swung around, but didn't let go of Mariah's hair as he quickly put Mariah between him and the gun pointed at him. Even before that, Darby couldn't have gotten a clean shot and Rafael knew it.

"I thought I killed you, cowboy."

"Not quite." But close. He felt weak. The room spun. It took all his strength to remain standing. He had to get Mariah away from this man. "Let go of her."

Rafael laughed. "Or what?"

Darby raised the gun. Angel had put down the shotgun he'd been holding, lowering it gently to the kitchen table and holding up his hands.

"I want none of this," the man said now as he backed toward the door.

"You take another step, Angel, and I will kill you myself," Rafael snapped. He still had his hand buried in Mariah's hair. Angel stopped, but only for a moment; he grabbed the doorknob, flung the door open and disappeared into the darkness. Cold air rushed in as the door banged against the side of the building.

"Let go of her. Now."

"You wouldn't dare shoot," Rafael taunted. "You could hit Mariah. She's cast her spell on you, hasn't she? Put her curse on you. And now you're willing to lose your life for her? She isn't worth it. Especially after what you did to her. You ruined her, didn't you?" the man demanded from between gritted teeth.

Darby could see the fury building in Rafael. He knew he was only going to get one chance. As weak as he was from the head wound and loss of blood, he wouldn't be able to defend himself against Rafael one-on-one. His only hope was to stop the man now before any more harm could come to Mariah— or to himself.

He aimed, knowing what Rafael had said was true. Taking a shot was more than risky. It was insane. But this situation was insane.

Rafael glared at him, daring him to fire. Darby could feel the gun wavering in his hand. He needed his other hand to steady it, but he couldn't raise it because of the gunshot wound in his side. He feared the pain would make him black out again.

"You might as well put down the gun," Rafael taunted. "You couldn't hit the broad side of a barn."

Darby pulled the trigger.

DISPATCH QUICKLY RELAYED that Deputy Harper Cole had called in for backup at the Stagecoach Saloon.

Two men, both armed, were inside the building. He was injured, unable to help. Situation inside the saloon unknown.

Flint turned on the siren as he quickly put out a call to all law enforcement. His heart pounded as he read between the lines. The situation inside the saloon was dire. For all he knew his brother and Mariah could already be dead.

The sky to the east was starting to lighten as he raced out of town toward the saloon. He had no idea what he might be walking into. Harp was wounded but had managed to call for help. If the men were still inside the saloon, then maybe there was a chance that Darby and Mariah were still alive.

He could only pray that they were. Other calls were coming in over the radio. Since the sheriff's department employed only a few men, when there was trouble, game wardens and border patrol could be called in. Both were trained law enforcement. Several were headed for the saloon.

"Stand down until I get there and can assess the situation," Flint said into his radio. Ahead he saw the turnoff to the saloon and turned off his siren.

HARP FELT HIMSELF drifting in and out of consciousness. He'd made the call for help, but now felt too weak to move. What would he do if the two men came out of the building and tried to leave in the patrol car?

He couldn't put up a fight. Not in his condition. Which meant he couldn't stay here. He glanced around the inside of his patrol SUV and suddenly remembered the compartment where he kept spare ammunition—and his .357 magnum pistol. He wasn't supposed to carry anything but regulation arms in his patrol SUV but he liked having the pistol with him as a backup even though he'd never used it. He'd even forgotten about it until this moment.

Opening the compartment, he expected it to be gone.

But there it was. With trembling fingers he picked it up. He kept it loaded. Cradling it in his lap, he considered trying to enter the building. Even for him, that was a foolish thought. He was still seeing double, still sick to his stomach, still too weak to even get out of the car and find a place to hide.

The rain had stopped, the sky trying to clear as light radiated up from behind the Judith Mountains. Soon it would be daylight. He couldn't just keep sitting here, waiting. As he considered what to do, he heard a sound as something banged and looked up to see one of the men running out the back door of the saloon.

From inside the building came the distinct sound of a gunshot. The man stopped as if confused which way to go, before he turned toward the patrol SUV.

THE BOOM OF the gunshot reverberated around the kitchen. Mariah flinched as if she'd been hit. She saw Darby's eyes widen in alarm and then they were both looking at Rafael.

He still had a handful of her hair twisted in his fingers. Blood bloomed on his temple. The bullet had grazed him, not taken him down.

He lifted his free hand to touch the bleeding wound and laughed. "You are one crazy bastard," Rafael said to Darby. "I would not have taken that shot, but you…"

Before either of them could react, he shoved Mariah toward Darby. She lunged to the side, but off balance went crashing to the floor. Her head hit the kitchen table leg as she went down. Stars danced before her eyes as she tried to get to her feet. Behind her came the report of another shot as Rafael rushed Darby.

She'd known Darby had been in bad shape even before he came to her rescue. His reaction time was off because of his injuries. He hadn't expected Rafael to move so quickly. Or to attack the way he did.

Rafael barreled into Darby, knocking the gun away. She was on her feet. She snatched up the shotgun, but not quickly enough to stop Rafael. He slammed his fist into the side of Darby's head and spun around to wrench the weapon from her.

Past him, she saw that Darby had slid to the floor and was out cold. Her gaze went to Rafael. He was bleeding from where the bullet had grazed him, but the second shot must not have hit him. Nor was the wound or the loss of blood going to stop him.

Mariah saw that he planned to end this. She took a step back, hit the wall and scrambled for the stairs, but he was too fast for her. He grabbed her arm, spinning her around and knocking her down onto the stairs. Leaning over her, his free hand went to the front of her T-shirt.

She heard the fabric tear. His gaze took in her exposed flesh, before lifting to her face again. His eyes locked with hers.

"Did you really think that your whoring around would keep me from taking you?" he demanded, wiping blood from his right eye as he bent over her.

Mariah felt her heart drop as he grabbed the front of her bra and tore it from her body. He looked down at her bare breasts through the tatters of her T-shirt and smiled as he lowered his head to bite at her nipple. She cried out and kicked wildly as she worked her hand down behind her leg to the top of her boot— and the knife she had put there.

He pressed his body against her legs to quiet them and caught her free hand in his larger one as he pushed her harder and more painfully into the steps at her back. He pulled hard on the waist of her jeans, unsnapping them and breaking the zipper. He jerked the jeans and her panties down, stopping to smile at her as he unzipped his own jeans.

She'd told herself that she would die before she'd

let him rape her. He'd thought that her other arm was trapped under her. But now with some of his weight off her as he began to lower his jeans, she drew her arm out.

He must have seen the flash of the knife blade out of the corner of his eye. But he couldn't move fast enough to protect himself as she went inside his arm with the blade. Mariah knew she had only one chance. She drove the knife into him up to the hilt, pulled it free and drove it in again.

HARP SLID DOWN in the seat of the patrol SUV as far as he could. Over the edge of the dash he could see Angel headed for the driver's side of the car. As soon as the man looked in, he would see him.

Fumbling to get the pistol ready, he waited, knowing he had no choice. If he didn't kill him... And yet the moment he fired, it would alert the other one—Rafael, the really scary one still inside the building. He felt like crying as he realized that he could be dead within moments.

Angel reached the SUV. But his gaze was on the back of the saloon as he opened the vehicle's driver's side door. He didn't seem to see Harp hunkered down in the seat. He didn't look surprised until he heard the loud report of the gun go off and looked down at his chest.

With two stumbled steps back, Angel fell, dropping to his knees, then keeling over a few feet from the patrol SUV. The wind caught the door and slammed it.

Harp sat up, but he couldn't see the man where he'd fallen. Didn't know if Angel would get up and come after him. Or if he had crawled back toward the rear of the building to warn Rafael. His gaze was on the back of the saloon. Either way, Rafael would have heard the shot.

Harp readied himself for the shootout that he feared would take his life. His head still ached, but he was seeing a little more clearly now that the sun had crested the Judiths. Which meant Rafael would be able to see him.

In the distance, he heard sirens and prayed they would get to him in time as he opened his car door and fell out onto the ground to wait.

RAFAEL LOOKED DOWN at Mariah in confusion. He grabbed her hand, slapping it away as he pulled the knife from his stomach. He stared at the bloody blade and then at her. For a moment, Mariah thought he would stab her. But he still seemed determined to rape her first. He tossed the knife aside on the stairs.

She lunged for it, but it was just out of her reach. Fighting to squirm out from under him, pummeling him with her fists and trying to kick herself free of him, she knew there was no hope against his strength—even injured. He caught both of her hands, held them over her head and leaned down, pressing his bleeding body against hers. She closed her eyes, turning her head away as she bit her lip.

All the fight went out of her. Maybe this was always the way it was going to end. All her running, all her fighting, it had been for nothing. Maybe this was inevitable from the time her uncle had agreed to the marriage dowry when she was fifteen. She squeezed her eyes shut tighter, telling herself that Rafael couldn't hurt her any more than he already had—knowing it was a lie.

But then Rafael shifted over her. He let go of her hands to try to pull his pants down farther. Now that it was within reach, her hand closed over the handle of knife on the stairs. But she closed her eyes, telling herself she didn't have what it would take to stab him again. Tears were running down her cheeks, hot and salty. She licked her lips, surprised to find herself crying.

At a sound, she opened her eyes. Past Rafael she saw Darby stumbling toward them. She knew that Rafael would hear him any moment. This time, Rafael would kill him.

Gripping the knife handle in her hand, she closed her eyes and drove the blade in Rafael's chest. Her gaze met his. She saw the surprise in his eyes, saw the light begin to dim in his gaze. Pulling out the knife, she started to stab him again when he collapsed on top of her.

As she struggled to get out from under the weight,

Darby grabbed Rafael's collar and with effort dragged him from her. But she could tell that Darby was barely able to stand.

She hurriedly pulled up her jeans as she heard sirens in the distance. Rafael hadn't raped her. But he'd come so close that she could still feel his weight on her...

"Did he...?" Darby asked, his words slurred. He leaned against the wall. She could see that he was having trouble staying conscious.

She shook her head as she looked down at the dead man at her feet. Then, as if the effort was all the strength he had, Darby stumbled back and slumped to the floor. "Darby!" He didn't move. He didn't answer.

Mariah shoved past Rafael. She knew he was dead but a part of her imagined his hand snaking out, grabbing her ankle, pulling her back to him. And what if this time she wouldn't be able to escape?

Rafael had been this evil threat hanging over her for so long that she couldn't believe it was over. He lay on the floor, unmoving. She took a step toward Darby, then another. To her surprise, the knife was still gripped in her bloody hand. Her fingers felt glued to it.

She reached Darby and dropped to her knees beside him. Opening her fingers she let the knife drop to the floor. She touched her blood-free hand to his chest, praying he was still alive. She felt the rise and fall of his chest.

He was still breathing. She could hear the sirens growing closer and closer. Outside a car door slammed. She looked over at Rafael. His eyes were open, but unseeing. He lay in a pool of his own blood. He wouldn't be coming after her ever again.

Slowly, she lay down beside Darby on the floor, curling herself around him. She closed her eyes. Inside the saloon, the only thing she heard was the pounding of her heart.

CHAPTER TWENTY-THREE

MARIAH HAD NEVER killed anyone before. She felt numb as she answered the questions from first the sheriff and then a crime scene crew out of Billings. It seemed that she must have repeated her story twenty times before they finally let her get cleaned up.

By then it was afternoon. Flint had insisted she come back to his house and try to get some rest. But she'd been too exhausted to sleep. She'd finally gotten up and gone to the hospital. She needed to be with Darby.

Flint had assured her that Darby was going to make it. He'd been shot, but no vital organs had been hit. He'd lost a lot of blood and he had a concussion, but the doctors were taking good care of him.

Mariah had to see for herself. She walked the few blocks from Flint's house to the hospital and entered the emergency exit. "I need to see Darby Cahill."

The nurse started to argue that she had to wait until visiting hours, but then stopped as if she'd finally taken in Mariah's injuries and realized who she was. Word traveled fast in a small town. The nurse's gaze became compassionate. "Come on. I'll show you to his room."

The hospital room was dark except for the medical devices Darby was hooked up to. She listened to the steady beat on the screen next to him as she moved toward the bed. His eyes were closed. He was breathing softly. She pulled up the chair next to the bed and sat down, lowering her head to the mattress as she took his free hand.

The nurse said something about her not staying but a few minutes. Mariah didn't remember anything after that. Listening to the machines and Darby's breathing, she closed her eyes and slept.

DARBY WOKE TO find Mariah sound asleep in the chair next to his bed. He felt a start until he looked into her face. She was all right. He couldn't remember everything that had happened last night. His head ached, he felt groggy and his side felt as if it was on fire.

All that mattered was Mariah. Her beautiful face was bruised, her lip bloodied and one eye black and swollen, but she was alive.

She opened her eyes, blinking as if surprised to see him awake. "Oh, Darby, I'm so sorry." She was on her feet and pressing her face into his neck, crying. He put his arm on his uninjured side around her.

"You're all right. That's all I care about," he said quickly.

She pulled back to look at him. "You saved me."

He smiled. "I'm glad to hear that. Truthfully, I don't remember much."

Mariah quickly told him what had happened. He listened, horrified at how close Rafael had come to not just raping her, but killing them both.

"What about Harp?" he finally asked.

"He's going to make it. Like you, he has a concussion. Flint said he's just glad to be alive."

"I know that feeling." He squeezed her hand. "And Rafael?"

She swallowed. "Dead. Angel too. Harp shot him." Tears filled her eyes. "Angel didn't want to be involved in this. Rafael…" She seemed unable to continue.

"Well, it's over now, right?"

She nodded, looking away as she did.

He felt something tighten in his gut. It *was* over, wasn't it?

"Good, you're back with us," the doctor said when he came in. "If you can give us just a minute," he said to Mariah.

She dried her tears and said she would be just down the hall.

"How are you feeling?" the doctor asked after she'd left.

"My head hurts." Darby touched the bandage.

"I would imagine it does. You suffered a concussion and were unconscious for quite a while. Do you remember what happened?"

"Bits and pieces. That's all."

The doctor nodded. "Your family is here, but I think it would be better not to have them all in here demanding answers."

Darby smiled through the pain. "Thanks, Doc."

"So I'll let them come in, see that you are all right and then send them on their way, how's that?"

He nodded, and then stopped himself. "I want to see Mariah, though."

The doctor smiled. "Just don't let her tax you too much."

Hawk, Cyrus and Lillie all came in along with Trask, Lillie's fiancé, but were quickly shooed out by the doctor. Flint came in last. He had on his sheriff's face so Darby knew it was bad.

"Mariah filled me in on what happened—at least what she knew," Darby said.

"You don't remember?"

"Not much. She said Harp has a concussion?"

"Yep, he's the town hero now." Flint shook his head. "How are you feeling?"

"I've been better. I'm just worried about Mariah. Are you sure there isn't anyone else out there from Rafael's family who wants to hurt her?"

"I've spoken with his family. Once they heard what he did… I don't think there will be any more trouble from them. Mariah's staying with me. Right now, the saloon is a crime scene. It will be a while before you can reopen."

He wasn't worried about the saloon. "Mariah told me that Rafael is dead?"

Flint nodded. "Mariah killed him."

"Did he…"

"She has a few scrapes and cuts, but she wasn't seriously hurt."

He thought of the bruises on her face. They would heal. The rest would take longer.

"You're going to be all right, the doctor said. The DCI will want to talk to you now that you're conscious."

"Is Mariah still out there?"

Flint smiled. "She hasn't left your side except when I insisted she try to get some rest at my house. As it was, she left to come down here. I found her sleeping in a chair next to your bed. I hope now that you're awake, we can get some food in her and she'll agree to continue staying at my house. I'll let her come in and say goodbye, but then I'm insisting she get some food."

Now that he knew Mariah was all right, Darby nodded. He closed his eyes again. He couldn't remember ever being this tired. Rafael was dead. So was his cousin. He hated to think what repercussions that would have for Mariah. Was she safe now? Or would other members of the Roma community want blood?

One thing was clear. She could never go back even if she wanted to. She wouldn't want to, would she?

VICKI FOUND HARP'S hospital room but didn't go inside right away. She stood just to the side of the doorway looking in at him. His eyes were closed and, as badly beaten as he was, he looked…peaceful.

She realized he would have looked like this in his casket. *He'd almost died.* That thought made her feel sick to her stomach. Actually just about everything did.

Now people were calling him a hero. If he hadn't saved the day, Darby Cahill and Mariah Ayers would be dead right now. She knew how proud he must feel. Wasn't this what he dreamed would happen? That he would show the sheriff that he deserved more respect? That he would finally get the recognition he deserved?

She was happy for him, but worried he would no longer be interested in some skinny waitress at Sue's Diner.

As if sensing her, his eyes opened. He looked surprised to see her, but seemingly happy too. He lifted a hand and waved her in, motioning for her to close the door behind her.

Hesitantly she entered with the little flowerpot she'd picked up and the piece of pie Sue had sent with her. Apple, Harp's favorite. She put the flowerpot and pie down on the table next to his bed.

He reached out his hand to her, and to her surprise, she saw tears well in his eyes. She took his hand. He squeezed hers so hard she almost cried out as he pulled her to his side.

"It is so good to see you," he said, sounding as if he was choking on tears. He cleared his throat. "You heard?"

She nodded. "You're a hero."

He grimaced, closed his eyes and shook his head. When he opened them, he said, "I'm sorry we didn't get to have that talk." His gaze searched hers. "Is it what I think?"

She swallowed the lump in her throat. "I'm pregnant."

He let out a laugh and for a moment she didn't know how to take it. "That is the best news I think I've ever heard." He squeezed her hand a little more gently. "We should get married."

"Really?" Vicki had heard him say those words, but only in her wildest dreams. She'd imagined this conversation going a few completely different ways. "You mean it?"

He nodded. "There's something I have to tell you first." Harp glanced toward the door, before returning his gaze to hers. "I'm no hero, so if you think you're marrying one…" His voice broke again. "You need to know the truth. Our baby…" He cleared his throat again and made a swipe at his tears with his free hand. "Promise you won't ever tell anyone?"

She nodded and took his hand in both of hers, bracing herself as she listened to his side of the story.

"Still, if you hadn't radioed in when you did—"

"I almost didn't. I was so scared. I told everyone that I went back into the trees because I thought it might be the man after Mariah and that I got jumped by them. I thought they were going to kill me."

Vicki leaned down to kiss his cheek. "Anyone would have been scared, Harp. You shouldn't be so hard on yourself."

"You think?"

"I know. You did the right thing. Maybe it didn't start out that way, but you helped save those people's lives."

He nodded and gave her a weak smile. "You won't ever tell?" He sounded as if he might already be regretting telling her the real reason he'd gone to check on the van parked in the woods. "The sheriff was by earlier. Thanked me. Actually *thanked* me. Usually he just cusses me out and threatens to fire me."

"Well, all that's changed now," she said. "You'll get the respect you deserve. He might even buy us a wedding present."

Harp met her gaze as if it was finally sinking in. "Right. A wedding. A baby." He took a shuddering breath. "Once I get on my feet. Could be a while."

"WAYNE, DO YOU have a moment?" Flint asked as he entered the office building that afternoon and caught Wayne Duma heading out. He had a lot on his plate, but he wanted to take care of this since it had to be done.

Duma was a large handsome man who had made a lot of money in the real estate business before settling in Gilt Edge, having an affair with Flint's wife and ultimately marrying Celeste.

The man looked at his expensive watch as if he had places to be, but then looked resigned. "Why don't we step into my office?" He ushered the sheriff in and closed the door. "I think I know what this is about."

"You do?" Flint took a chair even though Duma hadn't offered him one. Had Celeste confessed all? Flint could only hope, but it didn't sound like her.

Duma walked around his desk and sat down to lean forward as if it was a subject he didn't want to get into and wanted to make this quick. "Celeste mentioned that you stopped by last night, *late*, while I was away. I flew back this morning after her call."

Flint groaned inwardly, realizing from the man's tone that Celeste had not confessed anything. She'd lied. He shouldn't have been surprised, but somehow he was. "I'm not sure what she told you but—"

"She told me that you have been…stalking her, that you haven't gotten over her and that you're trying to get her back."

Flint couldn't help it. He let out a laugh and shook his head. "I came by because someone tried to set

Maggie Thompson's house on fire last night. She identified that person as your wife."

"I see. If that was true then I would assume you plan to file charges?"

"Wayne, we both know it would be Celeste's word against Maggie's, but this isn't the first time that Maggie's property has been vandalized. I know it's Celeste but I can't prove it and Celeste knows it."

Duma said nothing as he looked at the floor for a moment before returning his gaze to the sheriff. "Celeste seems to think that you might be dangerous."

"Okay, I've heard enough," Flint said sitting forward in the chair. "I see how this is going to go. I told her I was going to tell you about what she'd been doing. Apparently she can't stand that I'm getting serious with Maggie and has been doing everything possible to keep us apart."

"I really don't think—"

"Wayne, you don't know me, but other people in this town do. So ask around. I'm in love with Maggie. I'm going to marry her. I don't want anything to do with Celeste. I just want her to butt out of my life."

"Then why would she—"

"Tell you different? Because Celeste is the dangerous one. I suspect you might already know that. She *lies*." Duma started to interrupt, but Flint continued. "She lied that night you were hauled down to the sheriff's office, first saying you struck her, leading us to believe it wasn't the first time. She wanted us to believe that you physically abused her." He held up a hand. "I didn't believe her. But then I know her. And then magically it all came back to her, and no, she recalled that she'd fallen down *after* you left. She was ready to throw you under the bus, and all because she wanted to interrupt my date with Maggie that night."

Duma cleared his voice. "I find that—"

"Hard to believe? How about the vandalism at Maggie's shop?"

"I heard it was kids."

"Did you also hear what was written on Maggie's mirror—not Daisy's—just Maggie's. That sound like kids to you?" Flint got to his feet, his hat in his hand. "Celeste is sick and I'm afraid of what she might do next. She seems determined to keep Maggie and me apart. But no matter what fool thing she does next, Maggie and I are going to be together."

"I don't know what you expect me to do with this information."

"I'm just here to give you a heads-up. The next time I stop by your house, I fear it will be either to take your wife away in a straightjacket or arrest her for some horrible crime she's committed against Maggie. Think about that when you're sleeping next to her at night. Get her some help." He tipped his hat and left.

MARIAH WOKE TO SCREAMING. It took her a moment to realize the sound was coming from her lips.

Darby reached for her. She jerked back as the dream still had her in its grip.

"It was just a nightmare," he said quietly as he turned on the lamp next to the bed.

She blinked at the sudden brightness. It filled the deep shadows in the room illuminating the apartment and dragging her out of the dream.

She took a few ragged breaths, her body wet with perspiration, and began to tremble.

This time when Darby reached for her, she curled into him, feeling small. She was so thankful to have him home from the hospital. In the days since, she'd hoped the nightmares would stop. Unfortunately, they seemed to be getting worse.

She'd always thought of herself as strong. Right now, she felt vulnerable. Even with Rafael after her, she'd been confident that somehow she could escape him.

She'd underestimated him and it had almost gotten her killed—and Darby, as well. That made her question everything she'd thought about herself.

"You're safe," Darby whispered into her hair as she pressed her cheek into his bare chest. "You're all right, Mariah."

But she knew she wasn't. Rafael had followed her into her dreams. Every night he was waiting for her since the night he'd died, that horrible smirk on his handsome face, that murderous look in his black eyes.

Rafael and Angel were dead. Both were funer-

als Mariah wouldn't be attending. The tragedy of
Angel's life especially hurt her deeply. Why had he
gotten involved in this? Hadn't he known how badly
it would end?

She thought of her uncle. Maybe he hadn't arranged the marriage for the money. Maybe he really
thought Rafael would be a good match for her. Even
now, when she was trying to make sense out of all
this, she still couldn't believe that. He'd done it for
the money. Maybe he'd thought she could handle Rafael if any woman could. Not that it mattered now.

"Have you spoken to any of your family?" Darby
asked.

"I don't really have any family left. I talked to a
friend of mine. Everyone in the Roma community is
just glad that Rafael is no longer a threat. But they
are all sick over Angel. Not that they blame me."

But none of that helped when she closed her eyes
at night. Rafael was dead. She'd killed him. Mariah
wished she could wipe away the memory. She told
herself she'd had no choice. He was going to rape
her. For all she knew, he'd already killed the deputy.
Darby had been hurt badly, was maybe even dying.
She'd had no choice and yet it haunted her.

"How is Mariah?" Flint asked when he stopped by.
The saloon had been reopened once Darby was well
enough to work again. The regulars had practically

been waiting at the door. Of course, there were those who came to see where two men had died.

Darby had insisted Mariah wait longer to come back to work. He knew there would be those people who wanted to see the woman who'd murdered her former fiancé. The story had gone national.

"You look as if you haven't had any sleep in days," Flint said to his brother. "Are you sure you should be back at work so soon?"

"Doc gave me a clean bill of health. I'm fine. It's just been...hard. Harder on Mariah than me. But she's all right." He'd looked away before adding, "She's still having a little trouble sleeping though."

"I gathered that since you look the worse for wear. People often think that killing another human being wouldn't be hard if they had a good enough reason. They see it on television. But it's different in real life."

"Are we talking about Mariah now?"

Flint pulled off his Stetson to rake a hand through his thick dark hair. Given how messy it looked, it wasn't the first time he'd done that today. "I've only had to use my weapon once, but it still haunts me. I think Mariah should talk to someone," Flint continued. "I know someone who might be able to help her."

"*I'll* help her."

"Darby, she can't talk to you the way she can a stranger." He pulled out his phone and keyed in the information. "I sent you a text with the woman's name. Just think about it."

His brother nodded. "Thanks, but I'm sure she'll be fine. She just needs time."

But later when he went upstairs to check on her, he looked into Mariah's face. There were dark bruises under her eyes from lack of sleep. Those damned nightmares. He'd hoped that with time it would get better. But he saw the hollowed look in those beautiful dark eyes of hers and knew he had to do something.

"I was talking to Flint earlier," he said. "He thought you might want to talk to someone. Mariah, if you need to go home to your people for a while…"

She shook her head as she cupped his cheek with her warm soft palm. "You're my people now. I'm Romani, but I no longer want to live in that community. I haven't since my uncle arranged my marriage to Rafael. I know my grandmother would understand. She would never have let me marry him."

"But I think you need more help that I can give you. Flint said it helps to talk to someone. You know, a professional. He gave me the name of a woman."

"You told him about the nightmares?" She made it sound as if he'd betrayed her.

"No, I didn't have to. He said he knows what you're going through. He's been there. Mariah, I know how strong you are. But sometimes we all need help. In a situation like this…" He cupped her shoulders in his hands and looked into her eyes. "This kind of trauma… At least think about it. For your sake, please. Her name is Nancy Crest. Here's her number."

She bit her lower lip for a moment, eyes shiny, and finally nodded as she took the note from him.

SUE WAS WAITING for Vicki when she came out of the diner's ladies' restroom. "I'm going to do you a favor," her boss said. "I'm going to fire you."

Vicki thought she might be sick again.

"It's for your own good. You'll be able to draw unemployment because I'm betting your deputy boyfriend isn't going to be helping you out financially. That way you can stay home and take care of yourself until you are well enough to work again. If I can't put you on, I'll write you a good recommendation, okay?"

All Vicki could do was nod. Sue had been so kind to her. "I'm sorry."

Sue brushed that off. "I'll stop by occasionally and check on you. Bring you something decent to eat. Now get out of here."

Vicki walked out to find Harp leaning against his patrol SUV. Had Sue called him? Her car had run again after that night Harp had become a hero. But last night a thunderstorm had come through and it wouldn't start again. Sue had had to give her a ride home again. She'd called Harp and had to leave a message yesterday, but he hadn't gotten back to her.

"Here, give me your keys," Harp said now. "I'll see if I can get your car going for you."

"It often doesn't start when it's raining," Vicki said, so glad to see him that she'd given him a quick kiss on the cheek. He'd sidestepped most of the kiss, glancing toward the diner as if worried that Sue was watching. "The car will probably start now that it's dried out."

Sure enough, it turned right over. Harp left it running and climbed out. He seemed ill at ease around her now. They hadn't seen much of each other since he'd gotten out of the hospital. Was he sorry he'd told her the truth about that night? She'd never tell. Didn't he realize that?

"I guess I'll see you later. We can talk then about…well, everything," he said.

She nodded and smiled. "I've been thinking about it. I think you should move in with me. My apartment is small but it's all we need right now. We can save our money until the baby comes."

Harp looked as green around the gills as she often felt.

She had to laugh. "I know it's scary. I feel the same way. But as long as we're together…"

"Right." He nodded and looked toward the diner. "You going to keep working here until the baby comes?"

"No. Sue just fired me so I can collect unemployment. I haven't been able to work. Too sick." She shrugged. "But the morning sickness is supposed to only last three months."

"Huh. Okay." He edged toward his patrol SUV. "I guess I'll see you tonight, then." He looked so serious that she felt sorry for him. But she told herself that he'd be fine once he realized what a good wife she would be.

DARBY COULDN'T BELIEVE how much he'd seen of his brother Flint lately. He'd been by every day for one reason or another. So it was no surprise when he drove up again a few days later. Darby and Lillie were in the kitchen when he came in the back door.

"Thought I'd give you an update on Kendall Raines," Flint said. "I stopped by her apartment. She's long gone," he said as he joined Darby and Lillie at the kitchen table. Billie Dee was busy cooking up something that smelled wonderful and singing to herself.

"I'm not surprised she took off," Darby said, thinking he wasn't a very good judge of character. "Mariah told me that she saw Kendall going through Lillie's locker."

"I always leave my tips in there. That time she was out of luck since I'd taken them to the bank," Lillie said.

Darby sighed. "I figured that money was gone with her, as well." They would have needed proof in order to have Kendall thrown in jail—let alone get restitution. "Don't worry, I'll be more careful when I hire her replacement. I'll run the next one through an agency, I promise."

"Everyone loved her," Lillie bemoaned. "She was so good at her job."

"Apparently," Darby said.

"And to think that I tried to get the two of you together." His sister looked horrified at the idea now. "All the time she was stealing from us. You must have suspected her."

Darby laughed. "Nope. She just wasn't my type."

"Unlike Mariah," Lillie said, brightening. "How is she?"

"Still shaken. She's seeing a counselor. Flint's idea." He smiled at his brother.

"Everyone thinks that, if forced, they could kill," his brother said. "They just don't realize what it does to you, taking another person's life."

"Mariah's the one, isn't she?" Lillie said studying her brother.

"The one?" He let out a laugh and shook his head. The one? He didn't know about that. What he did know was that when she wasn't around he felt empty inside as if drained of whatever made him get up in the morning. Mariah challenged him. She made even the darkest days brighter. She brought something interesting into his life. Mostly, she'd made him want her like he'd never wanted any other woman. He smiled. "Yeah, she's the one."

Lillie laughed. "So what are you going to do about it? You can't let her get away."

He hadn't had time to think about the future. He was still dealing with the past, like Mariah. But the thought of her getting away, as Lillie put it, shook him. Would she want to go back to the Roma community now that she was safe from Rafael? She said not, but he knew it was what her grandmother had wanted for her.

Also he worried that he wasn't enough for her right now. Maybe she needed, if not family, then people she had known. Maybe she needed to go back to the Roma community to overcome everything that had happened.

At the thought, he felt hollow inside as if someone had carved out his heart. He had to talk to Mariah. He'd been waiting, waiting for her to get better. Waiting because he was afraid.

MARIAH HADN'T KNOWN what to expect. It had taken her a few days before she'd called the number that Darby had given her.

Nancy Crest opened the door holding a baby in one arm and a dog on a leash in the other. "Sorry," she said, looking past Mariah to the street as a car pulled up and a man got out. "My husband is running late."

The man ran up the walk, apologizing as he took

the baby, the diaper bag and the dog. He kissed his wife and left.

Nancy smiled. "It isn't usually this crazy here in the mornings." She laughed. "What am I saying? It's usually worse. Come on in." She stepped aside to let her enter.

Mariah was thinking what a mistake this was. She didn't want to talk about any of this with a stranger. Especially this harried mother.

But when Nancy led her out to a room off the back, she relaxed a little. The room was filled with plants and sunlight and comfortable colorful chairs. Nancy plopped down in one and offered Mariah her choice.

"I love this room," the woman was saying. "It gives me peace." Nancy breathed in deeply, closing her eyes for a moment.

Mariah looked around and found herself breathing a little easier as she picked a chair.

"I shot my first husband. It was an accident. We were arguing over a gun."

She looked into the woman's warm brown eyes and swallowed the lump in her throat.

"I was a mess. Couldn't sleep, couldn't eat. No charges were filed because there were witnesses. Not that it mattered. He'd wanted to kill himself—and me with him because he'd had an affair and the woman had dumped him. He blamed me." She smiled sadly. "Life just isn't fair sometimes."

Mariah said nothing as she thought of Rafael. He would definitely have killed her and Darby, as well. She'd never seen him so out of control.

"I couldn't believe I killed him. I was so angry that he forced me to do it. Mostly I felt such over-whelming guilt," Nancy said as she reached for a ca-rafe sitting on a small table. "Tea? I'm not a huge fan but for some reason this room requires it."

She couldn't help but smile and nod. She wasn't a huge fan of tea either but she felt a bond with this woman.

"Even knowing that he would have killed the two of us if I had let go of that gun... It didn't help. I'd taken a life," Nancy said as she poured the tea. "The life of a man I knew and had once loved. Whether you shoot someone on purpose or the gun goes off accidentally, the victim is still dead. But when forced to take a life, well that makes an enormous differ-ence in how you later reckon with what you've done."

"It's hard to talk about," Mariah said.

The woman nodded. "Nightmares?"

"I keep reliving it."

"I went through the same thing. The 'what if I had done this differently?' What if... All a waste of time. Can't turn back time."

"So what did you do?"

"At first I tried to handle it myself. Bottled it up. Told myself with time, I'd be fine." Nancy laughed and shook her head. "Finally, a friend talked me into seeing someone." She smiled. "It was amazing to just talk about it with someone who didn't know me or my husband. I can see you're skeptical. I was too. But there are other things you can do, as well."

Mariah took the cup of tea Nancy handed her and cupped it in her hands. The heat felt good. It did seem to go with the room.

"You can write everything you remember down. Surprisingly this can help you keep from reliving it in your brain. Just get it out. You would think that the greatest threat to your mental health would be the fear of dying. But it is the act of taking another person's life."

They sipped their tea in the quiet of the sunroom for a few moments.

"It also helps if you can talk to someone who understands," Nancy said. "If and when you're ready."

Mariah couldn't speak around the lump in her throat.

"I was so depressed, I felt so isolated, so…changed. I love this quote by Victor Hugo from *Les Misérables*. 'Every blade has two edges; he who wounds with one wounds himself with the other.' Humans are wired not to kill another human being.

"There is a suffering that comes from killing. I hope you'll let me help you through it."

They finished their tea, talked about the weather, Lillie's upcoming wedding and finally Nancy said,

"Close your eyes. Think of something that makes you happy."

Mariah complied. She thought of Darby.

"Something not connected with recent events."

She squeezed her eyes tighter and thought of her grandmother. She imagined her sitting in a chair smiling up at her. In her imagination, her grandmother reached for her hand. Mariah could almost feel the weathered warm skin, the strong grasp, the feeling that everything was going to be all right. She didn't want to open her eyes, didn't want to let go of the image or the feeling.

Hot tears welled behind her eyelids. A sob escaped as she felt her hand in her grandmother's strong, warm one. Another sob burst from her and then another.

ELY PULLED UP a stool and looked down the bar. "What's he draggin' for?" he asked Lillie, motioning in Darby's direction. The Stagecoach Saloon was quiet this morning even with the family gathered.

Lillie looked in Darby's direction. Her heart ached for him. "A woman."

Her father's eyes widened. "'Bout time he got serious about someone. So what's the problem?"

"Mariah's not from here. She's from a completely different culture. There's a chance she won't want to stay."

"So he'll have to go after her and convince her otherwise."

Lillie smiled and touched her dad's hand. Her heart was bursting with love for this irascible, strange, wonderful man. "How are *you* doing?"

"Fine." He was looking down the bar at Darby as if worried about him. She knew that feeling. She'd been worried about him too—until Mariah had come into his life. She'd never seen him happier. At least for a while. Now though...

"Don't give him a hard time," she said. She'd already warned Hawk and Cyrus. To her surprise, neither of them had stepped out of line. They had all been worried about Darby. Fortunately, the gunshot had healed and so had his brain after the concussion. Now the only thing that was ailing was his heart.

"I won't tease him," her father said. "So when's this weddin'? I'm just stayin' around for it. Once we get you and Trask married, I'm headin' back up into the mountains."

Lillie wanted to talk him out of it. But she could tell by the set of his jaw that Ely was having none of it. This was his life. She couldn't take that away from him and she knew her brothers wouldn't have much luck either at talking him out of going back into the mountains. "I'm just glad you'll be here for my wedding. I can't get married without you."

He looked at her then. His eyes were moist as he

squeezed her hand and said, "I wouldn't miss my daughter's weddin'. Not for nothin'."

He looked down the bar at Darby again. "Son, get off your duff and ask the woman," Ely called down the bar. "I can't believe I raised such lily-livered boys. Not one of them is going to make me a grandfather before I'm dead," he complained good-naturedly. "It's going to be up to you, Lillie Girl, the way things are going. I'm depending on you."

She laughed. "I'll do my best, Dad."

DARBY REINED IN his horse beside Mariah. He didn't know why he hadn't thought of a horseback ride sooner. She looked relaxed, the sun on her face, her gaze on the mountains ahead. A warm breeze stirred the pines and he could hear the creek babbling nearby.

"I don't think you have ever looked more beautiful than you do right now," he said.

She looked over at him and laughed. "Flatterer."

"I mean it. I can tell you're feeling better."

"I am, but getting out like this? I needed it. I love this place." She cocked her head at him. "I'm surprised you didn't want to ranch with your brothers."

"It's in my blood, that's for sure. But I guess I needed to find my own way. Being handed the ranch was too easy," he said with a self-deprecating chuckle. "I like to do things the hard way. Come on." He slid down off his horse and went to hers to help her down.

Together they walked to the creek. The clear water pooled around an array of colorful rocks like stepping stones across the stream. "I used to come here when I was a boy and dream about what I would do with my life. I saw myself with a wife but I could never see her face when I looked into the water." He drew her closer until their reflections appeared on the quiet surface at the edge of the creek. "But I can see her now."

Darby looked over at her. "Mariah, will you be my wife?"

MARIAH FELT TEARS burn her eyes as Darby dropped to one knee at the edge of the creek. Reaching into his jean jacket pocket, he pulled out a small velvet case. His gaze met hers and held it as he slowly opened the lid.

The ring was so beautiful and so right, that she let out a gasp of surprise. Set in a wide band of gold was a diamond-shaped onyx stone. He took it out of the case and slipped it on her finger. It fit perfectly.

She looked from the ring to Darby and then threw herself into his arms.

They fell over in the warm sand at the edge of the creek.

"A simple yes would have been fine," he said with

a laugh as he rolled her over until he was on top of her. "So you like it?"

"I love it. I love you." She looked into his gray eyes, seeing all the love and tenderness she'd known in this man. His look held a promise of a future she had never thought possible.

"So you're going to marry me?"

"You'd better believe it."

"I don't want to wait," he said, suddenly serious. "I feel as if we've been through so much…"

"I'd marry you right now."

He laughed. "That's what I was hoping you would say." He leaned down and kissed her softly on the lips. She felt desire rocket through her. They hadn't been together since that night before Rafael had showed up. All bound up with guilt, remorse, anger and depression, she'd thought she might never feel passion again.

But she'd underestimated what she and Darby shared. She wrapped her arms around his neck and pulled him down to her in a searing kiss. She'd never wanted him more than she did at this moment.

"What should we do to celebrate our engagement?" he asked, grinning.

"I have an idea."

FLINT STOPPED BY Maggie's house, not sure of what kind of reception he was going to get. They hadn't spoken for a few days. He knew she was still angry and frustrated after the fire. She felt he hadn't done anything about Celeste.

She opened the door in jeans and a shirt. Her feet were bare and her hair was pulled up in a ponytail. She looked like a teenager and he felt himself fall even harder for her.

Her cheeks were flushed as if she'd been doing something physical. He hoped she'd been packing to move in with him, but had a bad feeling that wasn't the case.

"Mind if I come in?" he asked.

"Sorry." She stepped back to let him in.

As he walked into her house, he saw at once that she hadn't been packing. She'd been cleaning. Rock music pounded out of the speakers and the house smelled of lemon. What struck him was how happy she looked.

"How is Darby? I heard what happened. How terrifying and after being robbed earlier in the month…"

"He's going to be fine."

"And Mariah?"

"She's working through it."

Maggie went over to the stereo and turned it down.

"You're not moving in with me, are you?" Flint said to her back.

Maggie turned to study him for a moment before she shook her head.

He nodded and had to swallow the lump in his throat. "Want to tell me why?"

She didn't look as happy as she had when she'd opened the door and he felt guilty about that. She sighed. "Would you like something to drink? I just made lemonade."

"Sure." He doubted he could swallow a drop right now, but he welcomed the distraction. It bought him time. Because he knew he wasn't going to like what she said and there wasn't a damned thing he could do about it.

In the kitchen, he watched her pour two glasses of lemonade over ice. She handed one to him but didn't pick up her own. As she leaned into the kitchen counter, she picked up one leg and rested her bare foot against her ankle. He could tell she wasn't as relaxed as she wanted him to believe.

The sad part was that he knew this woman. He ached to take her into the bedroom. Ached to hold her naked in his arms. To smell the scent of her. To feel her heart beating next to his.

"I can't do it. Not knowing that the only reason you asked me was because of your ex."

"That's not true. You know I want us to be together."

"I know. But moving in… It was too early for us to do that. We aren't ready. I'm not going to let Celeste run my life anymore."

Good luck with that, he thought. "I talked to her. I even talked to her husband," he said.

"She denied everything. I would imagine Wayne didn't believe it either."

He nodded. "So what do you want me to do that will fix this?"

Maggie shrugged. "Short of killing your ex-wife? I don't know. Maybe she'll tire of this if we keep seeing each other."

Flint grabbed on to that sliver of hope. "You still want to see me?"

She cocked her head at him, giving him a disbelieving look. "I'm in love with you. Have been for years."

He smiled and, remembering the cold, sweating glass in his hand, took a sip. "Good lemonade."

She smiled at that.

"You know I love you and don't want to spend another day away from you," he said. "If there was anything I could do to…"

"I know."

"You'll still be looking over your shoulder."

She nodded. "But I think it escalated because she heard we were moving in together. It would have been easy enough for her to hear since I had called about giving up my house when my lease was up."

He cursed under his breath. "So you're playing right into her hands."

"No, Flint, we weren't ready to move in together.

We were rushing it because of her. I'm happy here in my house. I'm not ready for that next step, I guess, otherwise I wouldn't let Celeste stop me."

"Okay, but I'm disappointed. I was looking forward to your moving in."

She smiled again, a smile that always seemed to bring sunshine into the room. "If our relationship can withstand your ex, then it will last. We just got back together after the last hurricane Celeste. Apparently we're going to have to live with her so maybe time is the only thing that will help."

He didn't think Celeste would tire of trying to control his life, but he said nothing as he took another drink of his lemonade. He knew Maggie was right. He'd asked her to move in on impulse and she knew it. He wouldn't make that mistake again.

"You're still going to Lillie's wedding with me, aren't you?" he asked as he put down his glass on the counter.

"Of course." She stepped toward him and, leaning into him, kissed him. "I have just the dress. It's blue. I think you'll like it."

"I'm sure I will. But I'm also a big fan of what you're wearing right now, though all I can think about is taking it off you."

LILLIE COULDN'T BELIEVE her wedding day was coming up so quickly. She'd dreamed about this day all her life. After falling for Trask Beaumont, she'd known that the only groom she wanted standing next to her was him. For those nine years he was gone, she'd thought she'd probably never marry. She definitely wouldn't fall in love again.

Then he'd come back for her. It still seemed like a dream, one she'd had many times while he was gone. But it had come true. Trask loved her, wanted to marry her, wanted to have children and raise them on the ranch he'd bought.

She couldn't imagine anything more perfect.

Now if she could just get through the wedding without crying. Lately, she'd been in tears a lot. She'd almost lost her twin. Her heart still ached when she thought about it.

"Lillie?" Trask asked when he saw her tears.

"I was just thinking about Darby."

"Darby is going to be fine," he said coming over to take her in his arms. She felt him falter. "This isn't about the wedding, is it? Are you getting cold feet?"

Lillie shook her head, unable to talk around the lump in her throat. She couldn't explain what she was feeling. All she could think about was that she'd almost lost her brother and she didn't think she could live without her twin in her life.

"Honey, if you're having second thoughts…" Trask began.

"It's not that," she managed to choke out. "I… I… I can't get married without Darby there."

"He will be there. He's mended, even back at work."

"That's not what I mean."

Trask looked lost. "Okay, why don't you tell me what you mean?"

"I have to talk to Darby first." With that she left her handsome cowboy fiancé looking confused as she rushed toward the door.

"The whole family is crazy," Trask said under his breath.

"I heard that."

"WHAT'S WRONG?" DARBY SAID when he saw his sister come through the back door of the saloon. It was clear that she'd been crying.

"I need to talk to you."

"Is it Trask? Is it the wedding? Is it—"

"I almost lost you."

He let out a relieved laugh. "I'm fine. You haven't lost me."

"Still, I realized something. I need you in my life."

"You got it." He pulled her into a hug. "Are you sure this isn't about the wedding?" he asked letting her go.

"In a way it is," she said.

He'd seen this look in her eye before. "Lillie?"

"You asked Mariah to marry you and she said yes, right?"

Darby nodded slowly, afraid where this might be headed.

"I want you next to me at my wedding." He didn't get a chance to ask what she was talking about. "I already spoke to Mariah. I told her how I felt about her joining our family and how I can't get married without my twin next to me." Tears welled in her eyes. "She agrees with me that there is only one thing to do. Have a double wedding! We're twins. Of course we should have a double wedding."

"Wait." Darby tried to argue that he didn't want to steal her thunder. "You don't want to share your wedding day."

"Don't be ridiculous. Getting married on the same day as you would only make my wedding day more special. It was meant to be, so quit arguing."

"But I need to talk to Mariah about this."

"I already did."

"Lillie."

"The only thing that wasn't settled between you two was when. I know you're anxious to tie the knot but you wanted to wait because of my wedding. So see, this is meant to be."

He quit arguing. He always gave in to his twin. He and Mariah had planned to elope as soon as Lillie and Trask's wedding was over. Mariah hadn't wanted a big wedding. Definitely not some big wedding dress.

"And after we're all married, I can help Mariah

furnish the apartment. She said the two of you are going to live there."

"Did she? Sounds like the two of you have everything figured out." He could see his sister and Mariah with their heads together. He liked the picture it painted. He could also see how Mariah would have gotten caught up in Lillie's excitement.

"We have it all planned. She and I will try to plan our pregnancies around our schedule at the saloon."

Darby laughed. "Good luck with that." But he couldn't help but imagine his kids and Lillie's playing together. He liked the idea and apparently so had Mariah.

"So what do you think?" Lillie asked.

He smiled. "I think I couldn't have been luckier than to have shared a womb with you."

She playfully slapped his shoulder. "I'm not sure you mean that, but I love you anyway."

CHAPTER TWENTY-FOUR

LILLIE AND TRASK had postponed their wedding day to give Darby and Mariah a little more time. As the days passed, Darby saw that Mariah was getting much better. She slept more and woke up less during the night. It had been weeks since she'd had a nightmare and it hadn't been one of the bad ones.

Now the double wedding was upon them. Darby had never seen his sister looking happier. He kissed her cheek and held her at arm's length. "You look beautiful and so grown up."

She smiled up at him. "You clean up nice, as well. Seriously, Darby, you look so handsome in that tux."

"Monkey suit. I can't wait to get out of it."

She hit him playfully on his shoulder and then winced as she must have remembered it hadn't been that long ago that he'd been shot.

"I'm fine," he assured her.

Lillie seemed to breathe a little easier. "Excited?"

"Very. How about you?"

She let out a breath. "Nervous. We have to watch Dad at the reception. He's been good for a while, but—"

"Don't worry about Dad. Cyrus has it covered." He glanced at the clock on the wall. "About time. Ready?"

She nodded, smoothing her beautiful wedding dress. He couldn't help but think of Mariah's first wedding dress. He quickly pushed the thought away. Lillie had gone with her to pick out a wedding gown. When they'd come back, his sister had told him the gown was beautiful—just like Mariah—and nothing like the other one.

Both he and Mariah were trying not to look back. They'd survived and now their futures lay ahead of them. Darby couldn't wait.

At a knock on the door, he turned to find Flint standing in the doorway. "It's time."

Darby quickly gave his twin a kiss on her cheek. "Break a leg," he said.

"You too."

He followed Flint out into the packed church and took his place next to Trask and his brothers. Lillie was right. They all looked good in their tuxes. It took a wedding to get them out of their jeans. But they all still had on their boots with their tuxes. Dress boots, but still cowboys at heart.

The organist began to play the wedding march. Darby looked toward the front door as first Lillie appeared and then Mariah.

His breath caught in his throat. He'd never seen a more beautiful woman. Mariah had her long dark hair pulled up. Her dress was simple and sleek, a pale silken honey against her olive skin.

Both women stopped for a moment, looked at each other and smiled then, holding hands, began the walk toward their grooms.

Darby had thought his sister had lost her mind when she'd suggested a double wedding. But now as he watched his beautiful bride and his beautiful and amazing sister coming up the aisle, he knew that Lillie had been right. Nothing could be more special than this.

He smiled at Mariah. She was glowing today. They'd put the ugly past behind them. He couldn't wait to make her his wife.

HAWK STOOD BACK watching the dancers at the wedding reception. Even Cyrus had gotten out there and was now doing the cowboy jitterbug with Lillie while Trask and the others clapped and cheered from the sidelines.

He couldn't remember the last time he'd been at a dance. Maybe Lillie was right. He and Cyrus were becoming cranky old bachelors. Well, at least he was, he thought as he watched his brother and sister dance.

"You forget how to dance, cowboy?" asked a distinctly female voice next to him.

He turned to find his high school girlfriend, Deirdre Hunter, smiling up at him. "I don't see you out there, Drey."

"I would be if you asked me to dance." Just then the song ended and a slow one began.

"Unless you're afraid you'll step on my toes," she teased.

"I *will* step on your toes. But you know me, I can't back down from a dare."

"That's the Hawk Cahill I knew and loved." She seemed to realize what she'd said. He saw color warm her cheeks.

Drey hadn't changed that much since high school, he thought as he looked at her. If anything she was prettier in a more confident grown-up way.

"Then I guess we have to do it," he said, motioning to the dance floor. "But you've been warned."

She said nothing as he led the way out into the middle of the fray. Once there, she turned toward him. She didn't look so sure now. He figured they both would have preferred a fast dance given how many years it had been since they'd been in each other's arms.

He stepped toward her and gently drew her to him. They were both stiff at first, but then it was as if the years had never happened, as if this was their senior prom, as if this was still the night he'd ask her to marry him—and she'd turned him down.

They moved to the music and toward each other as if drawn together by something much stronger than the two of them. She laid her head against his shoulder and he pulled her close, breathing in the sweet, familiar scent of her hair.

It transported him back to that night when they'd had their whole lives ahead of them. When he'd thought they would be making the journey together.

He felt a tap on his shoulder. It took him a moment to realize that someone was trying to cut in. Turning, he saw who it was and quickly let go of Drey.

"You don't mind, do you, if I dance with my date?" Junior Wainwright asked.

"She's all yours," Hawk said, and he left the floor.

"I SAW YOU dancing with Drey," Lillie said to her brother Hawk a while later. "Whatever happened with you two?"

"Nothing happened."

"Exactly. Why not?"

He shook his head, smiling patiently at his sister. "Isn't it enough that Darby is married now? Can't you leave the rest of us in peace?"

"You still like her."

"Lillie!"

"Oh my gosh, you're actually blushing."

"If I'm turning red, which I'm not, then it is out of fury. You are not going to play matchmaker with me. Do you understand? Stay out of my love life."

"What love life?"

"I'm warning you, little sis."

She grinned at him. "Now I'm more curious than ever what happened between the two of you."

Hawk groaned. He knew how tenacious his sister could be once she set her mind to something. Out on the dance floor, he saw Junior Wainwright spin Drey. The two were laughing. He turned away, but not before Lillie had seen his expression.

He'd thought she would be grinning but instead she looked sad for him. That was the last thing he wanted, he thought as he stepped to the bar for a drink.

Drey was his past. Better to leave her there. Anyway, she'd come here with Wainwright, the most eligible bachelor in town.

FLINT AND MAGGIE stepped outside to stare up at the stars. The clear summer night smelled of pine as a light breeze whispered in the nearby trees.

He looked out across the wide valley for a moment. The lights of Gilt Edge rose up into the night like the aurora borealis. Then he turned to take in Maggie.

"Did I tell you how beautiful you look tonight?" he asked.

"As a matter of fact, you did, but please don't let me stop you," she said with a laugh.

"I love that dress on you."

She smiled and turned in a circle. "I thought you might like it. Someone told me that blue looks good on me."

"Whoever they were, they were right," he agreed

as he pulled her closer. "You're radiant tonight." And she was. He knew part of it had to be that she felt good. Safe. He'd been worried that his ex-wife might do something to try to ruin this night, but he and Maggie had been dating for weeks and Celeste had done nothing.

He'd hoped that once Celeste realized that he was serious about Maggie, that would be the end of it. He was happy to have been right. Also, it probably didn't hurt that he'd talked to Wayne. Celeste wouldn't want to lose the money and prestige that came with being married to Wayne Duma.

Flint was just glad all that was behind them. He put his arms around Maggie and looked into her luminous brown eyes. He wanted to spend the rest of his life with this woman. He'd even thought about asking her to marry him tonight. He had the ring in his jacket pocket.

But this was his sister and brother's night, he told himself. He and Maggie had many more beautiful nights. When the perfect time came around, he'd know.

The sheriff kissed his beautiful date as the band played and fireworks lit the sky.

THE RECEPTION WAS held at Lillie and Trask's new home on the ranch he'd bought. Everything was perfect—just as Lillie had hoped. Tiny lights twinkled in the warm summer night as the band played on.

On the dance floor, Darby pulled his wife closer. His *wife*. He looked into Mariah's dark eyes. Sometimes he thought he could see the future there as if he was the fortune-teller in the family. He saw a home on the land his father had given him for a wedding present. It was a nice piece on the ranch away from everyone with a great view of the four mountains ranges that circled the valley.

He saw himself and Mariah with a half dozen kids running around. Fortunately, in this future, they weren't all theirs. Some were, but there were cousins galore. His and Mariah's had their dark hair, a couple with his gray eyes, a couple with her deep brown ones. Two boys, two girls.

"A penny for your thoughts," she said as they moved to the music of a slow love song.

"I was just thinking about our kids."

She raised a brow.

"Two boys, two girls. The girls look just like you. The boys—"

"Let me guess, look just like you?"

He laughed. "I can see the house we're going to build. We'll need a lot of bedrooms and a huge area for the kids to play. Their cousins will be over all the time. You do like kids, don't you?"

She smiled. "I love them. In fact…" Her gaze met his. "I was going to wait to tell you this…"

"Mariah?" His heart took off in a gallop.

She nodded and he let out a rip-roaring cattle call and swung her around, putting her down gently as the song ended.

"You might as well tell everyone," Mariah said with a laugh. "I can see that you are busting your buttons to."

He kissed her and then turned toward the crowd. "We're going to have a baby!"

Applause, laughter and congratulations filled the room.

Darby caught his sister's look and began to laugh. "Hold on, I think we're about to have another announcement." More applause, laughter and congratulations followed.

He watched his sister and Mariah, both laughing as they hugged each other. His heart soared with happiness as his family crowded around him.

Ely insisted they open more champagne because it wasn't every day he found out he was going to be a grandfather.

"To the Cahills!" Flint said, lifting his champagne glass in a toast. "There is nothing like them."

"Thank heavens!" someone called from the crowd.

The band began to play again as Darby took his wife in his arms. The luckiest day of his life was the one when he first saw this woman, he thought. The happiest was right now when the future spread out like a Montana summer day before them. "To luck and love," he whispered as he pulled her close. "Together, we have both."

* * * * *

SPECIAL EXCERPT FROM

HARLEQUIN INTRIGUE®

*The kidnapping of the McGraw twins devastated
this ranching family. Twenty-five years later, when
a true crime writer investigates, will the family be
able to endure the truth?*

Read on for a sneak preview of
DARK HORSE,
the first book in a new series from
New York Times *bestselling author B.J. Daniels,*
WHITEHORSE, MONTANA:
THE MCGRAW KIDNAPPING

Their footfalls echoed among the terrified screams and woeful sobbing as they moved down the long hallway. The nurse's aide, a young woman named Tess, stopped at a room in the criminally insane section of the hospital and, with trembling fingers, pulled out a key to unlock the door.

"I really shouldn't be doing this," Tess said, looking around nervously. As the door swung open, she quickly moved back. Nikki St. James felt a gust of air escape the room like an exhaled breath. The light within the interior was dim, but she could hear the sound of a chair creaking rhythmically.

"I'm going to have to lock the door behind you," Tess whispered.

"Not yet." It took a moment for Nikki's eyes to adjust to the dim light within the room. She fought back the chill that skittered over her skin like spider legs as her gaze finally lit on the occupant.

"This is the wrong one," Nikki said and tried to step back into the hallway.

"That's her," the nurse's aide said, keeping her voice down. "That's Marianne McGraw."

Nikki stared at the white-haired, slack-faced woman rocking back and forth, back and forth, her gaze blank as if blind. "That woman is too old. Her hair—"

"Her hair turned white overnight after…well, after what happened. She's been like this ever since." Tess shuddered and hugged herself as if she felt the same chill Nikki did.

"She hasn't spoken in all that time?"

"Not a word. Her husband comes every day to visit her. She never responds."

Nikki was surprised that Travers McGraw would come to visit his former wife at all, given what she was suspected of doing. Maybe, like Nikki, he came hoping for answers. "What about her children?"

"They visit occasionally, the oldest son more than the others, but she doesn't react as if she knows any of them. That's all she does, rock like that for hours on end."

Cull McGraw, the oldest son, Nikki thought. He'd been seven, a few years older than her, at the time of the kidnapping. His brothers Boone and Ledger were probably too young to remember the kidnapping, maybe even too young to really remember their mother.

"If you're going in, you'd best hurry," Tess said, still looking around nervously.

Nikki took a step into the room, hating the thought of the nurse's aide locking the door behind her. As her eyes adjusted more to the lack of light, she saw that the woman had something clutched against her chest. A chill snaked up her spine as she made out two small glassy-eyed faces looking out at her from under matted heads of blond hair.

"What's that she's holding?" she whispered hoarsely as she hurriedly turned to Tess before the woman could close and lock the door.

"Her babies."

"Her *babies*?"

"They're just old dolls. They need to be thrown in the trash. We tried to switch them with new ones, but she had a fit. When we bathe or change her, we have to take them away. She screams and tears at her hair until we give them back. It was the doctor's idea, giving her the dolls. Before that, she was…violent. She had to be sedated or you couldn't get near her. Like I said, you go in there at your own risk. She's…unpredictable and, if provoked, dangerous, since she's a lot stronger than she looks. If I were you, I'd make it quick."

Nikki reached for her notebook as the door closed behind her. The tumblers in the lock sounded like a cannon going off as Tess locked the door.

At your own risk. Comforting words, Nikki thought as she took a tentative step deeper into the padded room. She'd read everything she could find on the McGraw kidnapping case. There'd been a lot of media coverage at the time—and a lot of speculation. Every anniversary for years, the same information had been repeated along with the same plea for anything about the two missing twins, Oakley Travers McGraw and Jesse Rose McGraw.

But no one had ever come forward. The ransom money had never been recovered nor the babies found. There'd been nothing new to report at the one-year anniversary, then the five-, ten-, fifteen- and twenty-year.

Now with the twenty-fifth one coming up, few people other than those around Whitehorse, Montana, would probably even remember the kidnapping.

"There is nothing worse than old news," her grandfather had told her when she'd dropped by his office at the large newspaper where he was publisher. Wendell St. James had been sitting behind his huge desk, his head of thick gray hair as wild as his eyebrows, his wire-rimmed glasses perched precariously on his patrician nose. "You're wasting your time with this one."

Actually he thought she was wasting her time writing true crime books. He'd hoped that she would follow him into the newspaper business instead. It didn't matter that out of the nine books she'd written, she'd solved seven of the crimes.

"*Someone* knows what happened that night," she'd argued.

"Well, if they do, it's a pretty safe bet they aren't going to suddenly talk after twenty-five years."

"Maybe they're getting old and they can't live with what they've done," she'd said. "It wouldn't be the first time."

He'd snorted and settled his steely gaze on her. "I wasn't for the other stories you chased, but this one…" He shook his head. "Don't you think I know what you're up to? I suspect this is your mother's fault. She just couldn't keep her mouth shut, could she?"

"She didn't tell me about my father," she'd corrected her grandfather. "I discovered it on my own." For years, she'd believed she was the daughter of a stranger her mother had fallen for one night. A mistake. "All these years, the two of you have lied to me, letting me believe I was an accident, a one-night stand, and that explained why I had my mother's maiden name."

"We protected you, you mean. And now you've got some lamebrain idea of clearing your father's name." Wendell swore under his breath. "My daughter has proved that she is the worst possible judge of men, given her track record. But I thought you were smarter than this."

"There was no real proof my father was involved," Nikki had argued stubbornly. Her biological father had been working at the Sundown Stallion Station the summer of the kidnapping. His name had been linked with Marianne McGraw's, the mother of the twins. "Mother doesn't believe he had an affair with

Marianne, nor does she believe he had any part in
the kidnapping."

"What do you expect your mother to say?" he'd
demanded.

"She knew him better than you."

Her grandfather mugged a disbelieving face.
"What else did she tell you about the kidnapping?"

Her mother had actually known little. While
Nikki would have demanded answers, her mother
said she was just happy to visit with her husband,
since he was locked up until his trial.

"She didn't ask him anything about the kidnapping because your mother wouldn't have wanted to
hear the truth."

She'd realized then that her grandfather's jour-
nalistic instincts had clearly skipped a generation.
Nikki would have had to know everything about that
night, even if it meant finding out that her husband
was involved.

"A jury of twelve found him guilty of not only
the affair—but the kidnapping," her grandfather had
said.

"On circumstantial evidence."

"On the testimony of the nanny who said that
Marianne McGraw wasn't just unstable, she feared
she might hurt the twins. The nanny also testified
that she saw Marianne with your father numerous
times in the barn and they seemed...close."

She'd realized that her grandfather knew more

about this case than he'd originally let on. "Yes, the nanny, the woman who is now the new wife of Travers McGraw. That alone is suspicious. I would think you'd encourage me to get the real story of what happened that night. And what does...*close* mean anyway?"

Her grandfather had put down his pen with an impatient sigh. "The case is dead cold after twenty-five years. Dozens of very good reporters, not to mention FBI agents and local law enforcement, did their best to solve it, so what in hell's name makes you think that you can find something that they missed?"

She'd shrugged. "I have my grandfather's stubborn arrogance and the genes of one of the suspects. Why not me?"

He'd wagged his gray head again. "Because you're too personally involved, which means that whatever story you get won't be worth printing."

She'd dug her heels in. "I became a true crime writer because I wanted to know more than what I read in the newspapers."

"Bite your tongue," her grandfather had said, only half joking. He'd sobered then, looking worried. "What if you don't like what you find out about your father, or your mother, for that matter? I know my daughter."

"What does that mean?"

He'd given another shake of his gray head. "Clearly your mind is made up, and since I can't sanction this…" With an air of dismissal, he'd picked up his pen again. "If that's all…"

She'd started toward the door, but before she could exit, he called after her, "Watch your back, Punky." It had been his nickname for her since she was a baby. "Remember what I told you about family secrets."

People will kill to keep them, she thought now as she looked at Marianne McGraw.

The woman's rocking didn't change as Nikki stepped deeper into the room. "Mrs. McGraw?" She glanced behind her. The nurse's aide stood just outside the door, glancing at her watch.

Nikki knew she didn't have much time. It hadn't been easy getting in here. It had cost her fifty bucks after she'd found the nurse's aide was quitting soon to get married. She would have paid a lot more, since so few people had laid eyes on Marianne McGraw in years.

She reached in her large purse for the camera she'd brought. No reporter had gotten in to see Marianne McGraw. Nikki had seen a photograph of Marianne McGraw taken twenty-five years ago, before her infant fraternal twins, a boy and girl, had been kidnapped. She'd been a beauty at thirty-two, a gorgeous dark-haired woman with huge green eyes and a contagious smile.

That woman held no resemblance to the one in the rocking chair. Marianne was a shell of her former self, appearing closer to eighty than fifty-seven.

"Mrs. McGraw, I'm Nikki St. James. I'm a true crime writer. How are you doing today?"

Nikki was close enough now that she could see nothing but blankness in the woman's green-eyed stare. It was as if Marianne McGraw had gone blind—and deaf, as well. The face beneath the wild mane of white hair was haggard, pale, lifeless. The mouth hung open, the lips cracked and dry.

"I want to ask you about your babies," Nikki said. "Oakley and Jesse Rose?" Was it her imagination or did the woman clutch the dolls even harder to her thin chest?

"What happened the night they disappeared?" Did Nikki really expect an answer? She could hope, couldn't she? Mostly, she needed to hear the sound of her voice in this claustrophobic room. The rocking had a hypnotic effect, like being pulled down a rabbit hole.

"Everyone outside this room believes you had something to do with it. You and Nate Corwin." No response, no reaction to the name. "Was he your lover?"

She moved closer, catching the decaying scent that rose from the rocking chair as if the woman was already dead. "I don't believe it's true. But I think you might know who kidnapped your babies," she whispered.

The speculation at the time was that the kidnapping had been an inside job. Marianne had been suffering from postpartum depression. The nanny had said that Mrs. McGraw was having trouble bonding with the babies and that she'd been afraid to leave Marianne alone with them.

And, of course, there'd been Marianne's secret lover—the man who everyone believed had helped her kidnap her own children. He'd been implicated because of a shovel found in the stables with his bloody fingerprints on it—along with fresh soil— even though no fresh graves had been found.

"Was Nate Corwin involved, Marianne?" The court had decided that Marianne McGraw couldn't have acted alone. To get both babies out the second-story window, she would have needed an accomplice.

"Did my father help you?"

There was no sign that the woman even heard her, let alone recognized her alleged lover's name. And if the woman *had* answered, Nikki knew she would have jumped out of her skin.

She checked to make sure Tess wasn't watching as she snapped a photo of the woman in the rocker. The flash lit the room for an instant and made a *snap* sound. As she started to take another, she thought she heard a low growling sound coming from the rocker.

She hurriedly took another photo, though hesitantly, as the growling sound seemed to grow louder. Her eye on the viewfinder, she was still focused on the woman in the rocker when Marianne McGraw seemed to rock forward as if lurching from her chair.

A shriek escaped her before she could pull down the camera. She had closed her eyes and thrown herself back, slamming into the wall. Pain raced up one shoulder. She stifled a scream as she waited for the feel of the woman's clawlike fingers on her throat.

But Marianne McGraw hadn't moved. It had only been a trick of the light. And yet, Nikki noticed something different about the woman.

Marianne was smiling.

When a hand touched her shoulder, Nikki jumped, unable to hold back the cry of fright.

"We have to go," Tess said, tugging on her shoulder. "They'll be coming around with meds soon."

Nikki hadn't heard the nurse's aide enter the room. Her gaze had been on Marianne McGraw—until Tess touched her shoulder.

Now she let her gaze go back to the woman. The white-haired patient was hunched in her chair, rocking back and forth, back and forth. The only sound in the room was that of the creaking rocking chair and the pounding of Nikki's pulse in her ears.

Marianne's face was slack again, her mouth open, the smile gone. If it had ever been there.

Nikki tried to swallow the lump in her throat. She'd let her imagination get the best of her, thinking that the woman had risen up from that rocker for a moment.

But she hadn't imagined the growling sound any more than she would forget that smile of amusement.

Marianne McGraw was still in that shriveled-up old white-haired woman.

And if she was right, she thought, looking down at the camera in her hand, there would be proof in the photos she'd taken.

Tess pulled on her arm. "You have to go. *Now*. And put that camera away!"

Nikki nodded and let Tess leave the room ahead of her. All her instincts told her to get out now. She'd read that psychopaths were surprisingly strong, and with only Tess to pull the woman off her...

She studied the white-haired woman in the rocker, trying to decide if Marianne McGraw was the monster everyone believed her to be.

"Did you let Nate Corwin die for a crime he didn't commit?" Nikki whispered. "Is your real accomplice still out there, spending the two hundred and fifty thousand dollars without you? Or are you innocent in all this? As innocent as I believe my father was?"

For just an instant she thought she saw something flicker in Marianne McGraw's green eyes. The chill that climbed up her backbone froze her to her core. "You *know* what happened that night, don't you?" Nikki whispered at the woman. In frustration, she realized that if her father and this woman were behind the kidnapping, Marianne might be the *only* person alive who knew the truth.

"Come on!" Tess whispered from the hallway.

Nikki was still staring at the woman in the rocker.

"I'm going to find out." She turned to leave. Behind her, she heard the chilling low growling sound emanating from Marianne McGraw. It wasn't until the door was closed and locked behind her that she let out the breath she'd been holding.

TESS MOTIONED FOR Nikki to follow her. The hallway was long and full of shadows this late at night. Their footfalls sounded too loud on the linoleum floor. The air was choked with the smell of disinfectants that didn't quite cover the…other smells.

Someone cried out in a nearby room, making Nikki start. Behind them there were moans broken occasionally by bloodcurdling screams. She almost ran the last few feet to the back door.

Tess turned off the alarm, pushed open the door and, checking to make sure she had her keys, stepped out into the night air with her. They both breathed in the Montana night. Stars glittered in the midnight blue of the big sky overhead. In the distance, Nikki could make out the dark outline of the Little Rockies.

"I told you she wouldn't be any help to your story," Tess said after a moment.

Nikki could tell that the nurse's aide couldn't wait until her last day at this job. She could see how a place like that would wear on you. Though she'd spent little time inside, she still was having trouble shaking it off.

"I still appreciate you letting me see her." She

knew the only reason she'd gotten in was because the nurse's aide was getting married, had already given her two weeks' notice and was planning to move to Missoula with her future husband. Nikki had read it in the local newspaper under Engagements. It was why she'd made a point of finding out when Tess worked her last late-night shifts.

Nearby an owl hooted. Tess hugged herself even though the night wasn't that cold. Nikki longed for any sound other than the creak of a rocking chair. She feared she would hear it in her sleep.

Don't miss
DARK HORSE by B.J. Daniels,
available August 2017 wherever
Harlequin Intrigue® books and ebooks are sold.

www.Harlequin.com

HARLEQUIN®

INTRIGUE

EDGE-OF-YOUR-SEAT INTRIGUE, FEARLESS ROMANCE.

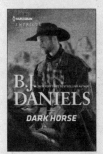

Save **$1.00**

on the purchase of ANY Harlequin® Intrigue book.

Available wherever books are sold, including most bookstores, supermarkets, drugstores and discount stores.

Save **$1.00**

on the purchase of any Harlequin® Intrigue book.

Coupon valid until October 31, 2017.
Redeemable at participating outlets in the U.S. and Canada only. Not redeemable at Barnes & Noble stores. Limit one coupon per customer.

52614848

Canadian Retailers: Harlequin Enterprises Limited will pay the face value of this coupon plus 10.25¢ if submitted by customer for this product only. Any other use constitutes fraud. Coupon is nonassignable. Void if taxed, prohibited or restricted by law. Consumer must pay any government taxes. Void if copied. Inmar Promotional Services ("IPS") customers submit coupons and proof of sales to Harlequin Enterprises Limited, P.O. Box 3000, Saint John, NB E2L 4L3, Canada. Non-IPS retailer—for reimbursement submit coupons and proof of sales directly to Harlequin Enterprises Limited, Retail Marketing Department, 225 Duncan Mill Rd., Don Mills, ON M3B 3K9, Canada.

U.S. Retailers: Harlequin Enterprises Limited will pay the face value of this coupon plus 8¢ if submitted by customer for this product only. Any other use constitutes fraud. Coupon is nonassignable. Void if taxed, prohibited or restricted by law. Consumer must pay any government taxes. Void if copied. For reimbursement submit coupons and proof of sales directly to Harlequin Enterprises, Ltd 482, NCH Marketing Services, P.O. Box 880001, El Paso, TX 88588-0001, U.S.A. Cash value 1/100 cents.

5 65373 00076 2 (8100)0 12281

HICOUPBJD0617

**Trouble comes to town for the
Cahill Siblings of Gilt Edge, Montana,
in this captivating new series from
New York Times bestselling author**

B.J. DANIELS

In the nine years since Trask Beaumont left Gilt Edge, Lillian Cahill has convinced herself she is over him. But when the rugged cowboy suddenly walks into her bar, there's a pang in her heart that argues the attraction never faded. And that's dangerous, because Trask has returned on a mission to clear his name—and win Lillie back.

When a body is recovered from a burning house, everyone suspects Trask… especially Lillie's brother Hawk, the town marshal. Will Lillie give Trask a second chance, even if it leaves her torn between her family and the man she never stopped loving?

Pick up your copy today!